# Irresistible Demise

*After Midnight Series*

Carly Spade

Published in the United States by Carly Spade.
Irresistible Demise. Copyright © by Carly Spade
www.carlyspade.com

Cover by Storywrappers
www.storywrappers.com

Formatting by Polgarus Studio
http://www.polgarusstudio.com

# CHAPTER 1

The irritating sound of my bedside alarm clock blared in my ears despite my best efforts at curling the pillow around my head. I groaned in protest. Slamming my fist down on it squelched the sound, and blissful silence greeted me once more. Reluctantly, I opened my eyes, glaring at the illuminated red numbers. 6:38 p.m. *Wait.* I leaped up, nearly tripping over a pile of laundry. Had I really been that tired? The snooze button must've been unintentionally pressed a total of twelve times because my intention had been to wake up at 6:00 p.m.

The coolness of the wooden floor beneath my bare feet sent a slight chill through my bones. Squatting near the pile of laundry and digging frantically, I held various articles of clothing to my nose and settled on a pair of pleather pants and a Guns N' Roses *Appetite for Destruction* tour shirt that was partially worn out due to overuse. I threw off the stained white tank top, slipped on a black push-up bra, and slid the T-shirt over my head. Not quite ready to succumb to the confinements of pants, I draped them over a nearby chair and made my way to the living room. It wasn't a far walk since my bedroom and living room were one and the same. Four hundred square feet of the finest living Pittsburgh had to offer.

I grabbed my Nokia cell phone. You know the one from year 2000 because who needed social media? Personally, I chose to believe the '90s never left. No missed calls. I could take my time. I grabbed the small controller from the kitchen counter and turned on the stereo. Dorothy's "Raise Hell" blasted through the small space, and I nodded my head in time with the bluesy rock goddess. I yanked open the green, rusted fridge door and ducked my head in for a peek. Frowning, I realized I had yet again forgotten to go shopping. A half empty bottle of mustard and an empty pizza box could hardly be considered breakfast.

Slamming the door shut, I let out a huff and proceeded to slip on the pleather pants and clunky combat-style boots, then ducked into the bathroom. I gazed at myself in the mirror, pulled the shirt off one shoulder, adjusted the girls, which were slightly visible through the varying slits in the shirt, and traced my fingers across the one-inch view of my stomach. I tousled my hair to make it presentable, threw on some eye liner, mascara, and lip gloss. Just enough to get by. The usual battle with the mirror ensued as I fought to keep my eyes from lingering too long on the scar on my neck. Smacking my lips together, I nodded in satisfaction and turned for the door.

I grabbed my keys from the key ring, slipped my phone into my back pocket, and shoved a half-empty Nicorette gum packet into the other. Stuffing three pieces in my mouth, I left my apartment.

It was an unusually chilly night for springtime in Pittsburgh, but I ignored the goosebumps littering my arms since work was a mere two blocks away. I paused at the crosswalk, slamming my palm into the button that would eventually allow me to cross the street without playing a real-life game of Frogger.

Chewing my gum extra enthusiastically as a means to expel every ounce of nicotine in it seemed to rub the guy standing next to me the wrong way. He stood nearly a foot taller than me, wore fancy, shiny shoes, an elegant gray trench coat, and a silk tie. *Late night at the office?* The man clutched a briefcase, his golden wedding band catching the moonlight. Sniffing the air next to him, I caught the familiar scent of a perfume my mother used to wear. For a moment, I'd forgotten my silent profiling, getting caught up in the memories the smell triggered.

"Are you on something?" The man's voice jarred me back to reality.

I blinked several times before glancing upward. The man eyed me as if my hands were growing out the sides of my head.

"No, I was just thinking how alarmingly feminine you smell." I shrugged. "But who am I to judge?"

Chomping my gum a few more times, I wasted no time when the walk sign illuminated. Booted feet carried me across the concrete threshold, the man's frantic voice fading behind me.

"It's—it's not what you think!" Mr. Innocent bellowed.

I raised a hand in the air, waving him off, and then shouted over my shoulder, "Not judging!"

The chill settled in while I'd been waiting for the light to change and I rubbed my arms. The illuminated sign for my home away from home, After Midnight, the bar I'd tended at for the past three years and where I met my best friend Rose, came into view. I gave a tilt of my chin to our burly bouncer Romeo, a tough yet gentle-as-a-teddy-bear African American fellow. He returned in kind, and I wrapped my hand around the oversized iron door handle.

Classic rock music flooded my ears. The bar wasn't the fanciest in the city, but it also wasn't a dive. Tables littered the main space, a small stage in the corner for when the occasional band would play, a pool table, darts, jukebox, and of course, at the front of it all, a long mahogany bar top complete with stools. My "office" six nights a week. I waved at Chad, who was the midday bartender. He looked relieved to see me. I *was* almost an hour late.

Chad was a young, twenty-something college student saving up for graduate school. He was tall, lanky, and made every woman that came into the bar swoon. Honestly, I didn't get it. But then again, clean-shaven, pretty boys were never really my thing. To each her own. I hopped onto the bar and swung my legs over, not bothering to use the proper route.

"Sleep through your alarm again?" Chad asked, cocking an eyebrow and drying a final glass with a rag.

"You've only been here two months and already know

me so well, Chaddy." I batted my eyelashes as innocently as I could, and he rolled his eyes in response.

He proceeded to inform me what each patron drank, slipped his tips for the evening from the register, and practically ran out of the bar. I shrugged, turning my attention to the three men and one woman who sat in front of me. None of them bothered to look up. Either they were too preoccupied with the television, or they were staring into their glasses of alcohol for salvation.

"Well, look who finally decided to show up," Rose's all-too-familiar voice boomed from the other side of the bar.

I grinned and walked over, running fingers through my hair. "Have I ever not bothered to?"

Rose shook her head, setting the small serving tray on the bar top. Her skin was tawny brown, and her hair was dark, thick, and wavy. Rose had such a unique look about her, it was impossible to tell her heritage. Considering that she told everyone something different didn't help either. She'd claimed to be a mix of black and white, Puerto Rican, Native American, Cuban, even Filipino. For all I knew, she could be all of the above, but I loved that she kept me guessing.

She smiled, her wide mouth further accentuating her angular jawline. "Table three needs a gin and tonic and something called a zombie."

Nodding, I grabbed two different sized glasses and went to work.

Rose pressed her forearms onto the bar, jutting her head toward a man sitting alone in the corner of the room. "What about that guy?"

Over my shoulder, I squinted into the darkened space. Shaking my head with a smirk, I returned my attention to the drinks. "Absolutely not. Just because he likes the dark doesn't make him one."

"What if he has a sensitivity to light . . . eh? He's only ever here at night."

"That would be photophobia," I started, setting the two drinks she ordered onto the tray. "And how many day drinkers do you see come in here?"

"Have I ever told you that your freckles make it harder to take you seriously?" Rose offered a charming smile, picking the tray up, her eyes twinkling with mischief.

"And have I ever told you that your ambiguous ethnicity continues to baffle me on a daily basis?"

Rose looked up, releasing a singular, "Ha!"

Chuckling, I cleaned up the small amount of liquid I'd got onto the bar top. Rose and I had a nightly ritual while we were at work. We would rib each other on our heritages, and Rose would try to spot a vampire. Yes, a vampire.

I'd had an encounter with one several years ago, and Rose remained convinced I was either full of shit or plain crazy. Neither of those claims were completely false. She turned my story into a joke, and I let it ride. It was far more exhausting convincing her otherwise. Besides, it was impossible for those same fangers to show up again . . . because they were all dead.

"I ain't never seen you before," a new man's voice piped up.

He was a portly, bald man. White tank top with obvious dip stains, black leather jacket, thick stubble, and already intoxicated. He had, in fact, seen me plenty of times. Normally, he came into the bar already sauced, so it was questionable how much he remembered on any given night.

"Well, I've never seen you before either," I feigned, crossing my arms over my chest.

A girl could have a little fun, right?

The man eyed me quizzically, taking a moment to survey my body. "What's your name?"

"Freya."

He smirked. "What kind of a name is that?"

"Scandinavian. You ordering a drink?" I slapped a cocktail napkin down in front of him.

"Beer."

I waited for an elaboration since none of the brands we served were simply named . . . beer.

After a momentary staring battle, I finally said, "Any particular kind of beer, or did you want what I could pour from the drip tray?" I referenced the sticky rubber laying underneath the beer taps.

He chuckled. "PBR, sweetcheeks."

I suppressed a shudder. It was uncertain whether it was my freckles, red hair, or younger appearance that inspired both men and women to call me all forms of cute nicknames. I may have sucker punched them all in the face if I were someone who cared what others thought of me. Clearing my throat, I turned my back on geriatric Mr. Clean and proceeded to fill a pint glass with beer.

"You want to open a tab?" I slid him the filled glass with the perfect amount of foam.

"Yeah," he responded before shoving his nose into the glass. When he resurfaced, his mustache dripped with foam.

I could barely contain my grimace and turned to punch the information into the computer. "Name?"

"Murphy."

I blinked. "Murphy . . . Brown, Robocop, Murphy's . . . Law?"

He smirked. "How old were you when *Robocop* came out, two?"

I stared at Murphy, deadpan.

Realizing he wasn't eliciting a response from me, he answered, "Phil Murphy."

Nodding once, I turned back to the computer. Rose walked up, moving the empty glasses from her tray.

"Table three. Seriously, look at him."

I turned and pressed my lower back into the counter. The man at table three was huge, scruffy, and puffed on a cigar.

"You mean Wolverine over there?" I snickered, idly grabbing the empty glasses to dunk into soapy water.

Rose cocked her head back and forth. "Huh. He does kind of have that burly mountain man thing going on, doesn't he?"

"That guy is more likely a werewolf over a vampire."

She slapped her palms onto the bar top. "There are werewolves out there too?" A smile tugged at the corner of her lips.

My head jutted backward in surprise. "I have no idea. It was a joke. You think I'm some supernatural expert or something?"

Raising an eyebrow, she responded, "Out of the two of us . . . which one has had a supposed paranormal encounter?"

I moved my hands to my hips, getting into self-defense mode. "You saw a ghost once."

"I was two . . . and it was my nanna."

My lips parted, trying to will a retort.

Rose threw her hands into the air before she ducked under the bar top and shoved the tray into my chest. "Go talk to him."

She had clearly gone deranged. "Excuse me?"

"I want to know. The only way I will is if you sniff him out. So go talk to him. I'll man the bar."

"This is the last one you get for a while." I pointed a finger in her face. "Don't ask me again next week."

Deep down, I think Rose wanted to believe my story, which is why the game continued. She wanted solid proof. Too bad she'd never get it.

She made a crisscross gesture over her heart, kissed her fingers, and then raised them to the heavens.

A defeated sigh escaped my lungs. "Fine."

Batting stray pieces of hair from my eyes, I pressed the tray into my side and approached Wolverine.

"Hey there. Can I get you anything?"

The man's gaze had been transfixed on something across the room and slowly lifted to my face once I'd approached. His brow furrowed so profusely his forehead looked like an atlas, and he removed the cigar from his mouth, leaning onto the table. He used his free hand to rub the short beard on his chin.

"I have a full beer," he said, pointing at the half empty bottle on the table.

Such a charmer, this one. "Considering how long you've been nursing it, I'd say it's warm by now."

The man leaned back, slipping the cigar back between his teeth. He motioned to the empty seat across from him. "You and I should have a chat."

It wouldn't be the first time a man flirted with me in the bar, nor the last, but this had been the most forward. "I'm working."

"You telling me you don't take breaks?"

You bet your ass I do. "Of course not."

The man chuckled between puffs on his cigar, calling my bluff.

I gripped onto the tray so harshly my knuckles turned white. "How about another beer? Bud work for you?" Turning away, I let the tray drop to my side.

His hand gripped my forearm, and instincts kicked in before I could stop them. I turned, grabbing his arm with my free hand, twisted it around, and shoved the tray to his throat, stopping before it collided with his Adam's apple. On another day, he may have walked out of here with a broken windpipe.

The cigar almost fell out of his mouth, his eyes turning downward, peering at the tray by his throat. He looked back up at me. "What are you?"

My chest heaved. "Me? I'm bored." I dropped the tray, taking a step back. "And what kind of question is that?" Waving him off and ignoring his perplexed expression, I shouted over my shoulder, "Romeo!"

The bouncer entered seconds later, glancing around the bar. I jutted my thumb toward Mr. Grabby pants. "Wolverine over there decided he's had enough for the night." Giving one final glance over my shoulder, I saw the man continuing to stare at me while Romeo escorted him out.

Rose stared wide eyed as I made my way back over to her. Flaring my nostrils, I hopped back over the bar top.

"Sorry, I didn't think it'd get that . . . intimate." She absently chewed on a red cocktail straw.

"He's not a vampire. But he asked me *what* I was."

"What kind of question is that?" The straw popped from her mouth.

"That's what I said." I bit my lower lip, putting Wolverine's facial features to memory for safekeeping.

The rest of the night went off without a hitch. Rose and I went through our normal routines, and she remained unusually quiet. I figured she'd felt bad that our little game turned into an attempted molestation, but it was nothing I couldn't handle.

Once we closed for the night, Rose and I stepped outside, and I bounced around on my heels for warmth as she locked up. She slipped the keys into her purse and eyed my bouncing legs.

"You sure you don't want a ride, princess?"

"Pfft. I'm fine. Seriously, it's two blocks away."

She shook her head. "You know they say that most incidents occur the closer you are to home."

"Well you know what I say about *they*."

"They don't know jack shit," we both repeated at the same time, grinning.

Rose made a clicking sound with her tongue before pulling me into a sudden embrace. I wrapped my arms around her, relishing in the heat radiating from her body.

"Mm, you're so warm." I locked my arms around her tighter.

Her chin rested on my shoulder, and her arms dropped to her sides. "You know, my car might be old as dirt, but the heater still works."

I stood straight, pulling up my big girl panties, and smiled in reassurance. "I'm good. Honestly. I'll see you tomorrow night, Rosebud."

"Goodnight," she said through a sigh.

Making my way back home, I slipped my hands into the undersized pockets of my pants. Honestly, why did people think women had no desire to ever use their pockets? A sound akin to *whoosh* grabbed my attention, and I stopped dead in my tracks. The encounter with the odd man in the bar had me a bit more on edge then I'd realized. Random fast food wrappers blew in circles on the sidewalk, and the night had worn on so long only dim lights shone from the buildings. But no creepy sounds, so I continued to walk.

When it happened a second time, combined with the hint of a shadow from the corner of my eye, I was no longer playing around. I gritted my teeth, breaking a piece off a nearby wooden fence with my booted foot, not caring it was from someone's yard. If a vampire was on the loose, they'd thank me. Holding the splintered piece of wood in my hand, I did several circles, eyes darting everywhere. I used to carry a stake on me every day for the last fifteen years, except a couple years ago when I'd decided I was no longer in danger. *Fool me once.*

My slower paced walk turned into a jog toward my apartment building, splintered fence post held tightly within my grasp. Once my building was within eyesight, I slowed down, walking backward, and surveyed the perimeter. No more sounds. No shadows. Was I officially losing my mind? I turned around, and a tall figure loomed over me. Without a second thought, I raised the wood in the air ready to strike.

"Freya!"

I blinked. Standing in front of me was my friend Adam. Tall, basketball player physique, baggy jeans, baggy plaid button-down shirt, and bleached-blonde hair that was longer than mine.

His eyes trailed up to the wooden plank I still held up. He half-heartedly pointed. "Were you . . . about to . . . stake me?"

I glanced up at the would-be weapon, forgetting I still held it, and let my arm drop to my side. "Yes . . . I mean no—not you per se, just that—were you back there just a minute ago?"

He slowly shook his head. "Nooo. I've been here waiting for you for the past fifteen minutes. It's Wednesday. AKA Whiskey Wednesday. AKA Odin's Day? We watch a favorite movie, you drink straight Jack, and I lace it with Coke, and you tell me what a pansy I am?"

My eyes closed in relief, and I let out a breath. "Right. Right. Sorry, I got caught up at work."

"Well, maybe this will help." He held up a DVD case, waving it back and forth.

I squinted. *Pulp Fiction*. One of my favorites.

"I'm going to need something livelier than Jack if I'm going to make it through that movie tonight."

"Got that covered too." He held up a box of Monster Energy drinks. The blue kind. Also, one of my favorites.

"You're too much." I gave his hair a light tug, and we turned for the apartment building entrance.

He walked over the threshold, and I paused, taking one last glance around. I wasn't convinced that what I heard and saw were just in my head. Pursing my lips together, I slipped the plank of wood into the back of my pants. Something told me it was time to start packing again. In case my worst nightmare in the form of pasty skin and extra-long canines had returned.

# CHAPTER 2

The world was black. The faint smell of copper leaked into my nostrils. My arms felt heavy, as if boulders rested on top of them. I blinked my eyes open, vision struggling to focus. Dizziness and nausea washed over me as I attempted to lift my head. I groaned, blinking several more times, willing my eyes to work. I rubbed my fingers together. They were moist, sticky, and stained red. My heart thumped against my chest, and my body involuntarily trembled.

Hesitantly, I sat up. Dead bodies. Everywhere. Blood covered the wood floor beneath me, the walls, the curtains. My breathing became shallow as anxiety took control. Turning my head caused me to wince. A sharp pain shot from my neck all the way down to my toes. I struggled to my feet, grabbing onto an overturned table for support. Glancing around at the bodies scattering the floor, tears began to well. My family. Each and every one of them . . . dead.

Interrupting my grief, a figure appeared before me from within the shadows. Her slender hand gripped my neck, and her stare locked my feet in place. I couldn't scream, couldn't move. All I could do was whimper and pray for mercy. The woman was beautiful. Dark, wavy hair, large, brown eyes, slender nose, and a rounded jaw. She canted her head to the side, eyeing me. She smiled. Full, pouty lips exposed perfectly white teeth and . . . fangs. My chest heaved, and I once again tried to run away but couldn't move a muscle.

She leaned in. "Hello, pretty one." And she struck.

*Wait this . . . this isn't right. This isn't how it happened.*

I jolted awake, gasping. Confusion dizzied my senses. A hand clutched my forearm, and I leaped to my feet, gulping.

"Freya! You were having a bad dream." Adam's deep voice flowed like a melody, calming me.

I took a deep breath. He sat on the couch, wide eyed, his hands clamped to my shoulders. *Pulp Fiction* still played on the TV, and I dragged my hands over my face.

"How long was I out?"

"You fell asleep during Walken's watch speech. I'm not sure I'll ever forgive you for that by the way. I mean, this is Walken we're talking about here."

I managed a small chuckle, knowing he was joking, well, mostly. But more so, I knew he was trying to bring me back down to earth. I sulked back onto the couch, letting my head fall into my hands. The voice of Bruce Willis faded away, and the faint sound of a remote resting on the table replaced it.

"You wanna talk about it?" he asked, hesitation lacing his words. "That one seemed especially fucked up."

"It wasn't right this time, Adam." My voice muffled against my palms.

"Care to explain?"

I lifted my head, resting my chin on my knuckles. "It was the same dream I always have. The one where I see them all dead, but this time there was a woman. It's not supposed to be a woman, Adam."

Adam's face scrunched. "Wait, so the vampire was a woman? What did she look like?"

Her appearance was singed into my brain like a brand. "Olive skin. Attractive. Eerie."

"Did she say anything?"

"She said, 'Hello, pretty one.'"

"Hello, pretty one? I'm so confused right now." Adam turned his gaze to stare absently at a nearby wall.

"*You're* confused?" I stood again, starting to pace back and forth. "I've had the same dream for over a decade, reliving that same night, and now all of a sudden some random chick appears in it?" Only it wasn't a dream. It was a genuine nightmare. An event I could never forget.

"I'm about to say something crazy, but hear me out." He paused, scooting to the edge of the couch. "What if it really was a woman all along? Traumatic experiences can screw with our heads. Maybe you're finally remembering the attack the correct way."

I stopped pacing, tossing him a glare.

He tapped his fingers atop his knees and slouched back into the cushions. "Or not."

"There was a guy at the bar tonight who also asked me *what* I was. Something's not right, Adam. I haven't felt this uneasy in a long time." I traced a fingertip across my lower lip, spacing out.

"Is that why you have a fence post in your pants? How is that comfortable?"

I'd forgotten it was there. Comfort had been the least of my concerns. I removed the wooden plank and tossed it around in my palms. "You're right. Stakes are smaller, easier to conceal, and not as likely to give me damned splinters."

"I mean, that's not what I meant but—" he started to say, but I was already halfway to my bed, resting the wooden fence post on the nearest surface.

I dropped to my hands and knees, knocking on each floorboard, and smiled when one board sounded hollower than the others. Digging my fingernails into the corners, I pried the board away and peered into the hole. I scooped the small black bag into my arms, like swaddling an infant, and made my way back to Adam. The bag landed on the table with a loud thud, one of the perfectly formed wooden stakes spilling out.

Adam gulped and rose to his feet, slipping the unruly stake into his grasp. "Been a long time since I've seen these."

"Didn't think I'd ever have to see them again. Can't say I wanted to." I dug my hand into the bag, removing another of the stakes. It felt foreign, yet so familiar. Not letting it consume my thoughts any more than it already had, I bent over, lifted my pant leg, and slipped the stake into my boot.

Adam watched me, a single brow raising. "You plan on sleeping with that thing?"

"Adam, how long have we known each other?"

"What, fifteen years now?"

"And in all that time have you ever known me to *not* be

slightly paranoid, judgmental, and untrusting of nearly everything?"

"Not ever."

"Then why would I not sleep with it given what's happened today?"

He nodded once. "Point taken, but aren't you the least bit freaked out at the idea of vampires being in town?"

My chest tightened. "Of course I am. I can't afford the time it takes to freak out if there really is something going on."

Adam's hand gripped my shoulder, his face frowning.

"I'm exhausted. I'm going to have to take a rain check on movie night."

Adam cocked his head to the side, gauging my expression. My eyes felt heavy, and my cheeks even more so. I hadn't one ounce of energy left in me.

"You want me to stay?"

"If you want to. Blanket is on the love seat." I pointed at the black crushed velvet two-seater with the red-knit blanket I'd had in my possession since I was a teen. I made my intentions sound aloof, but honestly . . . I did want him to stay. Having an extra body, an extra anything in the solitude of my apartment tonight, was exactly what I wanted.

Adam slowly nodded, gauging my expression again. "I'll slip out at sunrise. Won't even hear me."

I gave a half smile, unable to thank him. He knew though, he always knew.

\*\*\*

I awoke the next afternoon to a quiet apartment, completely alone, just as he'd promised. Making myself a cup of coffee with the grains I managed to sift from the bottom of the container, I spotted my yellow notepad sitting on the counter. I recognized the writing immediately. He always wrote in all capital letters, and I made fun of him because it looked like a serial killer's writing in the movies.

*Frey, I left the rest of the Monsters in the fridge in case you need an extra pick me up. Also, you need to go shopping. I almost ate some of the mustard, but even that has been expired since 2014. P.S.—And do some laundry will you? It smells like a locker room in here, and that's coming from me. Love, Adam.*

I chuckled to myself, clasping my hands around the warmth of the coffee mug. Letting the moisture from the steam collect on my nose, I willed my brain to prepare itself for the night ahead. It was Thursday, the bar's busiest weeknight due to our twenty-five-cent water-downed beers for an hour, and it just so happened to be a full moon. That wives' tale they say about a full moon making people crazy? Completely true.

Before heading to the bar, I took Adam's advice. I stopped at the laundromat and managed to fill half of my fridge with the essentials I needed to live. Bologna, cheese, sour cream, eggs, whipped cream, and green olives. Oh . . . and beer. Since it was finally clean, tonight I wore my favorite ensemble. Jeans with the knees torn open, boots, and a cut-off black tank top that had faded to dark gray from repeated uses.

Given the moon was in full form tonight, it lit my way as

I walked to the bar. It was an uneventful trip this time around, and I wasn't complaining one bit. The warmth of the neon After Midnight sign hit my cheeks once I reached the doors and pushed my way inside. Dozens of conversations hit my ears all at once. It was enough to make me shake my head, attempting to sort out the clutter of noise.

I adjusted one of my black bra straps, tossed my long locks over my shoulder, and moved behind the bar. The place was already packed, and I spotted Rose frantically moving from one table to the next. The old man I'd known simply as Henry took his usual corner seat at the bar. I'd always felt bad for Henry. Eighty-two years old, wife had been gone for the last decade, lived alone, no children, and every Thursday night he would come in here just to be around people.

"Hey there, Red. Do the carpet match the drapes?" Henry's mouth formed a near toothless grin.

I stepped over, tossing the rag onto the bar top, and leaned onto my forearms. "Now Henry, what do I tell you every time you ask that question?"

He chuckled. "A woman needs to have some mystery."

"That's right."

If it had been any other man, I would have slammed his face straight into the mahogany without a second thought. But this was Henry. He was harmless. He'd hardly ever talked about his past, but the anchor tattoo on his forearm, with words having morphed together into a black glob from age, suggested he was prior Navy. I'd be all ears if he ever felt compelled to share. He was probably quite the ladies' man in his formative years.

"Can I get an old fashioned?" Henry asked.

I nodded, going to work on the drink, and soon set the tumbler in front of him atop a napkin. "This drink suits you."

"Oh, because I'm old?"

"Nah. Just old fashioned." I grinned, unabashedly flirting with him. The way his eyes twinkled from my attention seemed like it made his night, so I was happy to oblige.

An unfamiliar gaze lingering on me caught my attention. Most people would quickly look away once they were caught staring, but not this man. I locked gazes with him, and a pair of the brightest eyes I had ever seen in my life stared back. He peered at me as if trying to consume my thoughts, my . . . everything. Blinking, I broke the moment and didn't give it a second thought. Just another customer trying to get my attention to order.

I plopped a napkin down in front of him. "What can I get you?"

The corner of his mouth twitched, and I took the briefest of moments to peruse his features. Messy brown locks of hair that stopped just below his earlobes. Slender nose, thin eyebrows, and a strikingly square jawline covered with a light beard. His gaze caught up to mine, his eyes glacial in color, almost ethereal, a thin scar starting above his eyebrow, continuing just past his cheekbone in a straight line over his left eye.

"Is that a trick question?" He spoke with a light accent, but as if it had faded away over time spent elsewhere.

"Considering I've never seen you in here before, I'd say it was pretty straightforward." Our eyes locked, and it intrigued yet unnerved me he could so comfortably make direct, silent eye contact with a complete stranger.

He rested his palms atop the bar, his eyes squinting. "I'll have scotch."

"Any particular kind?"

"The most expensive one you have."

"You really don't need to try to impress me. Let's just get that out of the way." I scoffed.

He leaned forward. "I would certainly do a lot more if I were trying to impress you. I simply enjoy a good scotch."

My pulse quickened. He squinted at me, and I started to wonder what this guy's deal was. My spider sense was tingling. I dragged my finger across the array of bottles, grabbing Johnnie Walker Blue Label and a tumbler.

"Over the rocks?" I didn't look at him this time, just spoke over my shoulder.

"Neat." His voice oozed like caramel over an ice cube. Warm and gooey at first but then clipped and frozen.

I poured the scotch into the tumbler, straight from the bottle. My ear perked, and I swore I heard the man say, "I can hear your heartbeat." I turned around, a crease in my brow.

"What did you just say?"

He shifted his eyes. "Excuse me?"

I set the tumbler down in front of him with a bit more force than intended. A drop of the amber-colored liquid flew from the glass onto the bar. "You said something. What did you say?"

He raised a single eyebrow, absently wiping away the

drop of alcohol with a napkin. "I can assure you, I said nothing." He canted his head, eyes roaming over my face.

Great. I was officially going crazy. "Sorry. All the voices in here, it sounded like it came from you."

He remained silent and instead lifted the glass to his lips, sipping.

I turned for the computer. "Did you want to open a tab?"

"I believe I'll be here awhile. So, yes."

*Oh, perfect.* "Name?"

"Marcus Syus."

I furiously typed, my thoughts jumbling. He could have been lying. Maybe he really did whisper such a creepy declaration and was so embarrassed by it he insisted it wasn't him. That had to be it. I turned, my elbow knocking into a dirty glass perched on the edge of the sink. My jaw clenched. I couldn't remember the last time I'd broken something behind the bar.

I dropped down to my knees, gracefully grabbing the bigger pieces. My finger pricked against a sharper edge, blood pooling at my fingertip. I hissed, sticking the injured finger into my mouth. Marcus's gaze lingered on me, his tumbler paused at mid-sip. I risked a glance, noticing the way his grip tightened around the glass. It was a subtle action, but all I needed to confirm why he felt so off. I grabbed a towel, applying pressure to the cut.

Marcus slowly placed the glass back onto the bar, staring at me while I rose to my feet. "Sorry. I should go take care of this. I'm a bit clumsy." I turned to walk away.

"You know what I am." Caramel over ice.

My blood froze. *Fuck.*

# CHAPTER 3

I attempted to hide my breath catching in my throat and gripped the towel tighter to my finger. Turning on my heel, I peered at him. He was grinning like a lion ready to pounce. "What you are? You mean an egomaniac with nothing better to do than sit alone at a bar drinking expensive alcohol?"

He chuckled, a lion's deep roar floating from the pit of his stomach. "Is that how you want to do this? I have all night."

*Until the sun comes up.* "I seriously have no idea—" I started before Rose slapped her tray onto the bar top, blowing a piece of hair away from her face with an exaggerated sigh.

"Table two. There is no way you can tell me no on that one." Rose jutted her thumb.

I widened my eyes, trying to signal to her without well . . . signaling to her, that the game was off for the night. Rubbing my earlobe and waving my hand near my neck did nothing. She simply watched and stared at me, blinking. Marcus turned to look at the referenced table.

"Vampires. I know, because I invited them," he said nonchalantly, turning back around.

Rose looked at Marcus, then at me, then back to Marcus. I knew the expression on her face. Curiosity. She moved before I had a chance to grab her, and my teeth ground together. She welcomed herself next to Marcus, shimmying her way between him and another man who didn't seem to mind her proximity.

"I'm dying to know your theory on vampires," she said, leaning her forearms on the bar.

He opened his mouth to respond, but I interjected. "He doesn't have one, because there's no such thing as vampires. Right, Rose?"

Marcus's attention focused on me, his finger tracing the rim of his glass. "Life would be so much more exciting if you just *gave* a little, Freya."

Since when could they read minds? I hadn't realized it, but my mouth fell open long enough for flies to make their way in. Marcus reached forward, slid a finger under my chin, and closed my jaw. His touch chilled me to the bone. At first it felt cold, deadly, but then it lit every nerve in my jaw on fire. I stumbled backward, my butt colliding with the sink. Chewing furiously on the gum still in my mouth, I willed every last ounce of nicotine to squeeze itself into my throat.

Rose glanced between the two of us again, grinning. It was obvious she didn't realize he was a vampire, otherwise she wouldn't have been acting so jovial.

"What's your name?" she asked.

He gazed at her, and I fought every compulsion to not

hightail it for the door. What good would it do me to venture into the night, alone? No. It was far better to stay put among a crowd, among witnesses.

"Marcus. And you?" His tone was beyond amused.

"Rose. Nice to have you at After Midnight, Marcus. Hope you stick around. This dive could use a few more pretty faces." She winked and trotted off.

Marcus chuckled, turning his gaze back to me. "Your friend is very lively."

I launched forward, tossing the towel aside, and gripped onto the bar, leaning in. "Cut the shit. *Why* are you here?"

He didn't flinch. "Am I not allowed in Pittsburgh? I must've missed the memo."

My patience dwindled quickly. "Your kind hasn't been here since . . . a long time." Think about puppies, rainbows, unicorns, anything but that night. Just in case he really can read thoughts.

"Oh? And how would you know that?" He took another sip of his drink, baiting me.

"You don't scare me."

"We both know that's not true. I can smell it on you."

I shrugged. "I forgot to put on deodorant this morning."

He leaned forward and snatched my arm with lightning-quick speed. The tip of his nose grazed up the inside of my arm. "And if I said I was dying to know what you tasted like . . . that wouldn't bother you?"

My heart thumped against my chest like a jackhammer. "I'd just call you a pervert. Besides, you wouldn't do that here."

"Why's that?"

"Too many people. You really want them all to know what you are?"

He grinned devilishly, releasing my arm. I cradled it with my other arm and took a step back.

"Why are you here?" This time, my voice was barely above a whisper.

His eyes dropped, staring at his hands before lifting back up. "Your city is about to get an unwanted visitor. I've come to find out why."

The skin on my forehead wrinkled. "Could you be any more cryptic?"

"The less you know, the better. Trust me."

I guffawed. "Trust is the furthest thing I feel for you, buddy."

He grinned. He let his fangs grow just enough so I could see them, which made his smile that much deadlier. "You feel something for me?"

My confidence returned, and I leaned forward on the bar. "Sure. Disgust. Distaste. Disapproval. Take your pick of disses."

He flicked the tip of his tongue against one fang before both disappeared and looked like normal incisors. "It's honestly never made you curious? What it feels like?"

I had a feeling I knew what he was getting at, but the mere thought made my stomach tie into knots. "What, what feels like?"

He caught my gaze, his pupils dilating, and his finger twitched against his glass. "The Kiss."

He didn't mean the tongue dancing, lips smacking kind of kiss. No . . . he meant a vampire's kiss. The illusive bite. Without realizing it, I dragged a hand down the scar on my neck, and my throat constricted.

"I have an everlasting reminder of your kind's kissing. Can't say I was impressed."

He frowned, eyeing the scar, and I draped my hair over it. Taking a quick, sharp breath, he stood from his stool and leaned as close to me as I let him. "He simply didn't do it right." His gaze caught mine, pupils reverting to normal.

My jaw clenched so tightly I thought I'd snap the crown on my molar in half, and I touched my chest, leaning backward. His confidence knew no bounds. An arrogant, flirty vampire. And an attractive one at that. How did I continue to get *so* lucky? Said me . . . never.

Changing subject. "And why did you have to bring your vampire posse with you?"

He smirked, retreating to his stool. "I have a lot of power, but even I cannot be in several places at once. I've brought them to help me investigate."

I glanced over at the table of four vampires. As always, they looked like normal humans. Humans that didn't get a lot of sunlight, but that wasn't so uncommon in Pittsburgh. Any other person would have been fooled by their appearance. You could tell by the way they moved there was something different about them. When they lifted an arm, it slipped through the air like melted butter. When they turned their head, it was like they were turning under water. It was a minute giveaway, but a giveaway I noticed every time. Except Marcus. I didn't realize he was a fanger until he reacted to my blood. That unsettled me.

"How old are you?" I blurted.

He rested the empty tumbler in front of me, using only his eyebrows and a jut of his chin to indicate he wanted another. I ought to have slapped him but thought better of it and refilled his drink.

"Didn't anyone ever tell you it's rude to ask one's age?"

I slid his glass across the bar, placing a hand on my hip. "Oh, you're a woman now too?"

He ran a hand through his messy, brown locks. "To tell you my age would tell you far too much information about me. Information you are far from earning."

My entire face widened. My eyes, my jaw, my skull—all of it. "Wow. Your ego surpasses the size of China."

He lifted his glass. "Cheers to that."

This bastard.

"What time do you get off?" He continued with casual conversation.

"Sunup." I made sure to emphasize the starchy dryness in my tone—and a pure lack of enthusiasm.

The lion roared with laughter, the back of his hand resting over his mouth. "Touché."

One of the other vampires, a tall, rail-thin female with bleached-blonde hair down to her hips walked up behind Marcus, all but glaring daggers into my eye sockets. She placed a pale white hand on Marcus's shoulder and dropped her head down to the crook of his neck. She didn't take her beady, dark eyes off me. Her irises were so dark you could barely make out her pupils. She proceeded to whisper something in his ear, and judging from his disappointed expression, I highly doubted it was sweet nothings.

"Give me a moment," he barked, eyeing her over his shoulder.

The vampiress stood straight, sliding her hand down his arm before releasing him. "Of course, my liege."

Her accent sounded European . . . German maybe? Translyvanian? She sauntered away, giving an exaggerated sway of her hips. She may have thought I was trying to poach on her territory. *He is all yours, sweetcheeks.*

"My liege? Wow, aren't you fancy?"

He bit down on his lower lip, suppressing a smile. "It would seem I have to depart sooner than expected." He lifted the tumbler to his lips, paused before drinking, and set it back down, sliding it toward me.

"Why don't you finish that? You know, after your shift is over and you're loitering until sunrise?" The lion's eyes glittered with mischief.

"I'm not a fan of undead germs." I scrunched my nose.

"Oh, come now. I'd hate to see it go to waste."

I impatiently tapped my foot, staring at the delicious alcohol. Little did he know, Blue Label was one of my absolute favorites, but I could never afford it. Sighing, I flicked my hand into the air. "Fine. But only because it's expensive."

He closed his eyes and nodded once. Standing from his stool, he moved so gracefully it looked like he floated. I noticed for the first time the way he dressed, which was nothing like the vampires I remembered meeting. He had on dark jeans, a dark gray V-neck shirt that fit snugly across his chest, and a collarless black leather jacket. I dare say he was casually chic? He was also tall—really tall. Like The Rock tall. I suddenly felt like the size of a mouse, and I was a reasonable five foot six.

"I *will* see you again, Freya."

My neck tensed. I really liked this job, this bar. I'd hate to quit because some vampire wanted to stalk me. Could you get a restraining order on an immortal? "Yeah, yeah . . . why don't you concentrate on paying your tab?" I turned to face the computer, choosing his name from the screen. "That'll be," I started, turning to face him. He was gone. Vanished into thin air.

"That son of a bitch." I was about to curse his very name when I spotted a wad of bills on the bar top along with scribbles on a napkin. How did he manage to disappear so quickly while also taking the time to write a damned note?

I picked up the napkin.

"My Dearest Freya—" Rolling my eyes, I managed to continue, "It was an absolute delight to make your acquaintance, and I look forward to proving to you that my bark is far worse than my bite. :)" He really did draw a smiley face. No joke. "PS—Keep the change. Maybe buy yourself a bottle. Something told me Blue Label is your favorite."

I dropped the napkin like it caught fire. Running a hand down my face in annoyance, I scooped the cash into my hand and counted. He overpaid by two hundred bucks. Who the hell did this guy think he was? Irritation washed over me in waves, and I was so mad it felt like my blood tried to boil through my skin. Picking up the tumbler, expensive or not, I tossed the remainder of the scotch right down the fucking sink. The cash however . . . I kept. A gal still has rent to pay.

# CHAPTER 4

Poke. Poke poke poke. What or who had the indecency to disturb my slumber? I pinched my eyes tighter, pretending I was still asleep, but the relentless torture continued against my back.

"Frey, I saw your eyes moving. Get up," Rose demanded.

Sighing, I opened my eyes, gazing at Rose from my horizontal perspective. I groaned, sitting up, and smacked my lips together. My mouth tasted like week-old beer nuts and tobacco, and the side of my face felt numb.

"Did you seriously sleep here all night?"

I wasn't in my apartment? That would explain Rose's presence because I didn't remember giving her a key. I rubbed the side of my face, feeling caked drool, and looked down at my bed. Blinking, I stared at the bar top.

"Going to take that as a yes." Rose shook her head and scooped her arms underneath my armpits. "Come on, Sleeping Drooly, time to go home."

"I honestly only meant to stay until sunup. I don't even remember falling asleep." Running my hands through my hair to make it somewhat presentable, I willed my brain to wake up. It was often a losing battle.

"Why sunup? Did you believe that guy? Vampires, Frey? Come on, we both know that's crazy."

I stared at a stain on the tiled floor. "Yeah, I mean you could be right, Ro. I didn't want to walk home last night is all."

Rose sighed, pulling me into a side hug. "Next time, would you please for the love of anything that's holy just ask me for a freaking ride?"

"Sure. I didn't want to both—" I started, but Rose's hand clapped over my mouth.

"No excuses. Just promise."

"I promise." My words muffled against the smoothness of her palm. How'd she keep her hands so soft working at a bar anyway?

"Alright. I'm buying you breakfast, and then I'll drive you home."

"You're too good to me." I half-smiled, my words genuine.

"Nah. I like projects, and you, my friend, are a *project*." Her wide eyes grew even wider, and she pointed to my head, to my feet, and back to my head again.

I guffawed. "What the hell is that supposed to mean?" Playfully, I punched her in the shoulder.

"Awful House good with you?" She ignored my question and proceeded to brush off the shoulder I'd punched.

"Is there any other choice for a hearty breakfast?" I grinned. We were in fact talking about Waffle House. We called it Awful House given its delicious but greasy food that surely clogged our arteries. But you only live once, right?

*\*\**

I wasn't sure what possessed me to walk to work that night. Had I thought about the fact that vampires were back in my life? Yes. So why did I still choose said form of transportation? Because I was tired of them ruling over me. For years I couldn't set foot out of the comfort and familiarity of my home without paranoia following me like a rain cloud. Every snapped twig, every water drip, every wind gust twisted my guts into origami. If one tried to bite me, the plan was simple. Stake them. Twice. Just to be sure.

I'd be lying if I said I wasn't still scared shitless. I pulled the sleeves of my leather jacket as far over my hands as they would go and clutched the fabric against my skin to prevent the chill of the wind from sneaking through. Every step I took caused the stake in my boot to rub against the side of my calf. The feel of the smooth wood pressing into my flesh gave me a bizarre sense of comfort. I eyed the first of three alleyways I had to pass on my trek to the bar and extended my hand, ready to grab the weapon if necessary.

Besides a screeching cat, the alley remained lifeless. I let out a breath I hadn't realized I'd been holding and curled my fist back into my sleeve. Alley two was the same scenario, so it was no surprise my guard was down a bit more passing the final one. I stopped dead in my tracks hearing murmurs echoing off the stone walls. Perking my ear, I made out the idle coos of a woman's voice and the deep rumbles of a man's. I rolled my eyes. Figures it was just two people more than likely having sex in an alley. Nothing like smelling urine and garbage while getting your freak on, but to each their own.

I started walking again, happy to be on my merry way, but the woman walked out from the alley and directly into my path. She almost bumped right into me, a dazed look on her face. She smiled faintly to herself, not bothering to glance in my direction, and I noticed blood staining the collar of her sweater, but no bite marks. What. The. Hell?

I bent down, scooping the stake into my grasp, and cautiously made my way into the alley. The second dumb idea I had for the night. I was on a roll. A tall silhouette leaned against one of the adjacent buildings, and my grip tightened around the wood in my hand. If it weren't for adrenaline, I may have pissed my pants. The shadow moved into the one solid piece of light cascading downward from a streetlamp, and I shuffled my feet, raising the stake.

"Freya," the black figure said, and I plunged the stake straight into his chest.

I staggered backward, staring at Marcus with a stake driven into him and still very much alive. He looked down at his predicament, clicking his tongue against his teeth, and then turned his gaze on me. The adrenaline started to dwindle, and my boots sank into the concrete beneath me like hardening cement. My mind could not communicate to my legs to move.

He used his thumb to wipe away a small amount of blood at the corner of his mouth. "You do realize you're an inch away from my heart?" He pointed at the stake before yanking it from his chest in one swift motion.

Vomit tugged at my throat, and I fought it back, watching the blood spray and gurgle in his chest cavity. He was right, though—I was rusty. Hadn't exactly stabbed anyone in the heart lately. "Yeah? But I bet it still hurt like a bitch."

He smirked, eyeing the stake like a priceless piece of jewelry. "This won't kill me if that was your intention." He tossed the stake at my feet. The hollowed sound of wood bouncing against stone ricocheted off the walls.

I slammed my foot atop it to keep it from rolling. "What do you mean?"

He stalked forward—the predatory lion, shoulders hunched, approaching its prey. "I am far too old. You would need other means."

I bent down, scooping the stake into my hand, trying to ignore the blood dripping onto my fingers. "And what means would that be?" I took a step back, holding the stake up despite the fact he just said it wouldn't work. It made me feel better.

He stopped right in front of me, sky-colored eyes peering down, dissecting me. "Why would I tell you and ruin all of our fun?"

I gulped, fingers tightening around the stake but slipping from the red liquid covering it. His height caused the back of my head to almost meet my shoulder blades. I had to tilt my chin up so high. My gaze fell to the corner of his mouth . . . dried blood. "Did you—did you *feed* on that woman?" My face scrunched in mortification.

He raised his brow. "Yes. Yes, I did. You do know that's what vampires do, correct? I figured with your experience and all. . . ." he trailed off, flicking his wrist into the air.

My lips parted, the contents of my stomach threatening to make an appearance. "You *disgust* me."

He shook his head, leaning in. "I don't believe you. In fact, I think I intrigue you."

Were vampires deaf? "That is the farthest possible thing from disgust."

"Quite the contrary. Oftentimes they coincide. You humans and your morbid curiosities." He leaned back, letting his upper lip curl back enough to show one of his fangs.

I'm not sure where the fear went, but suddenly it was gone. Replaced by an overwhelming urge to lop off a head. I changed my stance from defensive to haughty. "So just because you think we all have this morbid curiosity, it gives you the right to feed on us like cattle?"

He canted his head to the side, taking another step forward. "Between the two of us, who do you think is higher on the food chain?"

I clenched my jaw, knowing the answer but not willing to accept it or voice it.

"I'm a vampire, Freya. A predator. It's in my nature. Did I kill that woman? She walked away not remembering a thing."

I shook my head so violently my hair fell into my eyes. "That's not the point. The point is your kind *uses* us. We're not the only things on this planet with blood."

He lifted his hand and ever so delicately positioned some of my rogue strands back over my ear. His touch caused me to recoil and bat his hand away. Partly because he was what he was, and partly because his touch felt so . . . intimate.

"What would you have me feed on, hmm? Rabbits? Rats in the alleyway, perhaps?" As if on cue, a black rat scurried underneath a nearby dumpster.

"Well, why not? Why can't you live off animals?"

He sighed, a light rumble spilling from the depths of his throat that sounded similar to a growling purr. His eyes locked with mine, and I couldn't help but stare. "To ask me to feed on animals to survive would be like me asking you to drink water only when it rained."

Damn. I dropped my gaze, unsure of how to respond. My hand was suddenly intertwined with his. I tried to pull away, but he didn't let me.

"Good night, Freya." He pressed his lips against my knuckles, never moving his eyes from mine. He let one of his fangs graze the skin near a vein on the back of my hand with a devilish grin and vanished.

I stood there motionless, like an idiot, for what seemed like an eternity before I whipped out my cell and feverishly began to text. The first text was to Rose.

> Me: Call out sick tonight. ER. My place. 30 minutes.
> Rose: R U dying?
> Me: No. Just get someone to cover for you. 30 minutes.

Rose: U can be so weird sometimes, but ur
lucky I luv u. C ya in 30.

The second to Adam.

Me: ER. My place. 30 minutes.

Adam: Should I bring snacks?

I scrunched my face, but when my stomach growled as if on cue. . . .

Me: Doritos.

Adam: On it. See you soon.


Once back in my apartment, I paced back and forth, going over and over again in my head how I was going to ask my only two friends to help me kill an ancient vampire. I wasn't sure how for starters, not to mention I still needed to convince Rose vampires really did exist and it wasn't simply some form of PTSD on my part. This was going to be a long night. I hoped Adam brought the family-size bag. Cigarette. I could probably sneak a few puffs in before they got here. Buzzing brought my attention back to reality, and I nearly tripped over the couch, I was in such a hurry to reach the intercom.

"Yes?"

"It's me and some Indian lady. Do you know her?" Adam said, mockingly.

"Freya, how do you deal with this guy?"

"I asked you both over. Come on up." I released the talk button and pressed the button to unlock the entryway door. Waiting until I heard their feet shuffling down the hallway and saw their bodies filling up the peephole, then and only then did I unlock and open the door.

As soon as Adam stepped inside, I slammed the door shut. He yelped, jumping forward. "Jesus! You almost got my pants caught in the door. What the hell happened to you?"

I turned the deadbolt, slid on the chain, and faced them, pointing toward the couch.

"Sit." Eyeing the family-size bag of Doritos cradled in Adam's arm, I snatched it. "I'll have a few of these first, though."

They sat, eyeing each other sidelong. Adam extended his arm over the back of the couch like this was any other night, and Rose sat on the edge of the cushion, watching me.

I ripped open the bag like a starving raptor and shoved three chips into my mouth. Crumbs escaped at the corners of my lips in defiance. I tended to get the munchies when I felt threatened, or sad, or angry, and tonight I had the trifecta. I wiped the orange residue on my fingers against my pant leg. "I need your help to kill a vampire. A really, really old one."

Rose stared at me as if she expected to hear more, and Adam leaned forward.

"Wait. Since when did vampires crawl out of their holes? And here? In Pittsburgh?" he asked, pointing at the wooden floor like this apartment represented the entire city.

"I'm sorry, why is he here again?" Rose's head whipped in his direction.

"I've only been her best friend for over a decade. What do you got?"

I let the two of them tongue lash one another for a moment. Mostly because I wanted to eat more chips, and this gave me time to chomp on a few more.

"Only the woman she sees for eight to twelve hours a night nearly every day at work."

"Oh, right. The chick who chalks up her supernatural stories to her being weird."

Rose's jaw dropped, and her hands pressed into her knees like she was about to stand. I quickly tossed the bag of chips at the space between them, loud crackling noises from the plastic silencing the room.

"Hey! I just told you two I need help vampire slaying, and all you can do is debate on who is my BFF?"

They glared at one another and then at me.

"Okay, apparently reminder introductions are in order. Adam, this is Rose. Rose, this is Adam. Adam, orphanage. Rose, work. Adam, thirteen years. Rose, three. Adam, penis. Rose, vagina. Have I covered all the bases?" I held out my hands at my sides in a shrug.

They nodded at one another amicably, and I started to pace, pressing my palms into my forehead. "Marcus is a vampire, Rose. An *actual* vampire, not some figment of my imagination."

Rose looked at Adam, shaking her head. "Your scar?" She absently pointed at my neck.

"The story I told you about my family is one hundred percent true. No fabrication."

The color drained from her face. I reached behind me and grabbed the closest bottle of liquor, slamming it down on the coffee table in front of her.

"And this guy, Marcus? Has he hurt you?" The will to protect was evident in Adam's tone.

His question confused me. Marcus had plenty of opportunity to forcibly feed on me, to kill me, especially considering I hadn't hesitated to drive that stake into his chest, yet . . . he didn't. "No, he hasn't. I mean—he's messing with my head. He's arrogant, cryptic, and an all-around pain in my ass."

"Sounds like my ex-boyfriend," Rose muttered, taking a swig from the whiskey bottle.

"Did he say why he's suddenly in town?" Adam wasn't agreeing with me fast enough. My patience was wearing thin.

"He said something bad was coming, and he and his vampire clique are here to find out why." I flittered my hand in the air as if finishing my sentence with a "blah, blah, yaddah, yaddah."

"So let me get this straight. A vampire who has had every opportunity to kill you . . . hasn't, warns you about something coming, and your plan is to wipe this guy off the face of the planet?"

His ability to make sense irritated me.

"Hasn't tried to kill me *yet*. He's gotta go."

"I say we stake the bastard." Rose's words began to slur, and she rammed the bottle on the table, almost missing it.

Nonchalantly, I slid the liquor away from her. "Therein lies the problem. He can't be killed with a stake." I tapped my lip in thought. "Maybe thirty of them. . . ." Trailing the end of my sentence, I turned for my bed, flipping open the top of the chest at the base. I furiously shoved random articles of clothing, VHS tapes, and envelopes of old-school developed photos aside and peered down at the planks of wood I'd been saving.

A hand delicately touched my shoulder and I jumped, swatting it away. Adam cocked his head and grabbed each of my arms.

"Freya, you know I'd back you up on anything. You're my little sister whether it's by blood or not. I'd bury a body with you if it came to it. But this guy sounds dangerous and far more powerful than what you faced before. You survived vampires once—don't push your luck."

"Wow. Could you be any more of a buzzkill?" Rose draped herself over the back of the couch, her head resting lazily on her hand.

Any other time, I would've laughed at her comment, but Adam's expression forced my focus.

I gripped his shoulder, watching his face fall because he knew I was about to disagree with him. "I appreciate your concern. But I can't rest until this guy is sawdust, and I need you to help me."

He nodded, sniffed once, and ran a hand through his tattered blonde hair. "What do you need me to do?"

"Turn those into vampire killers." I pointed at the wooden planks and then turned to Rose. "Tomorrow, I need you to go to the library and research vampires like it's a part-time job."

"The library? Are you stuck in the 90s, Frey?" She waved

her cell phone back and forth. "I'll stay in my PJs and use this."

I half smiled. "Right."

"What are you going to do?" Adam asked, pulling the planks out of the chest one by one.

"Vampire-proof my apartment. Figured I'd get a crucifix for every entryway, buy out all the local grocery stores of garlic, see if the pawn shops have any cheap silver I could haggle for."

"Does any of that actually work?" Rose glanced up from her phone, leaning her elbow onto the back of the couch.

"I have no idea. Only one way to find out."

# CHAPTER 5

Have you ever walked through the check-out line at the grocery store and put ten pounds of garlic on the conveyor belt? The looks you get are astonishing. I didn't bother trying to explain myself at the pawn shop when I set four crucifixes of varying styles and a spoon on the counter. Walking down the street, my prized purchases snuggled safely into several plastic bags, I heard a low growl from a nearby alleyway. Me and alleyways didn't have a very good track record lately and I knew I should keep walking. Probably just some stray dog.

I waltzed right on past, confident in my decision, but then—what if the dog was hurt? Halting, I leaned back, peering into the alley. Nothing but a piece of newspaper floating in the wind and an odd, green-colored smoke wafting from a nearby vent. All seemed normal and I continued to walk.

"Freya," a gruff voice growled, and I nearly dropped my bags.

He stepped out from behind a car. It was Wolverine from

the bar the other night. Why was one of our customers seemingly stalking me, and furthermore, did he just try to lure me into an alleyway? He held his hands out to his sides, palms facing me. His height loomed over me like a skyscraper.

"You better start talking or I am thirty seconds away from doing something we'll both frown upon." I'd secured myself with three stakes this time and my fingertips already grazed the one stuffed down the back of my pants.

"We need to talk." He took another step closer.

"Considering I just threatened you, that's not very descriptive."

"I have information for you. About the vampires. You *cannot* trust them, Freya."

My name was about to go out of style, I'd been hearing it so much lately.

"And I am supposed to trust you? Who are you?"

He placed a hand on his chest, his motions slow and hesitant. "My name's Damian. All I need is fifteen minutes of your time. You'll really want to hear this."

"Fifteen minutes? So specific."

"This is serious," he growled, his patience obviously dissipating.

I ground my teeth together. This guy was my best lead yet, but I wasn't stupid enough to show him where I lived. "Meet me in the park in half an hour. I'll give you your fifteen minutes in a wide-open area, not a seedy alleyway."

I'd gone my entire life only ever leaning on Adam for help. I could count on one hand how many times I'd asked for it. Now there were several people not only trying to warn me about impending doom, but help me. Complete strangers. I'd always been able to take care of myself, but not gonna lie . . . it felt kind of nice.

He smirked, running a hand down the length of his beard. "Fair enough." His nose twitched. "Is that bag full of garlic? It absolutely reeks."

I shrugged. "I like Italian food." Turning on my heel, I continued walking.

"Thirty minutes, Freya!" His voice boomed behind me and I gave a thumbs-up without facing him.

\*\*\*

I felt like an absolute tool walking into a park with stakes as concealed weapons, but figured it was less conspicuous than a butcher's knife. *Oh, these? I'm on the way to repair a fence. Nothing to see here.* The wind gusted through the open, stone walkways surrounded by maple trees in Schenley Park. I passed by a group of older men playing a game of volleyball, and past them I spotted a single bench nestled underneath a tree where Mr. Scruffy himself sat.

I clenched my fists at my sides, slowly approaching, a bit astonished he turned to look at me when I hadn't been that close yet. The bench faced a perfect view of the Pittsburgh skyline, and the sun had started to set, casting a pink and yellow hue across the clouds.

"A mysterious meeting with a view. I like it," I said, peering at the buildings, taking a moment to appreciate the way it looked like a painting.

"Why don't you have a seat?" He motioned with his head

to the empty area on the bench beside him.

He wore a brown leather jacket that looked like it'd seen a fight or two, the collar folded over with Sherpa lining, and a dingy pair of blue jeans. He leaned forward, forearms resting atop his knees, and watched me as I passed him.

I sat as far away on the bench as I could, leaning onto the metal arm rest. "Is this one of those meetings where I'm supposed to stare straight ahead and pretend like I'm talking to myself?"

"People already seem to think you're crazy, wouldn't be too far off, hm?"

"Who are you, and why do you think you know me?" I sneered.

"I know you've been conversing with vampires, and I'm here to tell you it's a bad idea." His jaw tightened.

I sat straight up. "First of all, I literally ran into one the day *after* you showed up, and I am not willingly mingling with them. What's it to you anyway? Will you cut to the chase? I have things to do."

He dragged a hand through his spiky locks with frustration. "There's something coming. I don't know what and I don't know who, but somehow, you're getting mixed into it. None of this concerns you. If you knew what was good for you, you'd leave town—tonight."

I stared at him like his beard gave birth to a fur ball and then laughed.

"This isn't—why are you laughing?" He dragged his hand through his hair once more, pausing to give it a light yank this time.

I stood, still laughing so hard I had to wipe the tears from my eyes. "This has been a real slice, but I can't uproot my life because some complete stranger is concerned for my wellbeing. That's a bit creepy, by the way."

"Why don't you just tell her the bloody truth?" A female voice, smooth, sultry, and slightly British cascaded through the air. "This is getting us nowhere."

I dipped my hand into the back of my jacket, my other hand raising defensively. Damian let his head drop before glancing over his shoulder. The woman stepped out from behind a tree, and I whirled around, stake raised in the air. A large hand enveloped my forearm, stopping me in mid-stab. Damian glowered down at me.

"She's with me. She's my mate." He lowered my hand, glancing around to see if anyone noticed.

I let my hand fall lax at my side, canting my head. "I'm sorry. Your mate? I think you're taking this whole caveman bravado a little far."

She was tall, only a few inches shorter than Damian, thin, with chestnut colored hair, perfectly sculpted eyebrows, and a chiseled squared face. Her eyes were set apart at just the right width, delicately almond shaped, and their color reminded me of leaves turning yellow in the fall. She was an exotic friggin' masterpiece. She wore black skinny pants, boots, a cowl neck, droopy sweater, and a Van Halen T-shirt. Well, she had *that* going for her.

"We're werewolves," she said, raising one of those flawless brows.

Damian's head shot at her like a rocket. "Frankie!"

She crossed her arms over her chest, lackadaisical, and shrugged. "She would've bloody well found out eventually. Tip your toe in the pond and it ripples."

My palms began to sweat. Did some paranormal portal open somewhere I didn't know about?

I laughed a little. "Can we back up a moment here?" Raising the stake, I pointed between the two of them. "You turn into a wolf on a full moon? That's what you're saying?"

Damian snatched the stake from my grasp. "Would you put that away? You're the one who wanted to meet in the middle of a public park."

I snatched the stake right back, his look of surprise apparent, and stuffed it back into my pants.

Frankie sauntered to me, her walk nearly as exotic as her appearance, hips swaying, one foot crossing over the other in exaggerated flourish. "Not only the full moon. At any moment we can shed our clothes, grow fur, and prowl after our prey." She leaned forward, grinning, her eyes growing increasingly yellow.

I narrowed my gaze, holding my ground. She could've left the getting naked part out of the equation.

Damian's hand gripped her shoulder and coaxed her back. She frowned, her eyes morphing back to normal. "The vamps have been asking a lot of questions around town. From what we could gather, a rival clan is coming and soon. Your name has also been passed around."

I pressed a hand into my chest, beside myself. "Me? Why me?"

"We were hoping you could tell us." Frankie sniffed the air in front of me.

I wasn't sure what in my brain told me to do what I was about to do, but I'd trust something that could shift into a wolf over a thing that wanted to suck my blood. Licking my lips, I said, "I've killed them before."

"Vampires?" Damian looked at Frankie, who grinned like a serpent.

"Yes, but it was over a decade ago."

"Are you a slayer?" Frankie's tone became higher pitched.

I blinked. "No. No, no, no, no. I've killed exactly three— three very specific ones, and immediately retired. I haven't seen them since. Until just now."

"Specific ones?"

My chest tightened and I willed my hand to not draw attention to my neck. "A story you don't need to know."

Damian stared at me for a moment, the corners of his jaw popping, before he reached out a hand. "Give me your cell phone."

Reluctantly, I slid it from my back pocket and slapped it into his palm.

He held it like I handed him a scorpion. "Good Lord, where'd you buy this, RadioShack?"

"Ha, ha. It communicates fine."

He shook his head, fingers working quickly across the keys, and handed it back to me. "If you hear anything or need anything, just let me know. You have the support of our pack."

My eyebrows rose to the heavens. "Your pack? There's . . . more of you?"

They both grinned, Frankie slipping her arm into the

crook of Damian's, and they turned to walk away. "We'll be watching you, Freya."

I opened my mouth to retort, having had quite enough of being stalked by a vampire, let alone werewolves, but they were gone. The vanishing act was getting old. The sky morphed into colors of the sunset, crimson and dark purple. The sun would disappear within the hour, and I decided I'd lock myself in my apartment every night for the foreseeable future. Well, tonight anyway. I needed nicotine, whiskey, and a long, hot shower that would turn me into a walking prune.

After hanging so much garlic around my apartment it looked like it was snowing, securing crucifixes in all my windows and above my door, I took one of the longest showers I'd ever taken and didn't care how high it'd make my water bill. I deserved every last drop, just like the glass of whiskey I sipped. I perched myself on the windowsill in the living room, wrapped in a towel, and cradled a cigarette between my knuckles, letting the smoke tendrils escape out of the small opening.

"I expected you to lash out, but this is beyond anything I could imagine." Marcus's voice rumbled across the room, and I stood, the cigarette butt falling to the floor. With one hand I grabbed the towel, with the other, a stake.

"How the hell did you get in here?" If I were honest, I was lucky I didn't catch myself on fire.

"Have we not established that already?" He slipped from the shadows, the moon casting white glints off the tops of his polished shoes.

"I thought I had to invite you in?"

He nodded slowly, glancing around at the perimeter of garlic. "For you spending time with vampires, you really don't know a thing about us, do you? Garlic, crucifixes—all children's stories."

I gripped onto the towel like it held back my very soul. "I didn't exactly stop to interview one before I killed it."

He smirked, moving closer. The blue of his eyes looked more cerulean with the assistance of the moon. "I have to say, I find it rather amusing you decided to use one of your hands to secure the towel. If I were a true intruder, dropping that would have been quite the distraction." He grinned with a flash of fang.

"You *are* intruding. Why are you here, Marcus? This constant showing up out of nowhere is wearing thin."

His eyes dropped to the ground, and he crouched, returning with the burning cigarette butt. He made a *tsk tsk* sound with his tongue, squelching the flame between two fingers. "These will kill you."

"Says the immortal," I hissed.

He took another step forward, his moves swift and calculated yet graceful. "I've come to tell you we've found out—" he paused, sniffing the air. "Why do you smell like a wet dog?"

Gritting my teeth, I took a step forward, prepared to give him a piece of my mind, but the next moment he was behind me, his hand wrapped around my midriff, the other pressed over my mouth, and his lips dropped to my ear. I struggled against him, my life flashing before my eyes. I whimpered, realizing I couldn't move a muscle.

"Go into the bathroom, lock the door, and don't make a sound."

*Like hell.* I nodded only so he would let me go, and as soon as I was free, made a beeline for the door. He appeared in front of me before I could blink. Towering over me, fangs bared, he squared off his shoulders.

"Now, Freya!" he roared.

An actual roar this time that sent me writhing back on my heels.

I blinked a few times, thinking back to Damian's words. Don't trust the vampires. What choice did I have? He wasn't going to let me go, but why would he kill me now and not before? I retreated to the bathroom, shutting and locking the door behind me, carefully pressing my ear against the chipped wood. The sound of a boot slamming into my front door sent me reeling backward, narrowly missing the toilet.

# CHAPTER 6

I willed myself back to my feet, creeping up to the door.

"Well, well, it's our lucky day, fellahs. We get to kill us a vampire too," a gruff voice said.

The skin above my nose wrinkled. Too? My nails dug into the door, the sinking realization whoever was on the other side had come to kill me.

"I'd certainly like to see you try." Marcus's confident tone breezed like a melody. Calm, cool, and collected.

Several voices yelled obscenities all at once and feet trampled the floor. I counted three, maybe four. Sounds of slashing, throat gurgling, and gasping flooded through the thin pane of the door. I ground my teeth together, growing increasingly anxious. There was no reason to hide in here; I could handle myself fine. I gripped my towel and looked around the bathroom, thanking myself for consistently throwing clothes on the floor rather than in a hamper like they belonged.

I scooped up the Pantera T-shirt and a pair of lounge shorts, slipped them on, and let the towel fall away. The shirt was so large it fit me more like a dress. I whisked off the top of the toilet tank lid and grabbed the stake I'd hidden there. Taking a deep breath and counting to three, I opened the door, stake raised and at the ready.

I had to pause, allowing my brain to process with my eyes, and nearly dropped the stake. Three bodies bloodied and massacred lay at Marcus's feet. Marcus pulled his mouth away from the fourth's neck, letting the man slump to the ground, lifeless. He looked over at me, chin dripping crimson liquid, fangs still extracted.

"What the hell are you doing? I told you to stay in there for a reason," he growled, stepping over the bodies like he would step over a fallen log, then reaching for a roll of paper towels on the kitchen countertop.

My mind kept flashing back to the night I lost my family. The sight of the dead men staining my apartment floor frightfully similar. Marcus approached, ridding his mouth of blood with a paper towel. I turned, bringing the stake down toward his chest. I didn't care if it wouldn't kill him, I wanted to stab him regardless. He caught my wrists and re-directed them downward.

"Freya." He peered down at me, eyes searching my face.

"You had me lock myself in the bathroom so you could do *this*? It looks like the St. Valentine's Day Massacre in here, Marcus!" I tried to pull away from him, but he kept his grip.

"Either I killed them or they killed you. I figured you preferred the former, so I didn't bother to ask your permission."

Confused and mortified didn't begin to scratch the surface of how I felt. "Don't you think this is a bit much?" A pool of blood eked its way closer to my foot.

He looked down and picked me up like I weighed nothing more than a feather, sitting me on the countertop. He put a hand on either side of me, leaning onto the marble of the counter, caging me in. "Why were they after you?"

I blinked my eyes so quickly my vision blurred. "You're asking me? I have no idea! In fact, my entire world has become one big shit storm ever since I met you."

"They knew about vampires. Who did this to you?" He tossed my hair away from my neck, eyeing the scar.

"That was a long time ago. It has nothing to do with any of this," I said through gritted teeth.

He narrowed his eyes. "You sure about that?"

My nostrils flared and I pushed against the countertop, attempting to scoot away from him. He curled a hand around the back of my knee, pulling me toward him. A breath caught in my throat from his touch in that very sensitive spot, and I slammed my leg against the counter—and his hand—hoping it'd hurt him.

He flinched and retreated, a corner of his lips lifting ever so slightly. "You could be a little more thankful I saved your life."

"I could've handled it," I snarled.

He nodded, standing to his full height. I had to lean back on my elbows to look him in the face. "I believe you, but there's only a few very select ways I can die. I'd much rather risk my life over yours for that reason."

"Why? Why do you care whether I live or die? You don't even know me." I pulled at the hem of my T-shirt, suddenly feeling exposed.

He stared at me, widening his eyes, silent. "Go to work, Freya. I'll take care of this. No reason for you to see it." He turned, surveying his handiwork on my hardwood floors.

I hopped off the counter, careful not to step in any of the blood, or on anything else. "I have tonight off."

"Then go anyway." For a moment, I saw a softer side to him, but now the cold lion returned. He slipped a cell phone from his jacket pocket.

I stepped forward, yanking the cell from his grasp. That was a bit immature, I know, even for me, but I was beyond frustrated with life in general.

He rose an eyebrow and calmly turned to face me.

"You don't want me to see you what, cleaning up some blood? I think I can handle that and *try* to salvage what's left of my night."

"I have to dispose of the bodies. To do that, I'll have to get . . . creative."

Having watched the show *Dexter* a time or two, my stomach did flips. "Creative, how?"

Marcus sighed, peering up at the ceiling. "I'll have to dismember them."

And now my stomach sped into somersaults and pole vaults. "I'll go to work." I bit down on my lower lip. "Wait a minute. No. No. I'm not leaving some vampire in my apartment."

"The longer we stand here talking, the more blood sinks

into the floorboards." He glanced around, unenthused with the surroundings. "I promise I will not cause any damage to your charming abode."

My jaw dropped. "And now you're insulting my home?"

He raised his brow.

I clicked my tongue against the back of my teeth. "Okay. Fine. It's a dump, but a dump that puts a roof over my head, and that's all I need. I'm easy to please."

"Are you now?" the lion purred with a sensuous grin.

Pointing, I said, "Don't do that."

"Freya," he beseeched a bit more sternly.

I groaned, turning around. "What?" I yelled, clenching my fists at my sides.

"May I have that back?" He nonchalantly pointed to the phone in my hand.

I looked at the cell and held it out to him. He slipped it from my grasp. Rolling my eyes, I turned back to the closet, grabbing the first pair of pants and shirt I saw.

"I don't care if you've yet to have dinner, you need to get here now. We've got a cleanup. Tell the others," Marcus spoke into his cell phone, and I pretended not to listen while buttoning my jeans in the bathroom. I barely recognized myself in the mirror, the bags under my eyes doing nothing for my appearance, but I was too frazzled to care.

As I exited the bathroom, Marcus stood, plugging something into his cell, and glanced over at me. "I ordered you a car."

I walked past him, unsettled the sight of the bodies started to bother me less and less. Grabbing my pack of nicotine gum, and keys, I turned to look at him. "A car? It's only a few blocks away."

"A few blocks is plenty of time for someone to attack you. You have to be careful now more than ever." He slipped the phone back into his pocket.

I pursed my lips together, feeling imprisoned. "Fine. Seriously, do not touch a thing in here. No rummaging through my underwear drawer or anything." The keys jingled when I shoved them in my pocket.

He half smiled, running a hand through his tree-bark-colored hair. "I'll try to resist."

When I reached outside, a black town car that looked like a mini limo awaited me. I didn't know why I expected a taxi. Should I have really been surprised? I felt extremely underdressed. Not like I owned anything that would complement the snazziness anyway. A man in a black jacket exited the car and walked around to the back-passenger side door, opening it for me. I folded my hands together to keep myself from fidgeting. Taking one last glance up at my window, Marcus's form casting a silhouette against the curtains, I hoped I wasn't making a huge mistake.

It took us all of five minutes to reach the bar, but no one busted out the car window and abducted me, so I had that going for me. I offered an awkward wave to the driver and stood on the sidewalk staring up at the neon After Midnight sign. Everything that had happened in the past few days started to weigh heavy on my shoulders like a gorilla. Forget a monkey. Taking a deep breath, I walked inside, immediately turning away from the bar.

"Freya!" Rose's voice boomed across the room.

So much for sneaking in.

She bounced over, yellow notepad and pen in hand. "What are you doing here? Isn't it your night off?"

I gripped her arm, pulling her over to a less inhabited corner. "A group of guys, I have no idea who or what they were, busted into my apartment tonight trying to kill me."

Rose's eyes widened, her grip on the tablet so harsh it crumpled the top page. "Jesus, Frey. Are you okay?"

"Marcus is there cleaning up his . . . mess. That's why I'm here."

"Wait a minute. Marcus? Marcus is in your apartment? Why?"

I stiffened, still uneasy about him being there. "He showed up right before they got there. I didn't get a chance to find out why."

She bit the inside of her mouth, folding her arms. "Uh huh. Pretty convenient he was there in time to save you."

His timely appearance hadn't crossed my mind, and my face fell to my feet. "You think he—that he set it up?"

"Girl, I wouldn't put anything past anyone anymore. Just yesterday I find out all this time you've been telling the truth about vampires. What's next, werewolves?" She scoffed.

I stared at her, wide eyed. Should I tell her? Tomorrow. I'd tell her tomorrow.

"Anyway, I'm on break, wanna hear what I found out?"

My thoughts were anywhere but in the present moment. "Found out?"

She playfully tapped my forehead with her forefinger.

"Yeah. Remember you asked me to look stuff up on your fanged beings?"

Nervously, I laughed. "Right! Yes, absolutely. Tell me everything."

We situated ourselves at a nearby table, and she whipped out her cell phone. Her thumb swiped up and down, the light from the screen reflecting against her dark eyes.

"Apparently, though they don't know the exact year, the first vampire dates back to thousands of years BC. We're talking like mythological times here."

I'd only been half listening, slipping my own phone from my pocket. While she spoke, I'd found Damian's name and typed: Vamps in my apartment. 452 32nd St Apt 2314. I licked my lips, staring at the message, going over every encounter I'd had with Marcus thus far.

"Frey, are you even listening to me?"

I jolted in my chair. "Vampires date back to mythological times," I said, monotone.

"How are you not more fascinated by that? I wonder how old Marcus is. . . ." Her voice trailed off before her thumbs began furiously typing.

My own thumb hovered over the send button. Frustrated, I turned off the screen and slammed the phone onto the table. Honestly, why should I trust Damian at this point either? I furiously rubbed my hand across my forehead.

Rose's eyes remained downward, glued on her phone screen. "So, I didn't really find anything about how to kill a vampire aside from the usual junk. Wooden stake, sunlight, be-heading."

Killing Marcus. That's what I needed to focus on right now. "So basically you're saying our only options are to lure a really old vampire into going tanning or somehow lop off his head?"

"Or starvation? I read somewhere if a vampire goes long enough without blood, they sort of wither away." She shrugged.

I was a bit taken aback at how unusually casual she made the conversation. "Great, so we trap him in a cave or something. Simple enough." Sighing, I leaned against the back of my chair and stared at the ceiling.

"Hey." Rose's hand touched the top of mine.

I lifted my head, blowing out a puff of air, which caused some of my hair to fall in my face, and I left it there.

"We're going to get through this. As insanely messed up and crazy as it is. I keep pinching myself to make sure I'm not dreaming this all up." She half smiled, patting my hand.

"If this ended up being a dream, it would be the singular best thing that has happened to me in a decade." She frowned. "Except for you, of course."

A woman entering the bar caught my attention, and my eyes narrowed into slits. She was the tall, bleached-blonde vampire who called Marcus her "liege" the other night. I groaned under my breath, pushing away from the table.

Rose looked at the woman I'd been staring daggers into. "Who's that?"

"Another damn vampire, that's who." I grabbed my cell phone.

"Her? She looks like a supermodel." Rose cocked her head from side to side.

I glared at her over my shoulder. "Not helping."

"Today is a touchy day. Got it." Rose held her hands up defensively.

As I approached the blonde vampire, she spotted me and crossed her arms. "Oh, good, you're actually here. Saves me the trouble from traipsing around town making sure you're not doing anything idiotic."

"Why are you here?" I put my hands on my hips. A power move and I was freaking Batgirl.

"Marcus sent me to babysit you."

Figured. "Well, you can go on back to whatever hole you crawled out of. Things are handled here."

Her face appeared in front of mine, her hand wrapping around my throat. "Let me clarify something for you. The only reason I haven't killed you is because for whatever reason, Marcus deems your life important. Otherwise, I would bleed you dry." Her words melted off her tongue like spider venom.

I imagined that threat would've been accompanied by fangs if it weren't for the public setting.

She had a nose ring, a single loop in the center going from one nostril to the other, making her look like a raging bull. "Funny, Marcus said nothing to me about not killing *you*." Making it discreet, I removed the stake I'd hid in my pants and let the point of it poke her in the belly.

She glanced down, letting her hand slip from my neck, smirking. "You are to stay here until it's clear to leave. I'll be around." She flicked her wrist in the air, brushing past me, making sure to collide her shoulder into mine.

Gritting my teeth, I removed my cell once again. Pressing the delete button several times, I edited my previous message to Vamp at After Midnight. This time, I didn't hesitate to press the send button.

# CHAPTER 7

It didn't take long to receive a response from Damian. "Be there in 5."

Short, simple, and to the point. I smiled to myself, slipping the phone back into my pocket, and proceeded to walk around as if werewolves were not about to arrive. Whistling, I clapped my hands together lazily and found a wall, leaning against it. The blonde She-Devil, who had yet to share her name, perched herself in a corner, already talking up a male customer. I tensed, assuming she was checking out her menu for the night. *Not tonight, girly.*

My attention swayed to the door swinging open. It slammed into the wall, nearly splintering, and Damian stormed inside, chest heaving, fists clenching. The She-Devil shot up from her seat, clenching her own fists. Shit! Clearly, this had been a very bad idea. Leaping into action before they caused a scene, I ran over to Damian, pressing my palms into his chest. Good lord, he felt like a concrete pillar.

"Easy there, buddy. You really going to do this now? In here?"

I wasn't sure why I thought I'd stand a chance stopping a werewolf from walking forward, yet I still tried. He pushed at my hands like a linebacker, and my feet slid across the floor.

"It shouldn't be here. Stand back and we'll handle this." A low growl escaped from the back of his throat, his eyes growing increasingly yellow. That couldn't be good.

"Damian!" I yelled, punching my fists into his chest.

He snarled, turning his attention to me, and I felt my soul screaming. Frankie stepped from behind him, followed by a panicked Romeo, who they had eased right past.

"Did you not call us to exterminate vermin?" Frankie asked, lips curling back, and the nails on her hands growing larger.

This is what I got for acting on selfish impulse. "I called you because I don't trust what she'll do—I didn't call you to kill her. At least not right now . . . I mean I don't know." I peered around the tower that was Damian's body, eyeing Romeo, who stared wide eyed. "It's alright, Romeo. We were just about to take this *outside*." I attempted to growl the last word right back at the wolf and that got Frankie's attention. "Pretty please? You can smack talk to your howling heart's content, but not in here."

Damian let out a huff, pointing over my head at the blonde vamp. Her lips curled into a devilish grin, the slightest hint of fang, and she disappeared into the darkness. Damian and Frankie turned around so quickly my hair flew into the air. I was about to follow him when a hand gripped my arm.

"Freya, what's going on?" Rose asked, her eyes searching my face.

"I'll explain everything later. Right now, I need to stop a blood bath I accidentally, er, purposely caused." I ground my teeth together, ignoring Rose's perplexed expression and sprinted outside.

Once past the door, I frantically looked around.

"Do you have any idea how long it has been since I spilled wolf blood?" I heard the She-Devil's voice from a nearby alleyway.

When I rounded the corner, Damian and Frankie stood to one side, hands opened and tensed. She-Devil stood in a similar position, her fangs fully extracted, hissing.

For the love of— "Hey!" I shouted, moving myself between the two sets of supernatural beings.

"I'm going to rip your arms from your body and wear them like a shawl," Frankie said, inching her way closer.

My nose wrinkled. Um, graphic. They all acted as if I were about as invisible as cellophane. "We agreed on talking! Not dismembering!"

"For the last time, this doesn't concern you," Damian spat before he morphed into a huge black wolf, eyes the color of mustard and paws as big as my head.

I'd have taken a moment to process what I just witnessed, but he pounced toward She-Devil, his side launching into me as he leaped past. The impact felt like Superman punching me in the rib, and I fell back, my ass meeting concrete.

Struggling to catch my breath, I remained on the ground

and watched Frankie morph into an amber-eyed wolf, her snow-white coat sleek, shiny, and angelic. Her size slightly smaller than Damian's but still massive when compared to a normal wolf. They were the yin & yang of werewolves. She-Devil laughed, a blood-curdling cackle that would make ghosts wail in agony, and she moved so quickly my mere human eyes couldn't track her.

The wolves and vampire began to hack, slash, and bite at each other. Were they out of their minds? I couldn't imagine if someone peered into this alley right now. Grunting, I hoisted myself to my feet, gripping my side. That hit was going to leave a nice grapefruit-sized bruise. I pressed my back into the stone wall, the three of them rolling by in a fit of snarls, almost tumbling into me again.

The She-Devil let out a scream. The wolves had each of her arms trapped within their mighty jaws, pinning her. I winced, watching the blood ooze down her biceps, and wondered how they hadn't bit clean through. She growled like a grizzly bear, grabbing onto Frankie's neck and tossing her away like a garbage bag full of packing peanuts. She slammed into the wall right near my head, letting out a high-pitched yelp.

I looked around for a blunt object amidst the rubble surrounding the nearby dumpster. Settling on a wooden pallet, I scooped it into my palm and held it up, waiting for Damian to turn his head. He became momentarily distracted by Frankie's distressed shriek, and I smacked the pallet straight into the back of his skull. In the blink of an eye, my back was on the ground, his massive paws pressing onto my shoulders, bruising me. His snout dipped into my face, lips curled back, revealing large white canines the size of my fist. He snarled, drool dripping down and straight onto my cheek.

I grimaced, feeling paralyzed from his weight. "What the hell is wrong with you? Get off of me!"

His snarl only intensified. It was as if he had no idea who I was. The pressure on my shoulders disappeared, his body flying away and into the same wall Frankie had the pleasure of meeting only moments ago.

She-Devil stood above me, snatching me up from the ground. "We need to go before they wake up." The gnarled bite marks on her arms closed themselves up until only blood stains remained.

"What? No! We can't leave them here unconscious." I ripped away from her grip, but she appeared in front of me, grasping my shoulders.

"Are you really that much of an imbecile? I don't know what your relationship with werewolves is, but in that form all you are to them is a threat. We need to go *now*." Her eyes were intense, staring me down, fighting back the urge to snap.

"I'll leave, but I'm sure as shit not leaving with you." I pried from her grasp; her grip so tight her nails scratched me as I turned away.

Again, she appeared, blocking my way. "We can do this the easy way or the hard way. And I do so hope you choose the hard way."

My jaw squared. "Go to hell."

Her lips bent down to my ear and she whispered, "We're already there."

A sharp pain blasted into the back of my head and my entire world went black.

I moaned, blinking, my vision struggling to focus. The pain in my skull hit me like a tidal wave, followed by the sharp sting in my side, and it all started to come back to me. Werewolves and a blonde ho-bag knocking me out to take me—where was I? I most definitely was not in my apartment. A huge flat screen TV hung on the wall in front of me, surrounded by cranberry-colored couches. To my left there was a cocktail bar, the bar top made completely of glass and bordered by soft white lights.

I looked down, tracing my fingers down the abstract design of the comforter I sat on. The bed was huge. Had to have been king sized, possibly emperor sized, if they even made that.

"Look who's awake." His voice caused my entire body to tense, which only intensified the pain in my side.

I forced myself not to wince. "Marcus?"

He sat in a brown leather armchair. His legs were spread wide, gray dress pants hugging his thighs as he leaned forward, resting his forearms on his knees. He held a tumbler full of amber-colored liquid between two fingers, the white long-sleeved, button-up shirt causing his pale skin to look even paler. Each sleeve was rolled up to his elbow and the top three buttons of the shirt undone, giving just enough peek at his chest to bate me.

He stared at the tumbler before his glacial eyes shot up, instantly grabbing my gaze. "Why are you communing with werewolves?"

Well, he cut right to the chase, didn't he? "Why is that any of your concern, and where the hell am I?"

Despite the light beard peppered over his chin, I could see his jaw clench. "My hotel room."

My eyes widened, insides screaming. "Your hotel—this is *your* hotel room?"

He stood up, resting the tumbler on the mahogany nightstand by the bed, and shoved his hands in his pants pockets. "Answer me, Freya."

My neck felt clammy, beads of sweat formed on my brow, and I could feel the anger pushing its way through. I scrambled off the bed, ignoring how the entire left side of my body felt like a battered punching bag. "Where do you get off making demands or prying into my life?"

He stood still, his hands balling into fists within his pants, causing his forearms to bulge. "I told you I'd watch over you. I can't do that if you're"—he removed a hand from his pocket, flailing it about—"frolicking around with ignorant canines." His words were clipped and haughty.

I crossed my arms over my chest in a huff. "For your information, they came to *me* with some very interesting news." Okay, it wasn't that interesting, but he didn't know.

He rolled his eyes, sighing. "I highly doubt that."

I'd had just about enough of this and turned for the door. "I'm leaving. And don't get me a car, I'll call a friggin' taxi."

Marcus's hand slammed into the doorframe, his long arm

blocking my exit. "I know all of this is new, so allow me to educate you. When they turn into wolves, they become feral. They have barely any recollection of anyone or anything. If Celeste hadn't been there, they could've easily killed you regardless of your relation."

Celeste. So that was her name. I still preferred She-Devil. "I have a such a sparkling personality. How could they possibly forget me?"

Marcus huffed, his grip tightening on the doorway, causing the veins in his arm to thicken. I quickly looked away. "You cannot trust them."

"Funny, they said the exact same thing about you. Quite frankly, I'm over all of you." I ducked under his arm, turned the doorknob, and let myself out into the hallway.

He turned around, leaning forward, pressing each of his palms into the frame. "Over us or not, you *are* involved. I'm just not sure how yet. Don't be a stubborn mule."

I guffawed. "No. You're the ass here, Marcus. I'm simply an innocent bystander."

Turning away, I made my way down the carpeted hallway. The sound of Marcus's fist slamming into the door echoed off the walls.

Moments later I nestled into the greasy, leather seats of Pittsburgh's finest yellow taxi service. The car smelled like cigarettes, body odor, and pine from the thirteen car fresheners shaped like trees hanging all around the inside of the cab. I stared down at my phone, the white glow from the screen making my eyes squint in the darkness. Working my thumbs against the keypad, I texted Adam.

Me: You still awake?

Adam: Do you know me at all?

Me: Mind if I stay the night?

Adam: Everything ok?

Me: I'll explain when I get there.

Adam: Mi casa, su casa.

Me: Thx.

I pressed the power button with a sigh and leaned my head against the headrest. Regretting that decision given the gross state of the car, I lifted my head back up. I threw the wad of cash at the driver when he pulled up in front of Adam's apartment building.

My finger hovered over the buzzer, but the door popped open before I had a chance to press it. Given my paranoia as of late, I eyed the door as if a troll lived within it.

"Come on up, psycho." Adam's voice resonated from above. His head stuck out the window and he waved.

Smirking to myself, I pushed open the door and made my way upstairs to his place. I no sooner walked in, and not being able to contain myself, blurted, "Werewolves are real too."

His hand froze mid-air, letting the door close on its own. "Were . . . wolves? Werewolves?"

I ran my hands down my face. "Yes. Werewolves. I saw them *morph*. They're huge, mean, drooly." Biting at my cuticles, I stared at the ground, transfixed on both sides telling me not to trust the other.

"Okay. Well, that puts a whole new spin on things." Adam placed one hand on his hip and the other pulled out his cell phone. "What's their weaknesses again? Silver?"

"Please tell me you're not Googling how to kill a werewolf."

"Damn right I am. We need a contingency plan. Are they on our side?"

"I don't know. Both sides keep playing mind games with me. Can I go to sleep and have all of this be gone tomorrow morning?" I flopped onto his orange- and yellow-striped couch, the duct tape repair job in the seat cushion creaking. Groaning, I leaned forward and let my head fall between my knees.

"Here." Adam nudged my shoulder.

Reluctantly lifting my chin, I whined like a five-year-old brat in a toy store. He shoved a steaming mug of something into my hand and plopped down beside me. I gazed into the mug. It had brown-colored liquid with tiny marshmallows. Hot chocolate. Smiling, I lifted the mug to my nose, letting the steam cascade over my cheeks.

"Care to explain what you mean by both sides are messing with your mind?" He grabbed the remote control from the armrest and turned on the TV, sipping a can of Mountain Dew.

I stared at the ceiling, irritation tugging at my spine. "The wolves claim I've gotten in the middle of some paranormal uprising that is brewing, and it has something to do with the vampires. The vampires think I actually have something to do with said paranormal uprising and are pissed I talked to the werewolves." My grip on the mug tightened. "This is my life now, Adam. I am stuck in some crazy movie I can't get out of."

"So we're still unsure if we're Team Werewolf or Team Vampire?"

I ever so slowly turned my head toward him, glaring. "I will pay you to never say the word 'Team' in front of anything ever again."

He smirked. "I was only half joking. If something is about to happen like they all keep letting on, we have to pick a side. You're a badass, Frey, but you're only human."

I sighed, sipping my hot chocolate, then stared at it, mentally connecting the dots with the marshmallows floating in my drink. "I don't want any part of this."

Adam pulled me into a side hug and I instinctually rested my head on his shoulder. "Our lives have always been one step away from a mental asylum, but I'll admit that this takes the cake." He rubbed my arm. "What if you leave town?"

I sat straight up, furrowing my brow. "And abandon you? Abandon Rose? Screw that. If I'm somehow a part of this because of what I did to those fangers years ago, then I'll deal with it."

"You think that's what this is all about? Because you killed some vampires?"

I shrugged, downing the rest of the chocolate, and rested the mug on a nearby folding tray. "It has to be. Why else would I be involved?"

He dragged a hand through his long, greasy locks and then scratched at the blonde stubble on his chin. "True, but why now? Why not years ago?"

I pushed my hands against my knees, taking a deep breath as I stood up. "I have no idea. Damian thinks I am only involved because of the vampires, and Marcus thinks I'm involved for reasons he's unsure of. At least, he says he doesn't know. He could be lying straight through his pointy teeth."

"Are we still killing him?" Adam remained seated, cocking an eyebrow.

"Eventually. For now, I—" I closed my eyes, pretending to vomit in my mouth. "Need him. Need to figure out what he knows, but right now I need sleep."

He motioned with his head behind him. "You can take the bed. I'll sleep on the couch. Want to finish watching this, anyway."

I snickered at the television. "*Lost Boys*? Seriously Adam?"

He shrugged. "What? Could be good research."

A smile managed to tug its way at the corner of my lips. "Goodnight, knucklehead."

"Night, dweeb."

# CHAPTER 8

Reluctantly, I showed up to work the next night. Unlike the movies, randomly missing several days of work in a row was frowned upon in the real world. Even if there *was* a vampire apocalypse brewing. I'd love to see the look on my boss's face if I gave that excuse. A man named Bernie (Or was it Barney?) sat across from me talking about his wife leaving him and taking the dog. At least that's what I gathered from the small part of me that gave a shit. I had far more pressing matters on my brain. Like the fact every ten seconds I'd glance at the entryway waiting for "you know who" to show up.

I was absently cleaning out the same mug I'd been wiping for the past twenty minutes, glaring at the door, when Rose's voice made me jump.

"I need a Jack and Coke." Her eyes widened when my body jerked. "Wow. Jumpy today much?"

I felt my chest to ensure my heart still beat and finally set the mug down, leaning toward her to whisper, "Considering the past couple days I've had, can you really blame me?"

"Frey, you've kind of been MIA the past couple of days. If I were a bitter person, I'd say I was insulted, but I assume you have some good excuse?" She tapped her non-existent fingernails against the bar top, cocking a brow.

Scooping ice into a pint glass, I counted to two, pouring Jack Daniels next, and then topped it off with Coke from the dispenser. "Just dealing with Marcus, with werewolves, the usual deal for me this week." I set the drink on her tray, not noticing at first how she stared at me blankly. Right. Werewolves. Way to go, Freya.

"When the hell did werewolves become real too?"

"Did you want an actual answer to that?" I shifted my eyes left to right.

Her jaw tightened and she leaned toward me. "When were you going to tell me?"

"Today." I was never any good at thinking on my toes when conjuring a convincing lie. "I was going to tell you today."

"Balls. You have a lot of explaining to do after our shift, Freya Johansson." She pointed a finger in my face, whisked the tray into her palm, and walked away, glaring at me all the while.

I winced. She used my full name; that was never good. It was hard to piss off Rose. Could this week, this month, be over already?

"We need to talk."

For the second time that night, I nearly jumped through my skin. Whipping around, I faced Marcus, who sat on an end stool, dressed far more casually then he'd been last time.

Black leather bomber jacket and white V-neck shirt. His hair had that "just got out of bed but I still look fabulous" tussle to it and his blue eyes looked nowhere else but at me.

"Did you even come through the front door?" I ignored his statement, as well as the fear compressing my lungs, making it harder to breathe.

"We don't have time for you to go back and forth on if I am on your side or not. Trust me when I say it is far more dangerous for you to go at this alone." He interlaced his fingers, calmly resting his hands on the bar in front of him as if we were in a corporate meeting.

"Go at *what* alone, Marcus? Part of what makes me mistrust you is the fact you're so cryptic about everything. That and you could kill me in an instant." Hiding a shaky breath, I turned for the cooler, grabbing stool number three another can of Genny Light.

"What will it take to get you to trust me?" He ran a hand through his chestnut hair, and it fell messy in a perfect frame around his face.

Every time I did that my hair looked like a bird's nest.

I snorted. "An act of Congress." Slapping a rag onto the bar top right in front of him, I furiously began scrubbing, hoping he'd get the hint and leave.

Instead, he glanced over his shoulder and then back to me. "How good are you at pool?"

Considering I'd played a game nearly every night with the other employees, I'd say I was a regular Black Widow. "Decent." I clucked my tongue against the inside of my cheek. "Why?"

"I'll make you a bet. Beat me at pool, and I will walk away from your life forever. You will never see me nor hear from me again."

Color me intrigued, but there was always a catch. "And in the off chance you win?"

His gaze dropped to my neck before lifting to my eyes. "I get to taste you."

One second I paused. Only one. "No friggin' way. Nope. How could you ask me that knowing what I've been through?" I turned to walk away, and his hand launched out like a cobra strike, lightly grasping me.

"I told you we are not all as mindless and maniacal as those you encountered. I wish to prove that to you. And only if I win. If you're such a Black Widow with billiards, what are you afraid of?" The corner of his lips curved upward ever so slightly, and he stared at me, a challenge in his eyes.

Damn him. And how had he used the exact same reference I'd thought? Looking toward the pool table, I knew I had a good chance at beating him and ridding him from my life. He had no idea the hours I'd put into perfecting my game. "Fine. You have a deal."

He released his grip on my arm, smiling. "When are you free?"

"Give me a few minutes. It'll be my lunch break."

"I'll go make sure no one else takes the table." He made his fangs extract briefly, grinning all the while.

I squinted. "That's not funny."

He chuckled, retracting the pointy teeth, rose from his stool, and gracefully made his way over to the pool table.

With his ripped jeans and clunky black boots, he almost looked like a biker.

I topped my customers off with another round of drinks, wiped my hands on the nearest rag that happened to be wet (figured), and wiped my now damp hands on the front of my pants. As I made my way toward the pool table, Rose followed me with her eyes. She talked to a customer but still gave me a curious quirk of her brow. I jutted with my head toward the table, which caused her brow to arch even higher.

Marcus had racked the balls into the wooden triangle, and been expertly setting them when I walked over to the wall of cue sticks. He bent down, staring at the table from eye level to ensure all balls were even with one another. My nerves were slightly rattled. It was obvious he'd done this before. Grabbing my favorite stick, I turned around, flicking my hair over my shoulder. Marcus stood straight, eyes darting to my now exposed neck, and his nostrils flared.

"Dream on, Fang Boy." I chalked my stick, not gratifying him with a glance.

He leaned onto the table, pressing his palms into the polished wood. "Oh, come on now. You're more creative than that."

I shrugged. "With you I just seem to lack inspiration." I fluttered my eyelashes, resting the butt of the stick on the floor. "I'll give you a head start and let you break." Winking, I leaned part of my weight onto the stick, grinning at him like the sassy spider I was.

He nodded once, standing upright, and positioned his stick, leaning over the table with the grace of the lion I had officially associated him with. "What blood type are you? AB positive?"

The stick made a crisp *thwack* sound, colliding into the cue ball that sent all other balls flying. Two solids found their homes in opposite pockets, and a lump formed in my throat.

I stood up, not leaning onto the stick anymore, and he brushed past me to set up his next shot. He leaned toward me, sniffing the air. "No. AB negative. How rare."

My heartbeat increased. This thing knew my blood type from smelling me. Was I really that much of an idiot to bet him? He grinned, exposing some fang which pinched his lower lip, and shrugged off his leather jacket. He hung it on a peg behind me, and I tried not to eye his exposed, muscular arms that before tonight I hadn't seen.

He continued to look at me and pointed toward a corner pocket. "Back left." He then bent over, lined up the shot, and in it went. He had four more to go and I still had all seven. Sweat started to collect at the base of my neck. He moved around the opposite side of the table, eyeing the remaining balls like juicy gazelles grazing in an open field. "Back right." He bent over to take his next shot, and right when he slid the stick forward, Rose walked up.

"And just what is going on here?" She put her hands on her hips, looking down at the table.

Marcus grunted, barely grazing the cue ball, and it rolled forward a few inches.

Bless Rose and her glorious timing.

He stood up in a huff, tapping the rubber end of the stick against the floor. "Isn't it obvious?"

She crossed her arms over her chest and raised a single finger. "I'd watch how you talk to me. I still haven't been told *not* to kill you and there's a whole wall of ammunition." She pointed at the rows of wooden cue sticks.

He glared at her and took a step back, allowing me to step up and sink a few—hopefully.

I stepped between them. "Now, now, Rose. We're just playing a friendly, civilized game of pool here." Bending over, I lined up my shot. "Back left *and* right."

That's right. Trick shot. I had some catching up to do. And just like that, I sunk them both.

Marcus smirked, standing tall, holding the stick with one hand folded over the other. "Impressive."

I'm not sure why I did, but I sauntered past him, making my way to the other side of the table. "You have no idea."

He dragged the tip of his thumb along the underside of his bottom lip, squinting. "I'm beginning to gather." So the lion purred.

Rose smiled, bouncing back and forth on the balls of her feet. "Get him, Freya!" Ever my cheerleader.

I proceeded to do just that, making the cue ball hop over one of Marcus's to launch my own into a side pocket. Continuing to prove I was as good as I claimed, I sunk another three balls and had but one ball left on the table.

"One more and the eight ball and you never have to see me again." He stood in the exact same spot the entire time, with his legs spread wide, arms tensing every time I'd sunk a ball.

"Wait a minute. You guys have a bet on this game?" Rose scrunched her face.

I bit my lip, breathing shakily, and bent over the table, eyeing the last ball directly in front of the eight ball. Given just the right pressure I could launch the cue ball into the eight ball and use it to sink the ball I needed without going into the pocket itself. Tricky, but nothing I hadn't done before.

"Freya, what did you bet?" Rose stepped up beside me.

I glared at her, pausing in my poised position with the stick in hand. "Rose, I'm trying to concentrate."

She ground her teeth and changed her focus to Marcus, marching over to him. "You son of a bitch. What did she bet you?"

I chanced a glance over at the two, seeing Marcus raise a single finger to his lips to silence her. Taking a deep breath, I launched the cue ball. It collided into the eight ball, and it ever so lightly bumped the last remaining ball into the pocket. I stood up straight, laughing, and looked over at Marcus triumphantly. He grinned at me. It was when I heard the sound of a second ball falling into the pocket I felt the contents of my stomach gurgle. I scratched. Marcus won. He—won.

My arms felt so numb I couldn't tell if I still held on to the stick, and I had to sit on the edge of the table to keep from collapsing. He stepped up to me, dropping his face near mine, his lips centimeters from my ear lobe.

"Your place or mine?" he whispered, and it sent a shiver down my neck.

I gulped. "M—mine. Give me fifteen minutes."

He nodded once and retrieved his jacket from the wall. "I'll meet you there."

Rose's already large eyes grew even wider, bulging from

CARLY SPADE

her skull. "What the hell did you bet him, Freya?"

I felt like I was having an out-of-body experience, Rose's voice distant. Glancing at the table, I willed the eight ball to still be there, but it wasn't. I'd taken the risk and I lost. Now I held onto the shred of hope Marcus was the vampire he kept claiming to be and didn't drain me dry in my own apartment. I absently rested the stick on the table.

"Hey." Rose's hand gripped my shoulder and forced me to face her. "What. Did. You. Bet. Him?"

For a brief moment, I toyed with the idea of lying to her, but I hadn't the strength to think of a good one. "To let him feed on me."

She stared at me, her grip tightening on my shoulder. "Are you out of your mind?"

I threw her hand away. "I have to do this, Rose. He could've killed me numerous times by now. This is a way for him to truly prove himself, right?"

"At what cost? What if he's a lying asshole who wants to guzzle every last ounce of your blood?"

"Trust me on this. Please. Can you cover for me for the rest of the night?"

Her mouth fell open. "You're seriously going through with this."

"I love you. I'll call you tomorrow." I kissed her on the cheek and didn't give her time to protest any further.

***

I waited in my apartment, pacing back and forth, biting what bit of thumbnail I had left. A light *whoosh* came from the side window, and I turned to see Marcus lifting the pane and crawling his way in. Terror gripped me too solidly to wonder how he'd got up there in the first place.

I stood frozen, watching him stalk toward me.

When we stood toe to toe, I gazed up at him, and with a shaky hand I pulled my hair away from my neck and cocked my head to one side. "Just get it over with."

A sinister smile slid over his lips. He let his knuckles drag across the side of my head, my cheek, and finally my exposed neck. His other hand pressed into the middle of my back, coaxing me closer to him.

He dipped his face near mine, the tip of his nose brushing against my earlobe. "You don't have to be afraid of me, Freya."

My insides clenched, butterflies beating against my stomach. "And you made no mention of foreplay in our bet."

I felt his lips brush my skin when he smirked. "Would you rather me yank your hair and sink my fangs in? That defeats the purpose, doesn't it?"

My insides clenched even tighter. I had tilted the unscarred side of my neck toward him and resisted when his hand gently tilted my head the other way.

He dragged his fingertip against my scar and I hissed, "Not there, Marcus."

He pressed his cheek against mine, the feel of his ice-cold skin against the fever pooling in my face almost calming. "Shhh. Trust me."

I winced, preparing myself for the pain I'd felt the last

time a vampire claimed my neck. It stung at first, the feeling of two sharp objects sinking into my flesh. But unlike before, the pain only lasted a second before an overwhelming sense of calm rippled through me. I went limp in his arms, and his grip on my back tightened, holding me to him. My blood pooled against his lips, and I felt the occasional swipe of his tongue over my neck, coupled with his nose nuzzling my skin. I couldn't hear anything else save for the air escaping my lungs, my quickening heartbeat, and the subtle sound of suckling.

He groaned, his lips vibrating against my neck. His one hand massaged the back of my head while the other supported my weight, cradling me. The moment felt far more intimate than I could've anticipated. His bite far from predatory. He fed on me like I was his singular source of life. The feelings soon melted away, his fangs and lips disappearing.

I suppressed a whimper, already missing the euphoria I'd felt. Blinking and willing my vision to focus, I realized I was in his arms and stood upright, trying to regain my composure. He kept his hand on the back of my head, eyes searching mine. Somehow, his eyes had grown even bluer. The corners of his lips were stained with my blood. He licked it unflinchingly and I gulped.

With reluctance, he let his hands fall away, still staring down at me as if waiting for me to say something. There was no way in hell he'd ever know what he'd just done to me. The feelings it aroused. I'd never give him the satisfaction.

He lifted a finger to one of his fangs, pricking it. I furrowed my brow, watching him and wondering what he was up to now. He brought the finger toward my neck and I recoiled.

"May I?" He raised his eyebrows and didn't wait for a response, smearing the blood bead on his finger over the area he'd bitten. "My blood can heal humans."

I dragged a hand over my neck. No puncture wounds, and astonishingly—no more scar. The painful memory of my past erased in the blink of an eye. It wasn't just about the scar though, this moment right here in my living room had thrown my entire world off its axis. I stared up at him, letting my hand rest on my neck, almost protectively.

"A gift. You taste like nothing I've ever had before." His eyes burned with longing and my stomach fluttered.

I took a deep breath and exhaled shakily. "Hope you had your fill, because it's never happening again."

I squared my jaw. Had that been the truth? I was having a hard time even convincing myself.

He bit down on his lip. "Fair enough."

"Marcus, if you can heal scars, why do you still have one over your eye?"

When he opened his mouth to answer, the front door of my apartment shattered into a dozen pieces.

# CHAPTER 9

I barely had time to look toward the door before Marcus's looming form stood in front of me. His arm reached behind him curling me against his body, his fangs extracting.

"Step away from her, vampire." Damian's voice boomed.

I tried stepping from behind Marcus despite his hand trying to coax me back.

"Damian? I sure hope you're a damned carpenter." I kicked at one of the wooden shards that used to be my door.

Damian narrowed his eyes, air puffing from his nostrils, and he clenched his fists. Frankie soon followed in behind him, eyes already turning yellow.

"Don't you dare change." I pointed a finger in her direction, her teeth and nails slowly morphing.

"We saw this thing crawling through the window." Damian sneered at the floor like he'd been about to spit at Marcus.

Marcus growled behind me. He stepped forward, his arm brushing against mine. "Do you have any idea what I could do to you?" He sniffed the air. "You're but a puppy by comparison."

Oh, great. So much for trying to defuse the situation.

Damian's forearms tightened. "Can't remember seeing a vamp with a beard before. Secretly pining to be a were?"

Marcus chuckled. "That's what you got? Mocking my affinity for facial hair?"

Damian's eyes dropped to me, but to my dismay he stared at something from the corner of his eye. He whipped my hair over my shoulder, spying the blood stain on my shirt near my neck, and fumed. "Did he feed on you?"

Frankie lurched forward going into full transformation mode, and without thinking, my hand launched forward, grasping her by the throat. She stopped, eyes ablaze and fixed on me. "I said *don't* change." I let go, hoping she didn't rip my head off on the spot. That was bold, even for my taste, but I'd had just about enough of this.

Frankie reverted back to her normal human form, grasping her neck and snarling. She glanced up at Damian as if seeking approval to tear me open, but he gave none, only staring down at me.

"It isn't your business the how or the why of it, but I let him."

Damian returned his glare to Marcus. "Have you brainwashed her?"

My heart fell to my feet. "Can you do that?"

"A vampire's power is unique to the recipient and the one who makes them. I don't possess brainwashing capabilities."

My heart creeped its way back up to my chest.

"So you say," Damian countered.

"I'm certain I would have had her in my bed by now if I

possessed such an ability." He gazed in my direction, curling his lip in a mischievous grin.

Bastard. Right when you think you're starting to somewhat like a guy.

Damian cocked his head to the side. Marcus's reasoning seemed to squelch his skepticism for the moment.

"You need to start talking, wolf." Marcus retracted his fangs and folded his hands in front of him. "Your kind has an alarmingly keen interest in her, and my patience is wearing thin."

"The original vampire. She's coming. We think it has something to do with her—we're just not sure what." He referenced me with his hand like referencing a painting on the wall.

"Original vampire? What's he talking about, Marcus?" I found myself gripping his forearm.

Marcus's face grew grave and he stared at his feet. "Xochiquetzal is what she used to be called during the time of the Aztecs. She's gone by the name Isabela for the past century or so."

"I don't understand what any of this means. What has that got to do with me? Please tell me this isn't some 'Chosen One' thing, or I might honestly hurl." Given everyone's silence, my joke failed miserably.

"My pack has roamed the country for the past decade, investigating this rumor. Her return to the outside world could be catastrophic to immortals, mortals, weres, everyone. When Marcus found you, we thought he worked for Isabela."

"Do you always assume the worst if it involves a vampire?" Marcus's gaze caught fire.

"You're a predator. You hunt all other living things. Of course we do."

"And what do you consider yourself? A vegetarian? If Celeste wouldn't have been there the other night when you turned, you were ready to tear Freya apart." Marcus pushed past me, standing toe to toe with Damian now, fangs returning.

This was starting to get pathetic.

"He was under complete control," Frankie chimed in.

"I didn't think I was talking to you, She-Wolf." Marcus didn't bother looking at her.

I tried to shove my way in between the two tall and imposing alpha males but only managed to squeeze in my arm, grunting. "Would you two stop?"

"What in the Sam Hill happened to my damn door?" My landlord's voice sounded from the now very open doorway.

The entire situation calmed in an instant. Marcus retracted his fangs, Frankie's face softened, and Damian turned around with an eerily calm expression. They all almost seemed . . . normal. Weird. I stumbled from behind Damian and grinned.

"Sid! I am so sorry. My friends and I were kicking back a few brews, then a few turned into a dozen, got a little carried away, and these two decided to rough house." I motioned between both men, trying to act intoxicated. "Boys will be boys, am I right?"

Marcus grunted behind me.

Sid looked skeptically at our merry band of miscreants before eyeing the shattered wood pieces littering the floor. "You know I'm not payin' for this, right? I can bring in a crew, but it's gonna be added to your rent next month." He scratched his belly with his stubby sausage fingers. Sid was a fifty-four-year-old high school dropout, with gray hair that only grew at the sides of his head, a beer belly the size of Texas, and he always wore a stained white tank top. It was questionable on any given day if he'd be wearing pants. Fortunately, today was one of those days.

"That won't be necessary, Sid. Because you see, Damian here can do wonders with a hammer. I mean, do you see these biceps?" I grasped onto one of Damian's arms and couldn't help my eyes widening to the size of beach balls. "Good lord, do you bench press trucks?"

Damian smirked. "The door will be fixed, sir."

Suddenly the wolf was so formal.

Marcus stepped up behind me, his shoulder brushing into mine, and I let my grabby paws fall away.

Sid scratched the pepper-colored stubble on his chin, glancing at the doorway, which only had three lonely pieces of jagged wood on it. "I don't know. This job should be done by a professional."

Frankie sauntered forward, lifting a hand to drag across Sid's tubby face before holding his chin in her palm. "I can assure you he's fit for the job. That door will look better than it did before." She leaned forward, batting her disgustingly lush eyelashes.

Damian's forearm tightened, and I swatted him with my

hand. "Down, boy," I whispered.

Despite the sight giving me the heebie-jeebies, I could tell Sid was falling for Frankie's ploy with every passing second. He gulped, sweat beads forming on his forehead. He unabashedly let his eyes survey Frankie's features, and I had to cross my entire arm in front of Damian to keep him from losing it.

"I, uh, yeah—o-okay, sure. But if it looks shitty, Johansson, it's going to be on you." He pointed a finger at me, took one last peek at Frankie, and left.

Damian stalked forward with a growl. "Was that necessary?"

Frankie smiled up at him, her thin hands cascading over his chest before resting one on each of his shoulders. "It worked, didn't it? Calm down, love. You're mine as much as I'm yours."

Stifling an eye roll, I turned away from the two mated individuals and nearly plowed right into Marcus. I stared at his chest and trailed my eyes upward.

"That was quick thinking on your part." He grinned, dragging a hand through his hair.

"I'm used to it." I placed my hands on my hips, then crossed them, then let them fall to my sides, feeling uncomfortable.

"So you're a survivor, then?"

"Something like that," I muttered before turning away and clapping my hands together. "You all need to make a truce, right now. I don't care if it's temporary or conditional or whatever you want to call it, but we are obviously on the same side, and I can't afford to have my apartment trashed for a third time. So have at it." I stepped back, holding my hands outward.

Marcus's gaze turned on Damian, and they glared at one another for what seemed a solid minute.

"She has—a point." Marcus flicked a piece of lint from underneath his fingernail, clicking his tongue against his teeth.

"I'm willing to make a truce with you and any vampires directly beneath you, but any others we encounter, I won't hesitate to bite their heads off."

I scrunched my nose at that particular visual.

Marcus nodded once. "Fair enough. When you shift, if you or any of your pack threaten me, any of my vampires, or Freya, I will not kill you, but I *will* debilitate you." His fangs popped out.

Damian smirked. "Understood."

Clearing my throat, I stepped up to them. "Well, shake on it. Make it official."

Marcus grinned and Damian squinted. "Who do you thi—" he started, but I cut him off.

"Oh, shake on it already and get it over with."

Marcus extended his hand first, and he may have gained half of a point back for that. Damian rolled his eyes and they shook hands, all while I tried to avoid the sight of both of their forearms flexing.

Frankie laughed, folding her arms over her chest.

"What?" Damian scoffed.

"Nothing. I've never seen the Alpha subdued by a little human girl is all."

Marcus and Damian exchanged glances before Damian turned for the door, grabbing onto Frankie's arm to guide her away.

"I think we all know she's not just any human." Marcus purred.

"That's yet to be determined," Frankie countered, thinning her lips.

My face fumed. "Excuse me?" I took a step forward, the familiar sting at the base of my neck tingling when Frankie smiled at me over her shoulder.

Marcus grabbed my shirt, pulling me backward with little effort. "The truce applies to you too, Hellcat."

Hellcat. I kind of like that.

Damian led Frankie out the door but paused before leaving. "I'll be back in a couple of hours to fix the door." And they were gone.

"So are you going to answer my—" I turned to face Marcus but was met with an empty space.

The wind flapped the curtain from the open window, sending a cold draft throughout the apartment. I rubbed my arms, jogging over to shut it with a sigh.

I flopped down on my couch and leaned my head back, staring at the ceiling. My thoughts were consumed by the feelings Marcus feeding on me had stirred. An act that once repulsed me now caused my stomach to do a fluttery swoosh. Closing my eyes, I trailed my hand over my neck, reliving every second and relishing in the feel of the smoothness that now existed there. Tracing my hand over my collar bone, I bit my upper lip, moaning.

"Frey? What the hell happened?"

My eyes flew open, and I sat straight up with a gasp upon hearing Adam's alarmed voiced. I'd hoped to God he hadn't seen me practically feeling myself up on the couch.

"Jesus! Can you knock?"

He stood in the open doorway with raised brows, holding a grocery bag. "On what? The doorframe?"

I was an official idiot. Slapping my head on my forehead, I stood up. "Right, yeah sorry. Marcus was here and then Damian showed up thinking I was in trouble. It was just a big, fat mess."

Adam stepped inside, eyebrow quirking. "What was Marcus doing here? And Damian is—"

"The werewolf. Come on, keep up here, bud."

I yanked the ponytail holder off my wrist and secured my hair in a messy bun atop my head. Its weight started to feel like a boulder on my shoulders.

"And Marcus was here because?"

I bit at my thumbnail, pining for a cigarette. "Is that relevant?"

Adam shifted his eyes left to right and tossed the bag onto the couch. "Uh, yes. Considering last time we talked you were still unsure about killing him and wanted to know what he knew. None of which ever entailed him hanging out in your apartment."

Staring at him, I avoided the conversation by instantly going on a search for a box of cigarettes. I'd puffed my last one the other night, but maybe there was one hiding somewhere. Opening every drawer in the kitchen, checking between cushions, and underneath the couch, I found absolutely nothing.

He sighed. "What are you looking for?"

"A cig—my uh, my nicotine gum." I remained crouched on the ground, peering under the couch as if a magical cigarette would appear the longer I stared.

"Here."

Lifting my head with a smile, it soon faded into a frown upon seeing the pack of mint gum he held between his fingers.

"What am I supposed to do with that?" Standing, I grimaced at the package in his hand like it was a dog turd.

"Chew on it." He shoved it at me, rather haughtily, I might add.

I opened two pieces with a pout and placed them in my mouth, then sat on the couch.

"Talk, Freya." He widened his stance. Shit just got real.

"I stupidly bet Marcus I could beat him at pool. Somehow I lost and I had to let him feed on me."

*Chomp. Chomp. Chomp.*

"Wait, what? He *fed* on you? As in, he bit you?"

"That's usually how one feeds one's self, yes. Though in his case it was decidedly larger incisors."

"Are you out of your damn mind? Why would you do that?"

I huffed. "You know, I'm getting tired of everyone judging me. I made the bet. I knew the consequences. And you know what? He didn't kill me. He was able to stop, and quite frankly, I think that says a lot."

*Chomp.*

He stared at me. "You've officially gone insane."

"Been called far worse, Adam."

"Why don't you have any bite marks, and—" he blinked, stepping forward, peering down at my neck. "My God. Where's your scar?"

I slapped a hand over my neck, that spot feeling extra vulnerable all of the sudden. "He said his blood can heal humans."

"I have no idea what to say."

My leg bounced nervously. "Did you come over for a reason?"

He shook his head as if clearing away cobwebs and scooped the bag into his hands. "Yeah. It's uh—it's Wednesday. Thought we'd try to finish *Pulp Fiction.*"

I sighed, smiling in relief. "I could use every ounce of normalcy that can be mustered right now. Yes. Let's watch *Pulp Fiction.*"

# CHAPTER 10

I sat on my favorite bench in Schenley Park. Well, my favorite since a few days ago. Damian really had picked a great spot. Staring at the sun setting behind the Pittsburgh skyline, I tried to take a moment of clarity. I'd never been the type to meditate, do yoga or Pilates or whatever other crazy relaxing schemes were out there, but jumbling my head with thoughts? That I was good at.

Last night I managed to stay awake through all the glory Travolta, Jackson, Willis, and Walken could provide. It was just the escape I needed and lasted all of two hours before Damian showed up, as promised, to fix my door.

Adam fixated on him, asking questions like, "What does it feel like when you turn?", "Do you have canine tendencies when you're in human form?", "Can you turn someone into one or do they have to be born into it?"

Surprisingly, Damian humored him the entire time.

It unnerved me I had something to do with this— vampire invasion. Why me? Was it truly because I slaughtered several of them for murdering my family? If the

103

original vampire who started it all came back, it had to have been bigger than that. And why after all this time was she coming back now? So many questions and two hard heads who didn't want to fork over the information.

Irritation boiled in my core when I sensed a presence sitting near me on the bench. There were virtually dozens of other perfectly empty benches, and yet this asshole had to sit right next to me. My leg bounced and I shoved my hands into my jacket pockets.

"I'm sorry. Am I bothering you?" a man's voice cooed.

I eyed him sidelong. A young man, maybe early twenties? He was definitely a decade younger than me, if not more. I noted his sleek, pinstripe suit, shiny dress shoes, slicked back midnight black hair, and a pointy nose that resembled a goblin. Deciding I already didn't like him, I shifted my stance.

"Actually, yes, you are. I quite enjoy sitting alone. There's plenty of other benches."

I made sure to intentionally keep my body facing forward. This was a telltale sign to any normal person that conversation was not only uninvited but frowned upon.

The Goblin laughed, crossing one thin leg over the other. I scrunched my nose, eyeballing him out of the corner of my eye. This guy may have weighed less than me. Further dislike ensued.

"Very true, but this bench has the best view in the entire park. Surely, you're not so selfish to hog it all for yourself?"

I slammed my boots against the ground, hoisting myself to my feet. "The view is all yours, pal." Suppressing a curse word or two, I turned to walk away.

"You have a very unique look to you, you know?"

My face scrunched in confusion and I stared at him over my shoulder. "Who says that?"

"A person who can appreciate it." The Goblin grinned, his dark eyes dancing with a kind of mischief that made me uneasy.

"Okay. You enjoy the view, weirdo."

"I already am." His gaze locked onto me and my pace quickened into a jog.

A body emerged from behind a nearby tree, and my fist flew straight into his face. Pain shot up my arm all the way into my neck.

"Ow," Damian said, rubbing his scruffy chin.

"Ow you? Ow me! You're like punching a cinder block." I shook my hand, grimacing.

"Do you know that guy?" Damian jutted his chin behind me.

"Hell no. And are we going to skirt over the fact you have a tendency to hide behind things?"

Rubbing at my knuckles, I peered over my shoulder. The man still sat there on the bench, staring at me.

Damian's body stiffened, and he pressed a hand into the middle of my back. "Come on, let's get out of here. Sun's down anyway."

"What does that have to do with anything?" And then I stopped, the realization dawning on me. "Wait a minute, are you—are you guys taking shifts?"

Damian sighed, dragging his large fingers through his mousy brown hair. "Why does that surprise you?"

"It's not so much of a surprise as it is insulting. I don't need twenty-four-hour babysitting services." I started walking again, annoyed he and Marcus set up times to keep an eye on me.

"Think of us more as bodyguards. Besides, are you ready to take on a four-thousand-year-old vampire all by yourself? I'd pay to see that."

"Why not? I'll just lop off her head."

He chuckled. "You really are a spitfire."

"Oh? Who called me that?"

"Who do you think?"

I didn't want to dignify that with a response. Pausing again, I grasped Damian's forearm. "Damian, level with me. What do you know? You said you heard my name being passed around. In what context?"

Damian groaned, shifting his eyes before scratching one of his sideburns. "I really shouldn't be saying any of this."

"It's just you and me. I won't tell anyone if you won't."

The corners of his jaw popped multiple times.

"Do you want to pinky swear?" I held up my pinky, raising my eyebrows expectantly.

He smirked, batting my hand away. "We heard your name mentioned in relation to Isabela. That's all."

I threw my arms out. "Which tells me absolutely nothing."

"You sure?" He eyed me suspiciously, as if I were the one hiding something.

I cracked my neck and started walking again. "You people are impossible. The lot of you."

***

He walked me all the way to After Midnight, and as soon as he whisked away, Marcus appeared like a choreographed dance number. He casually leaned against the side of the building, hands in his pants pockets, the sleek leather jacket snug against his form. I gulped, memories of last night flooding my brain like an erupted dam.

Waving awkwardly, I spoke like a mouse. "Hey."

He took a step forward, the streetlights illuminating his face. "Hey."

"I was half expecting you to tap Damian's shoulder to 'tag in.'" Nervous laughter escaped my throat.

"I know you don't approve of us watching you, but it's for your own benefit." He clenched his fists within his pockets, canting his head to the side.

"Yeah, yeah. Do your thing. I'm uh—gonna go inside."

"Alright."

I stood there for a few more beats, unable to make direct eye contact with him. "Alrighty then. Off I go." Finally, I turned for the door and left him to his devices. Whatever bodyguarding a red-headed freakazoid like me entailed anyway.

Rose had barely given me enough time to pass the table near the door before her face shoved into mine. "You. Were supposed to call me."

I slapped my palm against my forehead. "Shit. Ro, I'm so sorry. Everything was—and then Damian showed up and then I—" Considering I was rattling off excuses, I cut myself short. "No excuse."

She thinned her lips and glared, then turned me round and round, examining me. "Well, you're not dead."

I let her look, holding my arms up to give her better access. "Astute observation."

"Seriously, Frey." She flicked her long, ebony locks behind her and then put her hands on her hips. "With everything going on, I'd appreciate being kept in the loop."

"You and everyone else. I got it."

I hopped behind the bar. If there were ever a night I desired to tend to all the drunk morons, tonight would be it. So far, there were only three people taking up the stools. An old woman with long, white hair and skin so tanned and leathery it looked like an alligator hide. A man with a receding hairline, wire-rimmed glasses, and a suit with the tie and top three buttons of his shirt undone. And a younger man with a buzz cut and University of Pittsburgh hoodie on.

"What can I get you all?"

"Another one of these," the man with the receding hairline slurred, holding a tumbler in the air, ice clanking back and forth.

I leaned on the bar top near him. "What's your name?"

The man hiccupped. "Larry."

Larry was clearly having a bad day. "How many of those have you had, Larry?"

"Two?" He shrugged.

I smiled and poured him another drink, but I doused it down with water. Setting it back in front of him, I winked. "This one's half off."

The man slowly blinked. "Well, gee. Wow. Thanks!"

Mr. College Boy swayed in his stool, holding the neck of his beer bottle by two fingers.

"What about you?" I asked, tapping my fingernails on the bar top.

"Isn't it obvious?" He scoffed, waving the Bud Light bottle back and forth in my face.

"So another Bud then with a side of spit?"

His face fell. "You wouldn't."

I shrugged. "How would you know?"

"I'm—I'm sorry, ma'am. It's finals week. I'm in my last year, just a bit stressed."

Biting the inside of my cheek, I opened the fridge, grabbing a bottle. I popped the cap off and set it in front of him, the momentary vapor-like smoke escaping from the top. "On the house." I was in a rather charitable mood today.

"We need to get you out of here, *now*."

Mood squelched.

I turned to see an alarmed Marcus hovering at the end of the bar. "Why?"

"A group just showed up. Damian and a few others are outside holding them off. We need to go." He flipped the top of the bar up, grabbing onto my shoulders.

"Marcus!" He ignored me and started to cart me away. I yanked from his grip. "Marcus! If you think for one second I'm okay with other people fighting my battles for me, you're gravely mistaken."

"Don't argue with me. Not now." Marcus grabbed onto my shoulder with conviction, and I shrugged him away.

"This isn't an argument. I'm going out there with you." I didn't give him a chance to protest further, turning away, hearing Marcus growl behind me in frustration before heading for the door.

"Rose, no matter what, I need you to stay inside until I tell you otherwise. Understand?"

She looked around, confused. "Oookay?"

I patted her arm and jogged over to Romeo by the front doors. "Once I walk out of here, I need you to lock all the doors and not let anyone outside or inside."

He narrowed his eyes. "What's going on?"

"I can't explain it right now, but will you do that for me?"

He gave a firm nod, and I was about to walk outside when Adam walked in.

"Hey!" He smiled, completely oblivious to the entire situation brewing outside.

"You come to the bar, what three times a year, and this is the night you decide to show up?" I said that a bit more exasperated than intended.

"Sorry? I just wanted to hang out."

I grabbed his arm, pulling him inside. "Stay in here, okay? I need to go take care of something."

"Well, I'll help you." He tried to push past me, and I pressed a hand into his chest.

"Adam. Please." I looked at him pleadingly, trying not to fathom the thought of losing him. "Stay here."

He studied my face. "Alright. I hope you know what you're doing."

"Do I ever?" I gave a half smile and ran out the door. The sounds of several locking mechanisms turning sounded behind me.

I ran down the street looking for a group of vampires and werewolves, who shouldn't have been that hard to find. When I rounded a nearby corner, right smack dab in the middle of the intersection, Marcus, Damian, Frankie, Celeste and a few other people I hadn't met yet were standing in front of one, single person. The Goblin from the bench.

"Were you really stupid enough to threaten us alone?" Celeste asked, glancing behind The Goblin at empty space.

He cackled, steepling his fingers. "Of course not. I was merely sent to lure you."

Marcus bit into his wrist. He held the bloody wound in front of my face.

I grimaced at the sight. "What are you doing?"

"Drink."

Staring at the blood oozing out of his arm, I shook my head frantically. "No. No way. Are you out of your mind?"

"Drink before it heals. If you insist on doing this, my blood will make you stronger." His tone demanding, he shoved the wound closer to my lips.

I opened my mouth, nearly gagging as I brought his wrist to my lips. Taking a deep breath, I did as he asked, sucking the blood down my throat. I'd expected the taste of copper but was shocked when it tasted more like . . . dark chocolate. Marcus grunted and pulled his wrist away, his blood trickling down my lips. I wiped my sleeve across my mouth. It wasn't a Popeye moment where I drank the blood and instantly grew muscles bigger than my head, but I definitely felt different. Fearless, even.

Grinning, I stepped up beside Marcus and he turned, pulling his shirt sleeve back over the now healed wound. They slunk from the shadows one by one until seven other beings surrounded the Goblin. They extracted their fangs in almost unison, and I slipped the wooden stake from my boot. Vampires. Splendid.

Damian, Frankie, and another werewolf morphed into wolf form, their clothes resting in piles beneath them. Both sides went on the offensive, the vampires moving so quickly I could scarcely tell whose side was whose. I stood still for a moment, mapping the space. Marcus ripped away one of the opposing vampire's throats with his bare hand. Holy shit. His eyes glowed before he moved on to the next victim.

One of them appeared in front of me, and I ducked when their clawed fingers reached for me. I felt quicker, far more in tune with my body. It had to have been Marcus's blood. Though the vampire's movements cut through the air like a shark hunting its prey, I'd been able to match move for move until finally I found my moment. I slammed the stake into the vampire's chest, hoping he wasn't ancient like Marcus. His body soon ceased to exist, and he remained nothing more than a pile of red goo on the ground. I winced, some of the blood splashing my eyes.

Damian and Frankie weaved through the vampires, timing it just right to pounce and attack their throats when the opportunities arose. Celeste moved with the grace of a ballerina, the blood stains on her mouth and trailing down her chin contrasting her beauty. Another vampire appeared in front of me. This one looked more like a demon than a glorified human. His face was distorted like torn flesh that never healed, eyes red, and instead of only two sharp fangs, he had a full row of pointy teeth. He licked the air in front of him before he launched at me.

He managed to knock me backward, and I landed on the concrete, the stake bouncing from my hand. I backpedaled, moving with the heels of my boots and my palms, but he kicked the stake away. Standing, I looked for another weapon. I spotted a thin piece of metal, but pain shot through my skull. He had a solid grip on my hair and yanked me backward.

"I was told not to kill you, but that doesn't mean I can't get a little taste," he hissed and licked my neck.

Willing my extra strength to support me, I slammed my foot onto his, then threw my elbow backward into his gut. He let go, giving me enough time to grab the metal. When he appeared in front of me again, I let out a battle cry and threw everything I had into a swing at his head. The metal sliced through his neck, lopping his head clean off. I huffed, tossing the metal piece onto his remains.

"Well, look at you," Celeste cooed, eyeing my dirty work.

"Can it, sister." My breathing was shallow despite the magical liquid coursing through my veins.

I hadn't seen the other vampire coming. Hadn't heard his boots scratching against the concrete. It all happened in slow motion, far too similar to the vamp who'd nearly ripped out my throat when I was a child. He pushed me against a nearby wall, pinning me. Despite my extra fervor, his weight felt like a rhino. Panic strangled me and I shut my eyes. I'd expected the pain of teeth sinking into me, but instead I heard Marcus's carnal growl.

I opened my eyes in time to watch the neck of the vampire in front of me disappear in a spray of red. Marcus stood there now, hands and face coated in fresh blood, shoulders rising and falling in fury. Looking down, I saw that I too was covered in blood, the sight not as alarming to me as it once was.

Marcus turned while the last remaining vampire attempted to run away. The ancient vampire appeared beside him, hand wrapped around his throat as Marcus held him in the air. The Goblin.

"Why are you after her?" Marcus shook the vampire violently.

The Goblin let out a gurgled cackle. "You honestly think I'd tell you?"

"I can crush your skull like a cockroach."

The Goblin cackled once more. "Her life . . . is the key to everything."

"Enough with the riddles," Marcus roared.

"That's all I am saying, Roman." The Goblin wriggled his fingers in the air.

Roman?

Marcus lowered him back to his feet and glowered down at him. "You tell Isabela she's not getting a hair from her head. Do you understand me?"

"Absolutely." He held back another cackle, and when Marcus let him go, he vanished into the night.

"What do you think he meant by that?" Damian's voice boomed.

My eyes bulged, taking in Damian's naked form. My gaze trailed below his waist, shot back up to his face, and then trailed right back down again.

"You do realize you're naked?" I asked and was completely ignored.

"It means she doesn't get near that witch, that's what." Marcus spat, dusting off his hands. He looked over at Damian and then grimaced. "Put some clothes on, wolf."

Damian snorted, scooping his clothes into his hand. I looked away when Frankie walked up beside him in her own birthday suit. Celeste approached me, her hands on her hips.

"You were somewhat good until you know, you almost died." She smirked, swaying her body back and forth.

I was about to answer with some form of witty response when Marcus stepped between us. He pointed at my face. "You're rusty."

"Well, thank you, Captain Obvious."

"If you want to be a part of this, of *all* of this, we're training. Starting tomorrow." He stared down at me, and I couldn't tell if the scowl on his face was anger or concern. Maybe both.

In an attempt to hide my growing embarrassment, I gave a meager nod. "Aye, aye Cap'n."

# CHAPTER 11

Amidst the piles of mangled vampire corpses, the realization hit me. This was happening whether I wanted it or not. I should've known better than to think it was over. Can anyone who's had an encounter with a vampire truly say it's over, even if they never ran into one again?

"Freya," Marcus's voice called for me.

I walked over to him as he stood up from surveying one of the deceased.

He opened his mouth as if to speak but looked taken aback once he saw me. "Oh, I was just about to come get you."

Didn't he *just* call out to me? Odd. "What's up?"

He eyed me curiously, squinting before he spoke. "I need you to go inside and keep them occupied. No doubt they've all got restless. We need time to clean this all up."

"How long are we talking here?"

"As long as it takes," Celeste uninvitingly chimed in, grinning. "Unless you'd like to try and explain the several piles of steaming cherry pie goo all throughout the street?"

She picked up what looked to be the remnants to part of an intestine and let it drop. It made a gurgling sound once it landed on top of the rest.

My mouth formed an "O" shape, and I held out my hand, ready to rant about what her problem was, but Marcus quickly intervened. "Please? Do a little human PR for us?"

I sighed, acting like this favor was putting a plane-sized dent in my plans for the evening.

"Fine. You're lucky Rose is in there. If anyone can convince an entire establishment of people to stay put, it's her."

He pressed his palms together, bowing his head. "Thank you. Your services will not go unrewarded."

The streetlamp glinted off one of his fangs when he grinned, and it made my throat constrict. I waved him off, masking the reaction, and turned for the door.

"Remember. Tomorrow night. We train. Meet me at my hotel room," he yelled across the street.

Clenching my fists, I turned on my heel. "Would you care to say that any louder?"

He shifted his eyes. "Meet me at my—" he started, much louder than last time, but I held up a hand.

"I got it. I got it! Sundown. I'll be there." I risked one final glance at his amused expression before I walked back into the bar.

I knocked on the door, pressing my ear to it. "Romeo, it's me. Let me in."

It creaked open and I slid through, shutting the door and locking it behind me.

"All good?" Romeo's deep baritone echoed off my very soul. His demeanor was calm until his eyes dropped to my shirt. His massive hands gripped my shoulders. "Jesus! Are you—"

"Not mine." After patting his hand, I held up two fingers. "I need a few more moments."

Rose stood in a corner, her arms held out to the sides, eyebrows raised. Adam surprisingly sat at the table near her like they'd been having a civil conversation.

I walked up to Rose, lowering my voice. "I need to keep these people distracted for a little while longer. Any ideas?"

She stared at my face and panned down to my shirt. "Is any of that blood yours?"

What big deal was blood after the chaos that transpired outside? "No. Just bad vamp blood. Focus here. Any thoughts?"

She grinned rather maniacally. "Absolutely." She climbed onto the table and cupped her hands around mouth. "Everyone! The next round is on the house!"

Cheers spread throughout the establishment, arms raising into the air, followed by the occasional belch.

I grabbed onto the back of her shirt and yanked her back down to reality. "Are you crazy? Do you want to get us fired?"

Rose smirked, reaching into the front of her shirt, and removed a piece of paper. "Relax. I may or may not have saved Marcus's credit card number. He's got one of those cards with no limits. I doubt he'll even notice." She turned, marching straight for the cash register.

"Did she say she stole Marcus's credit card?" Adam asked, rising from his seat.

I rolled my eyes and stormed after her, Adam right on my heels. Her fingers flew across the touch screen, and I leaned half my body onto the bar top, attempting to pry the paper away. "Why did you write down his credit card number, Ro?"

"This was back when we were on the 'kill Marcus' train." She glanced over her shoulder. "Is that train still chugging along, by the way?"

Flopping onto a stool, defeated, I flicked my hair from my face. "It's not derailed; it's temporarily down due to maintenance."

She turned back to the register. I knew that look. It was the look of "Whatever you say, sweetie." I hated it.

"So how was it out there?" Adam asked.

"Gory and unbelievable." I stared into my palms.

"Oh, come on. If you're not going to let me go out there, at least give me some details. Did you see the wolves shift?" He scooted to the edge of his stool, nearly falling off of it.

Cocking an eyebrow, I took note of his eagerness. "Yes."

"Well, what did it look like?" He nodded emphatically. "Did they have to take their clothes off first? Or did they just rip into shreds?"

"They're not the friggin' Hulk, Adam. And honestly, I never stopped to see if they take their clothes off. All I know is they are very naked when they shift back."

His jaw dropped. "Seriously?"

I eyed him curiously. "Why do you have such an interest in

the werewolves? You never ask anything about the vamps."

He flicked his hand in the air. "Because vampires suck. Pun fully intended."

Strangely, I felt defensive. "Wait a minute. Vampires are immortal. Some of them have lived through centuries' worth of history. That's pretty amazing, I'd say."

He smacked his mouth together, looking unimpressed. "They are also damned to darkness for all eternity and survive on human blood."

Rose leaned onto the bar top, biting her lower lip. "If Damian was that tall, scruffy guy with the beard, then I for one am more interested in hearing how he looked in the buff."

"Probably like a Greek statue. That guy is huge." Adam held out his arms to either side.

"He and Marcus are pretty much the same height." Rose and I shared a curious expression.

"Yeah, but like, Damian can shift into a wolf. Has to make him way more powerful."

"Adam, are you man-crushing on Damian?" Crossing my arms over my chest, I smiled.

He sat straight up, looking between me and Rose. "What? No. I can't find the idea of a werewolf fascinating?"

Rose held her palms up. "Hey. No judgments here."

Adam rolled his eyes, scooping his glass of what I'd assumed was whiskey and Coke into his hand. "I'm going for a walk. Around the—I'll just be back." He turned away, a bit flustered, and I knew better than to chase after him when he got like that.

"Now that I'm over being pissed at you, how was it?" Rose asked, wriggling her eyebrows.

"How was what?"

"Don't give me that shit. Ya know? The nibble?" She tapped the side of her neck.

My hands balled into fists, and I hid them in my lap. I gulped, willing words to form from my mouth. "It hurt—at first. Then it was—yeah."

She blinked slowly, waiting as if I were going to say more. "You're killing me, smalls."

And now she was quoting *Sandlot*. Perfect. I rubbed my lips together, leaning in to whisper. "It was—more . . . sensual than I thought it'd be."

One of her brows slowly rose before a devilish grin played across her lips. "Really? Like what?"

I rubbed my forehead, hating how she egged me on for details. "I—you know, felt that flutter in my belly and became completely swept up in it."

She stood upright, tapping her fingers against the wood, mouth open. "Wow. I would've never guessed. I mean, hickeys were always so annoying as a teen. Do you remember those?" She scrunched her nose.

I did in fact remember my first hickey. Robbie Thomas. Age thirteen in my second foster home basement. I'd hated it. "Not even close." My eyes met hers, and for the first time since I had to convince her vampires were real, I knew she believed me.

"Damn."

We stared at one another before Adam returned, jarring us back to the present.

"So what's the game plan? Is Marcus going to help you or what?"

Rose came around to our side of the bar, standing near us with her arms folded.

"Yes. I'm supposed to train with him tomorrow." I hoped they didn't ask anything beyond that.

"Training? Where? How?" Adam asked, widening his stance and squaring off his shoulders.

"At his hotel," I mumbled. "I'm to re-learn what I taught myself all those years ago. I agreed only because I almost got myself killed or captured or whatever it is they want with me."

"Almost got killed?" Adam asked while Rose said, "His hotel?"

Glad to see where their priorities lay.

Adam furrowed his brow, looking over at Rose. "She said she's going to his hotel?"

I threw my hands into the air. "It's a huge, swanky hotel. I'm sure they have a gym or something."

Rose smirked. "Wherever it is, I'm sure there'll be a lot of"—she wrapped her arms around me from behind, and lifted my arm up, assisting me with throwing a punch— "that. You know, showing you the ropes?"

I shrugged her grip away, stifling a laugh. "No. There won't be. He may be a vampire, but I can still kick him in the balls."

"Does he have balls, though? They can't reproduce, so what would be the point?" Adam asked, tapping his chin quizzically.

"Also, can we take a moment to appreciate the fact despite this stressful time right now, Freya hasn't mentioned the word 'cigarette' once?"

I loved Rose for changing the subject, but at the same time, she was right. Why hadn't I thought about it? Not so much as a nervous itch.

"Wow. Yeah, Frey. That's a milestone," Adam added, which I barely heard because I was lost in thought.

"They're done out there," I blurted.

"And how, pray tell, do you know that?" Rose asked, the skin between her brows wrinkling.

How *did* I know? It was more of a fleeting feeling I couldn't really explain.

"I mean, enough time has passed to clean up several dead vampires. It was a guess."

Rose curled her lip. "Uh huh."

I hopped off my stool. "I'm going to go check. You know, just to be sure."

I scurried for the door, undoing the locks, and peeking my head out. The street was so quiet a tumbleweed could have rolled past. They really were done. My fleeting feeling became that much more puzzling.

I shut the door, looking at Romeo. "All good."

Moseying my way back to my friends, I absently began to braid my hair, not meeting their gazes. "Coast is clear."

"How did you know that?" Rose's tone dropped to seriousness. A tone which sounded strange to me coming from her.

"I told you. A lucky guess. Adam, walk me home?" He

too eyed me suspiciously. Attempting to avoid an interrogation would have proved futile.

"What? I can't walk you home?" Rose threw her arms out to her sides.

"You need to close up." I gave a grin The Joker would have been proud of, showing all my teeth.

"Using that excuse again? What'll it be tomorrow?" Her tone held no inflection.

"I do have a lot of vacation time I haven't used."

She rolled her eyes. "You're lucky your life is a shit show right now. Get outta here. Tell Marcus I said 'Hello' tomorrow." She waved the paper with his credit card number back and forth, snickering.

I kissed the air, giving Rose a playful wink before Adam and I turned for the door. As we walked to my apartment building, I slid my hands in my pockets, bracing for impact.

"I'm worried about you, Frey."

Here we go. "You say that like it's a new thing."

He stopped walking and lightly grasped my arm, turning me to face him. "I'm serious. You're getting too wrapped up in all this."

I sighed, the cool night air turning my breath into smoke, making me look like a dragon on the brink of fury. Which wasn't too far off. "Like I have a choice? It's happening whether I want it to or not. Marcus is my best shot at surviving this."

His eyes widened, his hand releasing me. "Wow. You really do trust him now."

"Not . . . fully. Just more than I did before."

"You do remember you're dealing with a vampire, correct? Don't fall for his ploy, sis. Who knows what he's capable of?"

"How would you know what he's capable of? You've been so wrapped up in werewolves— have you bothered to research vampires at all? Even for me?" It wasn't often we fought, and it tied my stomach in knots.

"There you go getting defensive again. You like this guy, don't you?" His face scrunched like the guy he referred to was Ted Bundy.

I looked at the man standing across from me, who I considered a brother. We'd been through a lot together. You could call it some warped version of hell. Stepping forward, I simply hugged him, pressing my ear against his chest. He hesitated but soon his arms wrapped around me.

"I'm sorry. I don't want you to get hurt." His chin rested atop my head.

"I know. But, I'm a big girl now. I got this. I promise."

"That's what scares me the most."

I peeled away, peering up at him. "What do you mean?"

"You're such a hard ass. Well, you act like you are anyway." He playfully punched my shoulder. "Sometimes you take on more than you think you can handle. I wasn't there, but I do remember what you told me about those vampires you took out. How close one was to getting you?"

When I went after those vamps, my mind had been foggy. I'd gone after them for purely different reasons. Revenge. Justice. Call it what you wanted. The last vamp almost had me pinned, but the sun happened to be rising, and I was able to throw a rock into a nearby window. The smell of his body turning into ash flowed through my nostrils despite how long ago it happened.

"You love to bring that up, don't you?"

"Because it keeps you grounded. What makes you think this time is going to be any different?" He leaned his head down so I had to look him in the face.

"It will be." Lifting my chin, I stared up at him.

"Because of Marcus." He leaned back, rolling his shoulders.

"Because of Marcus." I repeated his words back to him, but my tone was decisively more optimistic.

He chuckled, dragging his hands through his long locks before gripping the back of his neck. "Do me a favor? Don't let him bite you again?"

I smiled, happy he joined my side of the boat. "Done."

We started to walk again, and he draped an arm over my shoulders. "You're gonna be the death of me yet."

"If it hasn't happened already, I doubt it ever will." I grinned and gave him a light elbow to the ribs.

# CHAPTER 12

I stood in the elevator leading up to Marcus's penthouse suite, nervously biting my lip. A gym bag was secured over my shoulder with a change of clothes inside. I'd settled on a sports bra, yoga pants, and put my hair in a high ponytail since I figured we'd be play fighting. The doors pinged open, and I hesitated long enough I had to throw my hand out to keep them from automatically closing. My sneakers touched the carpeted hallway and I stood in front of the door, staring at the gold number 1 nestled above the peephole.

I lifted my hand to knock and stuck out my bottom lip when the door opened. I stood there, fist still suspended in the air, when Marcus's face peered from behind the door.

"Are you going to come in or should we do this in the hallway?" He raised his brows, his eyes trailing from my face all the way down to my toes.

Immediately regretting my choice to wear only a sports bra and pants, I dropped my hand and rushed through the door. I felt his lingering gaze and threw my bag on a nearby table. Resting one hand on my hip, I turned around and leaned against the mini bar. My breath hitched in my throat at seeing Marcus dressed in nothing but a tight black tank top and a pair of torn blue jeans.

The lion prowled toward me, bare feet making impressions in the lush gray carpet. I eyed his arms that were far larger and more toned than I'd anticipated. We stood toe to toe and he grinned, lifting a hand to flick my ponytail.

"You planning on doing some rigorous activity?"

I narrowed my eyes, having a hard time deciphering if he meant it as innuendo. "You said we were training. I tend to sweat like most humans."

His eyes trailed down my chest and then to my bare stomach. "Oh, I don't mind at all."

I fought the urge to drape my arms across my abdomen. "Where are we doing this?"

He turned and started walking, motioning with his fingers for me to follow. "This way."

I followed behind him and my eyes dropped straight to his rounded ass, the jeans hugging it perfectly. Clenching my fists at my sides, I lifted my gaze to stare at his back instead, which was right in my line of vision. Not expecting him to stop so quickly, I ran into him. He gazed over his shoulder at me after I let out an "oof".

"Right here should be good." He turned around, extending his arms to each side.

"In the middle of the living room?"

"You don't need to perform acrobatics to best a vampire. You simply need to predict their moves. Be one step ahead."

"So what do you want me to do? Try to slap your hand before you slap mine?"

He walked over to my gym bag, running a hand through his chin-length chocolate-colored hair. Unzipping it without asking for one ounce of permission, he pulled out the stake I'd hidden.

"Figured you'd have one of these with you." He tossed it about in his palm, walking back over to stand in front of me. The sight of him barefoot made him seem so . . . normal.

"That was invasion of privacy, you know."

"Oh, really? Care to explain the thirty-two drink orders on my credit card?"

My throat tightened. *Note to self: Kill Rose in her sleep.* Nervously, I laughed and let my arms swing to and fro lackadaisically. "You noticed that, huh?"

"Little goes unnoticed with me." One side of his lips curled into a grin, his tone bordering on threatening.

I curled my finger around my ponytail like a twitchy schoolgirl. "It was a last-minute decision to keep everyone inside."

"I'm not mad." He chuckled, tossing the stake from one hand to the other, peering at me with a boyish charm that made me uneasy. "In fact, I'm amused. I've been around for over two thousand years and not once have I ever had my identity stolen."

My hand stopped mid-twirl, replaying what he'd said in my head. Two *thousand* years? I couldn't help my lips from parting in awe.

"I'll tell you more about my history at another time.

Right now, we have far more pressing matters." He held the stake out to me, and I curled my fingers around it one by one, still staring at him. He took a few steps away and bowed. "Try to stake me."

Blinking, I snapped back to the moment. "Stake you? That's it?"

The lion's lip curled back, revealing teeth in a devious smile. "That's it."

I gripped the stake, eyeing him suspiciously. He stood there like a statue. Gaze unfaltering. I lunged forward, faking a stab to his right side, spun and swung at his chest. His hand launched out like a snake strike. He gripped my forearm, turned me around, and pulled me toward him. My back collided with his chest, my arms crisscrossed over my breasts, still holding the stake. He held me still with one hand. With the other he tilted my head to the side and bit the air near my neck.

"Bon appetite for me." He released his grip and I tripped forward.

Turning on my heel, I peered at him. He paced back and forth, clenching and unclenching his fists. "Again." He pointed at the ground, his tone demanding and stern.

I contemplated spouting some flippant remark, but judging from the look on his face, it wouldn't be well received. Taking a deep breath, I darted forward, and just as I was about to strike, I spotted his arm lift. Dropping to my knees, I slid across the floor, now inwardly thankful I wore yoga pants. The move was intended to be a dodge, but his hand grabbed onto my ponytail, hurling me backward and onto my back. *No more ponytails. Check.*

He loomed over me and I lay there, staring up at him with my brow crinkled. "You're trying to be too fancy. Again."

I scrambled to my feet, gripping the stake with both hands. "I'm not sure what you want me to do. You're like the boss level of a video game compared to the vampires I fought. They weren't as fast as you."

He smirked, folding his arms. "And you're an expert in judging how long a vampire has walked the earth?"

I asked for that one. "They all died from a wooden stake, so I assumed—"

He appeared in front of me so suddenly I dropped the stake. He backed me up until my butt hit the nearest wall, my palms pressing into the ripples of the textured wallpaper.

His arms extended on each side of my head, caging me in. "You assume, you die. Even a baby vampire is going to be ten times quicker than you. A were will always be five times quicker. We have no idea what we're going to be up against."

To say I was terrified would've been putting it mildly. I didn't worry about Marcus hurting me, but the sudden change in his demeanor, the subtle undertone of the predator in his voice, reminded me though he was on my side, a lot more of them were not.

He pushed away from the wall. "Again."

I slid from the wall, wiping my now clammy hands against my pants. Scooping the stake into my grasp, I cut to the chase and stabbed right at his chest. Like every other time, his hand caught the stake mid stab. My knee instinctually went straight for his family jewels without a second thought. Marcus let out a grunt bordering on a gurgle, his hands falling to his knees.

Holy shit. That worked?

Not breaking for another beat, I stabbed the stake at his chest, but his hands shot up like fireworks.

My wrists caught within his grasp, he held my arms above my head and narrowed his eyes. "Exactly which part of that did you find to be a good idea?"

I sputtered a nervous laugh. "It was a theory?"

"A theory which will only further piss someone off." He spoke through gritted teeth.

"It buys me a second or two, right?"

He let go, shaking his head. "And if it were a female vampire?"

"Falcon Punch." I shrugged.

He looked at me as if my sports bra turned into spaghetti noodles. "Come again?"

"Falcon Punch. You punch her straight in the—" I started to take a knee, mimicking a forward punch, but spying the unenthused, judging expression on his face, I retreated.

He squared off his jaw, attempting to hide the adjustment of his nether regions. "Again."

I lunged forward, yet again, feeling like a broken record. Marcus stared at me annoyingly and turned his body to the side. Stumbling forward, I managed to stay away from the floor and blew out a breath in frustration.

"Are you even trying?" he growled, holding out his arms.

His biceps twitched and I focused my attention on the point of the stake, picking at it with my fingernail.

"What do you want me to do, Marcus? Tell me and I'll do it!" I was three seconds away from stomping my foot like a frustrated two year old.

"How did you do it last time?" He scratched the light beard on his chin, awaiting my answer. "You defeated three vampires by yourself. That's no easy feat."

"I don't know. I researched their weaknesses and then practiced stabbing a dummy repeatedly for years."

"Bullshit."

For whatever reason, his cursing alarmed me. "Excuse me?"

He walked forward, his hands resting loose at his sides. "We both know it takes more than that."

*You were afraid.*

A faint voice sounded in my head, and I found myself nodding in response to it.

"Fear." I stared wide eyed into the absent space in front of me. Fear had been what drove me that night. Under no circumstances would I have allowed myself to die. The fear of the deadly creatures was there, sure, but the fear my family would have died for nothing was another matter entirely. I finally met his gaze.

The skin between his thick eyebrows crinkled, perplexed. "Yes, fear. Even immortals have it. 'Courage is resistance to fear, mastery of fear, not absence of fear.'"

"Mark Twain." I smiled, half expecting him to be surprised I knew that.

He grinned back, eyes twinkling with intrigue. "Yes. Decide what you have to lose if she wins. Let it guide you."

A pit formed in my stomach. My family. They are what I'd lose all over again if this bitch got her way. Rose and Adam. I tossed the stake around in my palm. "Let's try this again."

Marcus dipped his chin and then retreated several feet away.

*Watch the hands, the legs,* that same voice said again, trickling over my brain like raindrops. Crazily enough, I allowed the words to sink in. This time when I lunged forward, I drew back my movement, watching Marcus's feet shift and his right hand lift. I deflected his striking hand with my opposite palm, twirled my body around, and stopped the stake just short of plowing into his chest.

Marcus peered down, the stake hovering over his torso. He eyed me curiously, but then nodded in approval. "Good. Let's try something else. Turn your back, and I am going to attack you from behind."

Trying not to get caught up in the words "from behind," I did as instructed. What did he want me to do? Sniff the air for his scent?

*Listen.*

My ears perked and I closed my eyes. His feet were barely audible against the carpet, but the sound of his arm swinging through the air caused me to duck. I quickly turned on my heel in a crouched position and stood, swinging the point of the stake below his chin.

He eyed me confusedly again. "That's a bit off from my heart wouldn't you say?"

"Not if I planned to lop your head straight off. That's how one of them died." I pulled the stake away and crossed my arms over my chest in a huff. "Why do you keep looking so surprised when I best you?"

He dragged a hand over his chin, the hair of his beard shifting. "I'm merely surprised you were able to turn your actions on a dime so quickly."

I shrugged, flipping the stake into the air several times. "I've got great instincts." And then I dropped it. Bending down, I scooped it back into my palm.

He smirked, watching me. "Uh huh. Well, let's make sure it's not re-beginner's luck."

He lunged at me so fast I almost dropped the stake for the third time that night. I leaped to the right and whirled around to regain my focus. He narrowed his eyes and rolled his shoulders.

*Right.*

He attacked from the right side, and I threw my forearm up to block him. We both stared bewildered at one another. He ducked his shoulder down, throwing it into my chest. I grunted, stumbling backward, and held a hand against the point of collision.

*Fake right.*

He lifted his right arm to swing, but I focused all of my attention on his left side, dodging out of the way.

His eyebrows furrowed so profusely it made his face look demonic. "How are you doing that?"

I would've loved to answer him honestly. "Doing what?"

"Predicting almost every move." His hand flailed about

as he spoke, but I couldn't hear him anymore.

An overwhelming desire to leave, to walk to a building downtown, consumed me. I turned away from him, sliding my feet across the floor to reach my gym bag like a zombie. Swinging the bag over my shoulder, I turned for the door. Marcus zoomed in front of me, the entire width of his body blocking my exit.

"Where the hell are you going?" he growled, staring down at me.

"Move." My voice didn't sound like my own. It came out harsh and seemed a thousand miles away.

"Over my dead body. There's clearly something wrong with you."

I attempted to duck under one of his arms, but he wouldn't let me budge. The resistance made me feel antsy. "Move. Now. We are done for the day."

I couldn't will my eyes to look up at him. They kept staring straight ahead.

His hand lightly but tensely grabbed my chin and forced my gaze upward. "Freya. Look at me." His ocean-blue eyes searched my own, and I may have noticed the concern in his expression if I hadn't felt so numb.

"I forgot I had a shift at the bar tonight. Let me pass." No, I didn't. I plainly remembered taking the night off.

He studied me further, the corners of his jaw popping. Dropping his arm, he stepped aside. He didn't speak another word as I passed him and walked out into the hallway. I wanted to turn around and ask him to help me, to tie me to a bed post if he had to, to keep me from going wherever I was going. But my feet were no longer my own, and my voice only spoke when whatever force controlled me allowed it to. *Please, Marcus. Don't follow me.* Surely my destination was not the dog park on a sunny afternoon. No sense in us both being in trouble.

# CHAPTER 13

I ended up in front of a shady looking building in one of the worst parts of downtown Pittsburgh. All I wanted to do was arm myself and get the hell out of dodge, but my will was no longer my own. And so I stood there, staring at a rusted, metal door in only a sports bra, yoga pants, and shoes. I'd probably stepped on a used needle or two on my way through the alleyway I had shuffled through.

The door ominously creaked open. It was pitch black inside, but my feet carried me forward. Goosebumps littered my skin, and all I felt like doing was hugging my midriff. Despite being blinded, I turned and walked through a doorway. The room lit to life with candles outlining the entire space. A woman sat in the corner, seated upon what looked like an old English throne covered with red velvet and bordered with dark wood. She sat cross-legged, her long hair the color of dark chocolate draped around her shoulders.

She stood and slowly closed the distance between us, crossing one foot in front of the other like she was on a catwalk rather than a dirty concrete floor. Her blood-red top with black floral accents flowed over charcoal skinny pants that flared out at the bottom, skimming black, open-toed heels. As her face grew nearer, illuminated by the dancing orange glow of the flames, a breath caught in my throat. It was the woman from my dreams. But how?

She circled me, and every time I tried to look at her, I became increasingly frustrated I remained frozen in place.

"My, my, you *are* quite beautiful," she said.

Her accent sounded exactly as I dreamed it. Exotic. Ancient. Aged like a fine scotch.

She stopped in front of me, her arms crossing over her chest. Even though she wore heels, I still towered over her by a good four inches.

"I'm going to release you, as I wish to speak with you freely. Do not try to run for the door." Her hand snapped forward, grabbing onto my chin, her painted red nails that matched her blouse scraping against my cheek. She tilted her chin upward, a pair of fangs extracting. "I'm much faster than you. Do you understand?"

I couldn't move. What was I supposed to do? Blink once for yes, twice for no?

Her hand slid from my face and her fangs retracted. Dark brown eyes bored into me, and I was able to move again at will. I really had thought about running for the door, but I never was the brightest crayon in the box.

"Who the hell are you?"

She smirked and started to pace, her heels making light clicking noises with every step she took. "Your great, great, times a hundred or so grandmother."

I felt frozen again, but this time it was intended. A laugh involuntarily escaped from my mouth. The lunatic granny squared off her jaw, clearly not getting the joke.

"How is that possible? We look nothing alike." My skin was so pale it was damn near luminescent.

She smirked, flicking something from beneath her fingernail. "Cross breeding tends to occur over thousands of years."

The word "breeding" made me shiver. "Okay . . . Grandma, who are you?"

"I go by the name Isabela now, but a long, long time ago I was known as Xochiquetzal. Goddess of beauty, power, and fertility." Her true name flowed from her tongue like a practiced melody.

A lump formed in my throat. This was the woman—the thing that came to town to wreak havoc. *Play it cool, Freya.* My fingers plucked at the seam of my pants.

"So how long have you known about me?"

She ran a single finger across her plump, glossy lips. "I tell you that you're a descendant of a goddess, and that's what you ask?"

She had a point. What exactly did that mean for me? "I'm more of a cut straight to the chase sort of gal."

A laugh comparable to the wicked stepmother from *Cinderella* flowed from her mouth. "We are most certainly related."

She said this like it was a good thing. "Uh huh. Listen, Izzy. May I call you Izzy? I appreciate the whole family reunion vibe we got going on, but I really do have to get back to my life. And preferably change my clothes."

Her form appeared in front of me faster than Marcus himself could move. "Let me clarify something for you. You are my sole remaining relative. Your birthday is extraordinarily well-timed, and I need you for a very good cause."

I found myself leaning backward with each word she hissed up at me. "That was horrible clarification."

Her lips thinned and my body froze in place again. She looked to her left and then caught my gaze. "Sit."

I tried to fight her compelling command, but my body turned and sat in a wooden high-back chair across from her red-velvet throne. She soon followed, sliding into the seat, and leaned into it like we were getting ready to have tea and crumpets and discuss politics. She waved her hand and my body relaxed.

"I really wish you'd stop doing that," I growled.

She crossed her legs and let her hands delicately place atop each of the armrests. "And you would willingly have taken a seat?" One of her thin, dark eyebrows arched.

I clicked my tongue against the back of my front teeth. "Point taken. Why am I here?"

She grinned. A sinister curl that would have put The Grinch to shame. "Do you have any idea how unique your birthday is?" She emphasized the word "unique" with a flick of her tongue.

I stared at her, waiting for her to tell me just how special it was. "Because it was a leap year? Plenty of people are born on February twenty-ninth."

"True." The "r" rolled off her tongue in a wave, and she

leaned forward, mimicking my position. "But how many are not only born on that date in a given year and also on a night where both a lunar eclipse and super moon occur at the same time?"

I puckered my lips, staring at the ceiling. Satisfied with my deduction, I nodded my head once. "Yeah, still doubt I was the only person born that night."

She appeared in front of me so fast my ponytail flew up into the air from the wind gust. Pressing her hands onto each of my armrests, she leaned her face into mine. She seemed tougher when she didn't have to crane her neck to look up at me.

"You were the only being of my bloodline born on that very special night. And for that, I do not intend to let you out of my sight."

I pressed the back of my head into the high-back chair, watching her eyes roam all over my face and down my body. She smelled like vanilla and cayenne pepper. The proximity started to make me tense.

"So this is a kidnapping then?"

She pushed off my chair, the legs squeaking as it moved back an inch or two. She stood straight and placed her hand atop her chest. "Why would I kidnap my great granddaughter? I merely wish to protect you. Do you have any idea what is about to occur in this town?"

I absently picked at the wood of the armrests with my nails, eyeing her suspiciously. "Funny. I was told *you* were about to happen to this town."

She chuckled and gave a flick to her raven colored hair.

"Of course they would say that. I am the most powerful vampire in the world. The first. Those who do not fear me resent me."

It unnerved me her words made sense. "You said you're a goddess. How are you also a vampire?"

Sighing in frustration, she dragged both her hands through her hair. "A story for another time. All I will tell you for now is that I was cursed by a fellow god because I would not betray my husband for him." Her eyes glazed over and her fist clenched at her side. A soft spot. "This was a very, very long time ago."

"That's a hell of a curse just because he wanted a tumble in the sheets." I smirked and half snorted.

She appeared in front of me again, the fury quite obvious on her face. "He got what he wanted by force. How do you think you came into existence?"

I was a descendant of both a goddess and a rapist. You don't hear that every day.

"I think it is time you rested." Her palm touched my forehead, cool as an ice cube.

\*\*\*

I groaned, forcing my eyes to focus in the darkness. Sitting up, I held my head in my palm, grogginess consuming me. I rubbed the backs of my hands over my eyelids, attempting to speed up their acclimation to the dark. Reaching my hands out in front of me, I felt nothing but empty space until they collided with cool metal. I explored further, wrapping my palms around what felt like prison bars.

No. Frantically, I felt the ground beneath me. Dirty concrete. She threw me in a damn cage. My eyes began to adapt to the ominous darkness that surrounded me. The cell couldn't have been more than four feet on any given side, and the space was void of any windows.

"You're finally awake." That voice would have chilled my bones days prior but now gave me a sense of relief. Of hope.

"Marcus!" I stood, peering at the entrance of the cage.

"Over here." His voice sounded emotionless from behind me.

I turned around, moving to the bars that separated us. He sat slumped in a far corner, caged like I was.

I collapsed to my knees. "You idiot. You followed me, didn't you?"

"Of course I did. Did you really think I'd let you blindly walk off?" He had one knee up, his forearm lazily resting on top while the other leg stretched out in front of him. His body pressed against the only wall with stone blocks instead of bars.

"Well, how'd that turn out for you?"

"You continue to underestimate me." His eyes seemed to glow, peering through the bars at me with a squint. "I find it irritating and intriguing all at once."

"Why are we still sitting here? Don't you have super strength? Bend the bars."

He sighed, thudding his head against the rock behind him. "I can't."

*Fucking silver.* The words flittered through my head, but I couldn't process them.

The bars looked like any other metal I'd seen. "Why?"

"The bars are made of silver." His hand flippantly referenced the bars surrounding us.

How had I known he was going to say that? And furthermore—"Silver? I thought that was a werewolf thing." I'd based that on virtually every werewolf movie I'd seen and not any other source of information.

He sighed again. "All forms of paranormal entities are weak to silver. Some it affects more than others. Conveniently, Isabela is immune."

Rising to my feet, I stared at the bars and remembered what Isabela had told me.

"What are you doing?" Marcus asked deadpan.

"Maybe I can do it. Apparently, I'm a quarter demi-goddess or something." I grabbed onto the bars and pulled at them with all my might.

Marcus stared at me unenthusiastically as I pried and pulled to no avail.

"How's it going over there, goddess?"

I gritted my teeth and gave it one last shot. I let out a huff and blew away a strand of hair that had escaped from my ponytail.

He canted his head to the side. "Are you going to explain why you think you're anything more than human or simply leave that little tidbit hanging out there?"

I flopped back down to the floor in defeat. "Isabela apparently is—my great, great, times whatever grandmother."

His posture changed and he moved across the ground with predatory ease. "You are her descendant? Did she say how many of you there are?" His eyes were frantic, and he lifted his hand toward the bars but let it drop.

His sudden change in demeanor caught me off guard. "She claims I'm the only one. Why does it matter?"

He dragged a hand over his beard in frustration. "She obviously needs you for something because of that."

"If it weren't for her throwing me in this cell, I might have guessed she was thrilled to find a living relative."

"We can't let you anywhere near her," he growled under his breath.

"I'd say we're off to a pretty bad start."

"I've got that covered. I informed Celeste of where you were before I came in and told her to come after us if I didn't return after a certain amount of time. I told her to bring the rest of our crew, and seeing as I had no idea what we'd be up against, the werewolves and—"

"You're having people come who can't touch the bars we're trapped in?"

". . . And Adam as well." His eyes shot to mine.

I sat up straight, cocking my head to the side, praying he didn't just say what I thought he did. "You didn't."

"He told me if you were ever in any kind of danger and we needed his help, to ask him. He's the only one who will be able to touch the bars."

"How could you? He's going to get himself killed!" I shot to my feet, pacing the length of my cage.

"You tend to underestimate people at every turn. Why is that?"

"You don't understand. He's not like me, he's—" I didn't know how to phrase it.

"He's what?"

Staring off into space, I whispered, "Fragile."

Marcus chuckled, leaning back. "And you're not?"

"My body, sure. But my mind—that's long since been screwed up. Adam is too sincere, too good to get involved in all this. I'd never forgive myself if something happened to him."

"I won't let it." His voice dropped an octave, and I turned to look at him. He stared at me with an intensity eerily similar to after he'd fed on me.

I walked back to our shared bars and slowly knelt down, sitting back on my heels. "Who are you, Marcus? How did you become this?"

He cast his glance away before nodding. "I suppose we have plenty of time for that particular tale. I could tell you, but I'd much rather show you. Give me your hand."

Hesitantly, I lifted my hand from my lap, holding it up mid-air. I reached it through the bars with uncontrollable trembling. His cool hand intertwined with my own, the calluses on his fingertips surprising me. He closed his eyes and soon I was no longer in the prison cell.

Men and women dressed in togas shopped food stands and pottery markets. Men in golden armor and helmets ran past me, chasing a man in rags, apples falling from his shirt. Buildings as tall as skyscrapers with columns at the front were off in the distance and then, I saw a familiar face. There was Marcus, but olive-skinned, no scar, and dressed like the other soldiers I'd witnessed, except his helmet had a horizontal red plume on top.

"Welcome to ancient Rome," his voice said in my head.

# CHAPTER 14

My body tensed as I took in the unfamiliar surroundings. It hadn't fully registered in my brain yet Marcus said we were in ancient Rome. I stared at a different version of him, clad in shiny armor and what I knew wasn't a skirt but didn't know the actual name for.

"Marcus how is this possible? And why do I feel like I am actually here?" I tried to lift my hand but couldn't. A toga draped itself over my body and my skin was tanned. My skin never tanned.

"Because you are there." He fed his voice into my mind. "I'm projecting your mind into another's subconscious so you can experience it in its real form. This person has no idea you are in there, and fortunately, they can't hear you."

Marcus grabbed onto one of the passing soldiers, one hand resting on the hilt of a sword on his left side. "Where is Caesar?"

"Caesar? As in Julius Caesar?" I asked, beside myself.

"The one and only."

"Were you two BFFs or something? This is absolutely insane."

"Shh. Pay attention."

The soldier pointed behind him, and Marcus glanced over his shoulder, nodding. The other soldier scurried off with the rest and Marcus walked past me. The world seemed to dip into slow motion as he passed. He was fierce, intimidating, and focused. His eyes landed on me, and I had no idea if he was seeing me or whoever I was embodying, but he nodded a greeting. It was strange to see him like this. He still resembled the cool and calculating vampire I knew, but the way he carried himself was different, and the look in his eyes held a different kind of determination I wasn't used to seeing.

I blinked and was no longer in a Roman market. Now, I stood in a vast room surrounded by soldiers. In the center of the space was a large table with a map spread over it and wooden marker pieces. As I walked toward the table, the metal of my armor made light clanking sounds. I realized not only was I a man, but one of the soldiers.

I projected my thoughts to Marcus. "You do realize the compulsion to touch my own private parts right now is extremely difficult to ignore, right?" Color me curious. How often does one get to be a man in ancient Rome?

"You can't move in any of these bodies, you're merely using them as a vessel."

How disappointing.

One soldier leaned over the table, moving the pieces around on the map. Marcus approached, standing at attention. He extended his right arm out, palm down, fingers touching, and held his chin into the air.

The man at the table looked up, nodding to his presence. "Ah, Scaeva. Just the soldier I wanted to see."

"Liege?" Marcus asked, stepping forward and removing his helmet. He held it with the crook of his arm and supported it on his hip.

The man at the table stood straight. He had an angular jaw, clean-shaven, with near jet-black hair cropped short. His eyes were dark and set close together, nose sloped straight downward, thin lips, and slightly sunken in cheeks.

"Is that—" I started.

"Yes."

Holy. Shit. I was standing in a room with *the* Julius Caesar. If I could have pissed myself, I may have.

"We are moving our camp closer to Pompey's on the other side of the bank in Dyrrhachium, where he will not suspect us. I want you to be part of our next attack along with the senior Centurions."

Marcus stared down at the map, rubbing his bearded chin. "I am honored. I will leave at once." He saluted Caesar once more and turned to leave.

"Scaeva," Caesar beseeched.

Marcus paused and glanced over his shoulder.

"Do not be tempted to hold the front lines. It will surely be suicide."

Marcus smirked, rolling his shoulders. "With all due respect, my liege, you know that is something I can never promise, for it would be a lie."

Caesar squared off his jaw, moving from behind the table as Marcus turned to walk away.

"Scaeva!" Marcus didn't stop this time. "Scaeva! Gods dammit."

I blinked and now touched shoulders with armored soldiers amidst a battlefield. A wooden javelin was in my right hand, and my left held a shield nearly as tall as I was.

Marcus stood at the head of the group and turned around to address the hundred men surrounding me. "Today. We fight for Rome! For Caesar! For Mars!" Marcus held his sword in the air, a feral look in his eyes, and then proceeded to beat the sword's hilt into his shield.

The men all hooped and hollered, including myself, and we all beat our javelins against our shields in unison. We charged forward, sandaled feet digging into the ground beneath us. Marcus stayed on the front lines, just as Caesar predicted he would. I'd seen plenty of bloodshed in my time, but to be amidst a battle of this caliber was another matter entirely. Men lost limbs, their bellies ran through with swords and their bodies pummeled with arrows. I used my shield in conjunction with the grace of my javelin several times, warding away enemies who neared.

The sounds of swords clashing, bones breaking, and agonized screams flooded my ears. Several men with the same style of helmet as Marcus fell to their deaths. Pompey's men seemed to be singling them out. One of them slumped to the ground right near Marcus, and he glanced down, yelling something I couldn't make out. He looked around; his face already stained red with the enemy's blood. He shoved his sword into the air, letting out a guttural battle cry.

"Keep moving forward! Do not back down! We. Are. Romans!"

The way he took charge and captivated the men made my chest swell. I wasn't sure what fascinated me more—the brute strength he exuded or the courage and bravery. Glancing skyward, I caught sight of a golden eagle attached to a rod raised high above us all. It was held by a singular soldier whose only job was to keep the symbol upright.

We continued to push, and Marcus never backed away from the front of the charge. While he was distracted battling an enemy, an arrow soared past him, grazing me in the arm. It was strange to see something strike you but not be able to feel the pain. Another arrow launched, landing straight in Marcus's left eye.

"Marcus! Holy hell! How did you not die?"

"Keep watching."

Marcus staggered forward, angrily yelling into the wind. He gripped the stick of the arrow and gave it a hard yank, tossing it, along with the remnants of his eye, to the ground. The entire left side of his face was now a bloodied mess, and I couldn't speak. He held his shield up and pushed forward, running ahead of the rest of the soldiers. The enemy would release a barrage of arrows, and he'd drop to his knee, covering himself with his shield, then continue to push forward, killing any enemy who crossed his path.

He continued this same pattern until eventually his shield had so many arrows sticking out of it, it looked like a pin cushion. Soon, the enemy began to retreat, but Marcus continued his frenzy, and the men around me cheered in triumph.

I blinked and appeared back in the same war room as before with Caesar standing in front of a battered and bruised Marcus. A rag was wrapped around his missing eye, cuts and scrapes littered over his arms and legs.

"I have never come across any other soldier with such conviction, such dedication and passion for his fellow soldier and for his country. That is why I am promoting you, Marcus Cassius Scaeva to Primus Pilus over the Legio Fretensis."

Marcus bowed his head. "You continue to honor me, my liege. I will not disappoint you."

I was now in a quiet alleyway at night, and I had become so captivated with Marcus's life, I'd neither remembered nor cared what person I was anymore. Marcus walked through the alleyway, dressed in his armor, sans helmet, and a leather patch lay over his eye. A woman with strawberry-blonde hair, elegantly pinned in waves atop her head, slunk from the shadows. She had a thin, long face, full lips, and a nose that tilted slightly upward. She wore a white toga adorned with shiny, gold accents, and she was skinny as a rail.

"I've been watching you, Marcus," the woman said, tracing her finger down the armor secured over his chest.

"Who the hell is this, Marcus?" I asked, feeling a knot form in my throat.

"You sound jealous."

"Not jealous. Intrigued."

"Maybe if you listen instead of talking to me in your head, you'll find out."

"Fine."

"May I ask who you are, miss?" Marcus formally asked the woman. He stood rigid, one hand resting at his side while the other played at the hilt of his sword.

"My name is Catalina. A man with your strength, your power and skills should live for all eternity. Your life is wasted in this useless mortal shell."

As she talked, she walked circles around him, eyeing him up like a piece of meat. She dragged fingertips across the armor over his stomach, and when she reached the front of him, she cupped his cheek with her palm.

"I am flattered by your words, but I am afraid I do not understand what you speak."

Catalina stared at him, unflinching. "Walk with me, Marcus."

He nodded and followed her.

"What the—why are you going with her? Marcus stop!"

"You realize I can't hear you?"

"Regardless, why are you following her?" It dawned on me, watching Marcus disappear into the darkness, following Catalina like an obedient dog. "She made you."

I appeared now in an empty room, save for several torches hanging from the walls. Catalina stepped in front of me, and I peered down at her. She raised a hand to my face, brushing a piece of hair from my eyes with a warm smile.

"You know I'm going to be able to say I've been inside you now, right?" I said, smirking.

"There was no other way to show you this final piece. I'll have to live with it."

"I am going to make you immortal. You will be stronger,

154

faster, and far more powerful than you could ever dream of, my love. And we will be together forever." She grinned, extracting her fangs, and without missing a beat, plunged them into my neck.

My body soon slumped to the ground and my vision blurred. A small, bloodied wrist appeared in front of my face.

"Drink and be who you were always meant to be." Her voice was a command I couldn't deny, and I drank. It started as a few licks at first, but then grew ravenous and greedy.

Catalina tried to pull away, but I wouldn't let her, digging my fingers into her thin arm, demanding more. She hissed and finally pulled free.

My body began to writhe, and I curled into the fetal position, screaming in agony. I clutched my stomach, then my head, and rolled back and forth on the stone floor. The pain was non-existent for me, but the way I jostled around, it had to be excruciating for Marcus at the time. And then I stopped. I sat up, no longer under her control, and wiped my arm across my bloody lips.

"What did you do to me?" Marcus's angered voice boomed from my chest.

"I already told you. I have made you into the man you were always meant to become. And that is not a man, but a powerful creature of the night." She grinned maniacally.

I stood to my feet, launching my large hand around her tiny throat, squeezing. "I did not ask for this! What gives you the right to play Queen of the Gods?"

She laughed despite my attempt to choke the life out of her. I growled, realizing my efforts were in vain, and let her go.

"With time, you will see this is the true you." She lifted a hand, swiftly removing the patch from my face.

I blinked rapidly, realizing I could see out of both eyes.

"And now to make that beautiful face whole once more," Catalina said, pricking her finger with one of her fangs. She lifted her hand to the scar on my face, but I pushed her away, stepping backward.

"No."

She looked at me, confused. "No?"

"I do not want it fixed. If I am to be this . . . thing for all eternity, it will be the only shred of humanity I shall have left."

She frowned, licking the blood bead from her fingertip. "If that is what you wish, my love."

"I am not your love, nor will I ever be. Have you not done enough damage?"

"Marcus, for years I have watched you, debating if you were the one I wished to roam the earth with forever. I chose you. Now we are to be together." She stepped forward, and I too stepped forward, dipping my face down to hers.

"I did *not* choose you, and I never want to see your pathetic face ever again. If I do, I *will* kill you. Do you understand me?"

Tears welled in Catalina's eyes, her jaw dropping, and she began to stammer. "But Marcus—"

I turned and walked away.

"You do not know how to survive as what you are!" she screeched.

I paused at the darkened doorway, not looking in

Catalina's direction. "Is that not why you picked me? I *always* survive."

I gasped, reappearing as myself in the cell. My hand was still wrapped around Marcus's, and his eyes were cast downward. From the way his jaw popped, I could tell he held back something. Instead of saying anything, I gave his hand a gentle squeeze through the bars, but in truth, I wouldn't know what to say anyway. What Marcus showed me put a whole hell of a lot of things in perspective. Things I wasn't ready to voice out loud. Marcus's life was stolen from him by vampires . . . just as mine was.

# CHAPTER 15

We sat there in silence for what seemed a lifetime, and surprisingly, he didn't try to pull his hand away from mine. He sat staring at the ground as if continuing to recall his past without my intrusion.

"So . . . Marcus Cassius Scaeva, huh?"

He sniffed once, lifting my hand to his face, studying my fingers. "Yes. Glorified Roman centurion reduced to an eternity in the shadows within the blink of an eye."

"Marcus . . . Syus. C. S. Clever."

His chilly fingers traced around my knuckles, making me uncomfortable, but I let him continue for now. "I figured it wouldn't arouse as much suspicion. Not many people go by three names nowadays." He smirked, pressing our palms against one another. Nearly twice the size, his hand engulfed mine.

"Did you ever see Catalina again?"

His face fell and so did his hand. I recoiled mine like he'd cut off one of my fingers.

"Twice." He clipped the word, picking up a random

pebble from the ground.

"And how'd that go?" I was half afraid to ask.

"She was obsessed with me. I thought I could kill her on a whim, just as I had so many soldiers on the battlefield, but something held me back. I felt compelled to warn her a second time after she draped herself over me whaling like a damned banshee. That was ten years after she made me. I didn't see her again for another two hundred years." He threw the pebble outside the bars with such force it cracked an outside wall.

"I'm guessing it wasn't a happy reunion?"

"I killed her. It was the only way to be free of her." He wouldn't make eye contact with me.

"Isn't there some vampire code or something? Not killing your own kind?"

Marcus laughed. A deep, throaty chuckle, causing his shoulders to bounce. I'm glad he found me so amusing, but for once in my life, I'd asked a serious question.

"The dead putting laws on the dead . . . that's a comedic notion, really." He finally looked at me, blue eyes somehow twinkling even within the darkness.

I could tell talking about the one who made him caused feelings to stir he didn't feel like dealing with. Not now in this vulnerable pit of hell. "You yelled 'For Mars.' Did you worship planets?"

He halfway smiled. "I believe you know the Greek name for him: Ares. We worshiped similar gods but called them different things. It was long before the spread of Christianity."

"God of War," I mumbled, staring off into space while I tried to do quick math in my head. "You've been around for thousands of years. You must've seen so many things, Marcus. I've got questions like you wouldn't believe."

"And I'd be happy to decide which ones I'll gratify with an answer." He winked, that devilish grin spreading across his lips.

"How did you figure out what she turned you into? I mean, you didn't ask her what, if anything, could kill you."

"I learned things the hard way. It doesn't take one long to figure out they cannot walk in the sun. When you can smell your own flesh burning and hear the sizzle, that's usually a bad sign."

My nostrils flared, imagining what it would smell like. "And the blood?"

"Ah, yes. As a new vampire, that was the most difficult part without guidance, I'm afraid. You become absolutely ravenous for it. It consumes you. I accidentally killed my first two humans. Though something tells me Catalina would've relished in watching me kill. Two humans may have turned into two hundred in a decade." He stared at me, tapping his fingers against his propped knee. "Does that upset you?"

His question surprised me. "I can't say it makes me happy, but it was such a long time ago, who am I to judge?" I stared back at him, recalling my time in ancient Rome, watching highlights of his life. "You're a survivor, then?"

His words repeated right back to him. We were more alike than I cared to admit.

He grinned. A genuine smile that made me feel all fuzzy

inside. "Something like that."

"Marcus—" I started, thinking over my words carefully, methodically.

His eyes shifted before returning to me. ". . . Yes?"

"How does a vampire's power work? You said it's dependent on who made them. Catalina was about to heal you; clearly you got that from her—and some form of mind control being able to erase recent memories like with the woman in the alley. Do you develop anything of your own?" I bit my lip, hesitating to straight-out ask if he could read my mind.

"I can't read minds. It's more like a glimpse, and I never know when it's going to happen."

"Did it happen right now?"

He offered a lopsided grin. "Yes, it did."

I clapped my hands together in triumph. "I knew it. I freaking knew it!"

"You seem to share in the gift yourself, do you not?"

My mental victory lap came to a screeching halt. "Not that I know of. Why?"

The door near our cages burst open. Both Adam and Rose stumbled inside, slamming the door behind them.

"Rose, go! I'll keep a lookout." Adam pressed his ear against the door.

Marcus and I both leaped to our feet as Rose approached my cage.

"Rose?" I gripped the bars, my words rushed and fuming. "Why the hell are you here? It's bad enough Adam insisted on coming."

She pulled a hacksaw from within her jacket and started cutting away at the bars, holding onto one of them for leverage.

"Did you honestly think I was going to play cocktail waitress while you and Adam saved mankind?" Rose peered at me through the cell, hacking away with the saw and waiting for an answer.

"Saving mankind is a bit of a stretch. Let's not make this into something of epic proportions."

Marcus paced the length of his cell like the caged lion he was. He ran his hand in frustration through his hair and over his beard several times.

"Oh, I think we've gone beyond epic proportions, Frey. You should've seen what we just saw out there. Celeste and Frankie are going ape-shit on a bunch of demon-looking things." Her eyes grew wide, and then there was a metallic clinking sound, followed by the door of my cell opening.

I rushed out, yanking the saw from Rose's grasp and quickly got to work on Marcus's cell. The wooden door near where Adam stood started to bounce, and he pressed his back into it. "Um, guys. I think we're about to have company."

My forearms burned as I worked the saw back and forth as quickly as I could.

"Faster, Freya!" Marcus bellowed, glaring at me through the bars.

I knew what he was doing. Pushing me by suggesting I was doing a shoddy job, only to push *myself* to prove him wrong.

"Seems to be working." He grinned.

I yanked the door of the cage open once the saw went through and cocked my head at him. "*Don't* do that."

Marcus scurried out, sneering at the silver bars. "It's adorable you think you can tell me what to do." He looked at me for a moment but not long enough to catch my seething glare. He guided Adam away from the door.

"Everyone move back."

We shuffled backward and I found myself protectively holding each of my arms out to move Rose and Adam further back.

"Are you going to take them all out by yourself?" Adam asked, looking at Marcus and then at me. "Is he crazy?"

I thought back to Marcus on the battlefield, cutting through the sea of soldiers like butter despite an arrow going through his eye. "He knows what he's doing, trust me."

Marcus lifted a leg and slammed his boot into the door. Wooden splinters flew everywhere, leaving an empty doorway with four creatures standing on the other side. They were vampires, but similar to the more goblin-looking creature from before, they looked more demonic than human.

Marcus launched forward, grabbing one creature by the throat, and hurled him into the other three. "Get out of here, all of you! I'll hold them off."

I sprung to action, grabbing onto Adam's and Rose's hands, pulling them behind me whether they wanted to move or not. We scurried past Marcus as he dipped, dodged, pushed, and threw the four vampires every time they tried to advance on us. Near the end of the hallway, another jumped out in front of Rose.

She shrieked, throwing a fury of punches at it. I pushed past her, and sliced at its neck with the hacksaw. It tore clean through, and the headless body stood still a moment before toppling over.

"Holy freaking shit, Freya!" Adam's hands flew to his head.

Rose stared at my face, which undoubtedly had blood splattered over it now. Ignoring both of their stunned faces, I grabbed their hands and yanked them further down the hallway. My chest hummed as I watched Marcus battle the four vampires. He looked fearless, but it concerned me the vampires weren't dead yet.

As I disappeared around the corner, bodies flew left and right further down the hall. I could make out Damian, who had yet to morph into wolf mode. His eyes were so yellow I could see them from where we stood. His chest heaved, and the veins in his arms bulged so profusely they looked like worms.

Damian spotted us and pointed with one of his burly arms. "Stay there!"

His body slammed in the wall nearest him, one of the vampires repeatedly biting the air in front of him like a snapping turtle on crack. Damian shoved it away, and in one swift motion dropped his pants, showing a moment's glance at his ass before morphing into his wolf form. His shirt shredded and tattered, fell to the ground.

"He just—" Adam started, standing there dumbfounded.

"Yes. He shifted, Adam. Try not to get a stiffy over it." I shifted my stance, starting to get antsy with this whole "stay here" business.

"Did anyone else see his ass or was that just me?" Rose asked, staring at the large wolf fighting the demonic vampire.

"Screw this." I gripped the hacksaw and marched forward.

Adam grabbed onto my elbow. "Freya, don't! Look at what they're up against. You can't take that on."

I gazed down at his hand before concentrating on the expression he wore. He looked scared out of his mind, but more for me than due to the insane creatures mere feet away from us. "Both of you stay here. Please. It's enough you're both here in the first place." Prying my arm from his kung-fu-like death grip, I continued my march.

"Has she always been this stubborn?" Rose's voice mumbled behind me.

"Since the very first damn day I met her."

The vampire threw Damian into the wall, the wolf landing on the ground with a thud, shaking its massive head.

"Hey!" The vampire turned to look at me, and within an instant appeared.

I took a deep breath, eyeing its movements, letting Marcus's words seep through. Instead of looking at the vampire's face, I watched its hands and feet. It was quick. Very quick. He slashed with his pointy fingers at my right shoulder and managed to scratch me as I dodged to my left. If he would've got that strike in at full force, I'd probably be missing a chunk of flesh right about now. Not having time to regain my composure, I shifted my stance and bent backward as it slashed at me again. When I stood back up, I brought the saw with me, slamming it into his abdomen. With one swift motion upward, I sliced him straight in half.

Adam ran up behind me, a rock the size of his fist resting in his palm. He held it above his head and stared down at the splayed-open vampire with horrified eyes. "Did you do that?"

"Maybe it was the wind." I gave him a sardonic look before dropping to my knees. The saw hadn't gone all the way through its skull. I yanked the saw through its neck, separating the head from the body for good measure.

Adam still stood there with his arm raised in the air, frozen.

With a gentle, but firm tug, I brought his arm down and snapped my fingers in front of his face. "You gonna be alright there, champ? We still have to get out of here."

He blinked once. "Yeah, yeah, I'm good. How are you not freaking out right about now?"

"I save the freak outs for when my ass isn't on the line anymore." I gave his one arm a light squeeze and then motioned for Rose to join us so we could continue to find a way out.

Wolf Damian and Marcus were now behind us keeping the other vampire attackers at bay. As we rounded the corner, Celeste and Frankie stood back to back, attacking vampires as they approached. As before, Celeste looked like a witchy ballerina, matching them move for move. I was surprised Frankie hadn't shifted into a wolf and wondered if they weren't as strong against these particular vamps.

"The entrance where we came in is around that corner! Go now while we have them distracted!" Celeste's white blonde hair flew in cascades around her as she continued to fight while willing us to move our asses.

We scurried past them, making a beeline for the corner. Distracted by my desire to be free from this place, I let my sense of awareness falter. A vampire leaped from the shadows and tore into the flesh above my knee with its monstrous claws. I screamed and fell to the ground. The saw launched from my grasp and scraped across the concrete floor.

"Shit. Shit. Shit!" Rose screeched, scrambling to pick up the saw.

I gritted my teeth, trying not to look at the gash in my leg, but the pain surging through my body made it impossible to forget. Using my hands, I scooted myself away from the vampire standing over me. He had no interest in anyone else but me and took one step forward for every scoot back I took.

The vampire grinned with its rows of pointy teeth, reaching down when a white blur leaped in front of me, launching the vampire through the air. Frankie had shifted into her wolf form and attacked the fallen vampire, lips pulled back in a snarl. I let out a breath, trying to keep myself in a sitting up position. Adam slid on his knees, hands trembling over my gaping wound.

"What can I do?" The fear had dissolved from his face, replaced now with determination.

"Marcus will heal her! Keep her awake," Celeste, the

mistress of multi-tasking, shouted our way while shoving one of the vampires into a splintered piece of wood sticking out from a nearby window frame.

Groaning, I tried to stand, but Adam put pressure on my shoulders to keep me put. I felt about as useless as leather underwear. The white wolf loomed over the vampire she'd attacked, and her head kept dipping down, returning upward with red staining her teeth.

"Is Frankie eating that vampire?" I squinted, doing anything I could to distract myself.

Adam glanced over and then back to me, making a gagging sound. "Yes, yes she is."

Rose stood with the saw in her hands, frantically glancing back and forth as more vampires piled into the room. Adam draped his body over mine. I wanted to shove him off so I could at least see my fate coming.

"Enough!" a familiar accented voice resonated throughout the room. Isabela.

The vampires halted and quickly retreated, vanishing into the darkness with shrieks and wailing.

"It is exhausting when one must do everything themselves." I could hear Isabela's heels clicking against the ground as she walked.

Adam's body pressed harder into mine, and then he was gone. Isabela had thrown him off of me, and I watched as his body fell into a near lifeless slump on the ground.

"No!" I winced, trying to stand.

Rose ran over to him and my tense muscles relaxed when she lifted his head and his eyes flittered open.

"My, my . . . you have not had the best day, have you?" Isabela peered down at me, motioning nonchalantly toward my wound.

The white wolf charged after her, and without so much as turning her head, Isabela reached her hand out, catching the wolf in mid-air by the throat. Frankie shifted back into a human while still being choked, grasping at Isabela's hands, her naked form dangling off the ground. Celeste appeared near her, a piece of splintered wood in her hand. Isabela snatched the wood from her hand. She hovered it up in the air, ready to strike Celeste now instead.

"You think wood will harm me, you infant?" Her eyes blazed with red.

"Isabela!" Marcus's voice sounded across the room like a thunderclap.

She turned to the doorway, opening her hand to release Frankie, who fell to the ground gasping. Damian appeared from behind Marcus and ran to her aid, dressed only in his pants.

"Marcus Cassius Scaeva. It has been a while." Isabela's lips curled into a mischievous grin.

"We need to talk." He stood rigid, clenching his fists at his sides.

"About the girl? I am afraid her fate has already been sealed, handsome." She craned her neck skyward to smile up at him.

"You'll want to hear this out. I assure you. Let's talk somewhere . . . private." He smiled devilishly down at her, motioning behind him.

*Will heal you later.* Marcus peered at me, concern flooding his face.

Isabela walked past him, draping a greedy paw over his chest. I nodded, knowing now the flitters of voices in my head belonged to Marcus. He turned away and disappeared with Isabela.

Adam stood and slipped his arms underneath me, preparing to lift. Damian grabbed onto his arm. "I can move faster than you. Let me."

Adam blinked, disappointed Damian was right, and stepped back. Soon, I was draped over the arms of a half-naked werewolf and being carted away to Marcus's fancy hotel. What exactly Marcus was doing with Isabela unnerved me. Why had he smiled at her? And why did she act like they had been all chummy back in the day? Or maybe it was the blood loss talking.

# CHAPTER 16

I lay limp in Damian's arms, drifting in and out of consciousness as the adrenaline wore off. Soon, I felt softness beneath me and wanted nothing more than to curl into a ball and sleep away the throbbing pain in my leg.

"She's lost a lot of blood. We don't know how much longer Marcus is going to be," Rose voiced from somewhere near me.

"And do any of you happen to have a tourniquet in your back pocket?" Leave it to Celeste to be sarcastic even while I remained there bleeding my little heart out. We had a bit more in common then I cared to acknowledge.

"Here." Adam's voice was stern, and I forced my eyes open enough to form slits.

He stood over me shirtless and proceeded to tie the shirt around my thigh, pulling it tight.

Moaning, I pinched my eyes closed again. Any thoughts of resting were but distant memories carried off in the wind after that. "Celeste, why can't you heal me?"

"Healing is not one of my gifts." She stood near me, her

arms crossed casually over her chest.

"Convenient," I mumbled, opening my eyes to stare at the ceiling and counting the tiles.

"Besides, I get the feeling you would much rather suck on Marcus than the likes of me."

I threw her a glare. A smug grin plastered across her face, and she rotated her torso back and forth like she'd just got away with something.

"If all vampire's blood tasted like chocolate, I wouldn't care who gave it to me right now." Moving my body wasn't such a grand idea, but my butt was on the verge of falling asleep. Pain washed over me in waves, and I immediately regretted my decision.

"Chocolate?" Celeste's arms dropped to her sides. "What the hell are you talking about?"

"Is playing mind games with me really necessary right now?"

"Our blood tastes like eating a penny, like the rest of you." She cocked an eyebrow and Rose came to the rescue, shoving past her to get to me.

"You're probably just going crazy. Well . . . crazier." Rose smiled, taking my hand into hers and kneeling on the floor.

"Where in God's name is he? What is he doing? Screwing her?" Adam walked back and forth, the jeans hanging low on his hips, clearly visible now that he was without a shirt.

"I'll certainly make sure to file a complaint with him when he arrives." Celeste smirked, sitting down in one of the two chairs at the small table near the bar.

"Go ahead! I'm sick and tired of dealing with his bullshit. He couldn't take three seconds to give her blood before disappearing with Isabela? He's warped her brain, fed on her, and who knows what else."

Celeste quirked her brows. Apparently, Marcus hadn't told her about our wager.

"Adam, calm down." Rose gripped my hand and I squeezed hers back.

"Why? You know as well as I do the guy is a complete asshole."

As if on cue, Marcus swept through the door. A chorus of anxious butterflies went off in my belly at the sight of him, and I clenched Rose's hand even harder. She winced, scrunching her face at me.

"Referring to me, I presume?" Marcus purred, slipping off his jacket. "This asshole is about to ensure your friend doesn't walk with a limp for the rest of her life."

"Yeah, something they could've done at a hospital." Adam scoffed.

Marcus shook his head, approaching the bed and rolling up his sleeve. He glanced at Adam's half-naked form and then at Damian. Rose stood up and backed away wide eyed. Marcus sat down on the bed beside me with a crooked smile.

"Would you feel more comfortable if I too were shirtless?"

I fought the compulsion to roll my eyes straight out of my skull. "Would you just bite your wrist?"

His grin turned predatory. "My, my, haven't we grown greedy?"

He kept his eyes locked on mine and bit into his wrist. As he hovered it over my mouth, a single drop fell, staining the white bedspread beneath us. Unlike before, my lips engulfed the wound without hesitation. I didn't close my eyes and instead caught his gaze. Nobody else existed in the room, and I kept drinking, gripping onto his forearm. Slowly, I sat up, the pain diminishing with every ounce I took down my throat.

Marcus reached forward and brushed his knuckles down the side of my cheek before pulling his arm away. Reluctantly, I let go and continued to stare at him. What the fuck happened? I blinked several times, willing my brain to work. Looking around the room at everyone's faces told me they were as bewildered as I was.

Adam looked concerned bordering on pissed. Rose had her hands on her hips, eyebrow cocked. Frankie and Damian didn't look like they gave a rat's ass, but their expressions suggested nausea. Celeste seemed flat-out annoyed. Marcus reached forward, brushing his thumb against the corner of my mouth and then under my lip. When he pulled his finger away, the tip was stained red, and he licked it. The sight made my stomach feel like a hummingbird was caged within it.

Marcus untied the shirt from my thigh. Save for remnants of blood, my leg was healed. He held the shirt out in Adam's direction but never took his eyes off of me.

"You look chilly," he said as Adam stepped forward and tore the shirt from his grasp.

"Thank you." My voice sounded foreign to me, like a confused little girl.

"Any time." He grinned, canting his head to the side.

*The way you craved me right then was . . .*

My brow crinkled, not seeing Marcus's lips move but hearing his fleeting thought.

"Was what?"

His expression melted. "Interesting." I wasn't sure whether he was saying that to finish his thought or to refer to the situation.

"Liege." Celeste's voice broke our moment, and Marcus stood from the bed, walking to the center of the room.

"I managed to buy us some time with Isabela," Marcus said, staring at the floor and stroking his hand over his beard.

"What does that mean?" Damian asked, leaning against the wall, crossing his feet at the ankles.

I moved my legs off the bed, turning my body to the side, and Adam trotted over to me once Marcus was a safe distance away. He placed a hand on my back between my shoulder blades and looked down at my leg. I noted the way he bit the inside of his cheek. After patting his hand to reassure him I was fine, I stood up, relieved when a pain didn't dart up my entire body.

"She vowed to no longer summon Freya so long as we keep her from harm's way." Marcus walked to the bar.

"But she will still come for me."

Marcus's finger traced across the bottles lined up in the back of the bar before settling on one. He grabbed it and used his other hand to spin the top off in one fluid motion. "We—*I* won't let that happen. It buys us time to figure out a solution." He poured some of the brown colored liquor into a tumbler.

"The solution?" Rose asked.

"How to bloody well kill her, I hope," Frankie said, peculiarly placing a hand over her belly.

Marcus took a sip from the tumbler, nodding. "At the very least . . . entrap her."

"You made a deal with her, didn't you, my liege?" Celeste asked, her nostrils flaring.

"What? Is she right, Marcus? You made a deal with her?" I asked, my fists clenched.

He stared down into the contents of his glass. "Yes, I did."

"And what did you promise her?" Celeste asked, her eyes unflinching.

He didn't say anything at first, simply taking another sip of his drink.

"Out with it, vampire," Damian's voice boomed across the room.

"Me." Marcus gulped down the rest of his drink and delicately placed the glass back on the bar top.

My heart ached, and I felt tears threatening to leak out. I ran to the bar and slapped my hands down. "No, Marcus. No! I won't let you do this."

"I wasn't asking for permission." He squared off his jaw, letting the tough-guy bravado take over.

*I can't let her take you.*

His stare burned into mine, and I pressed my palms into the marble bar to keep them from shaking. "There has to be another way. We don't even know what she wants with me."

"It can't be for anything good," Damian said behind me,

his feet sliding against the carpet as he neared us.

A world without Marcus seemed strange. He'd worked his way under my skin, and the thought of not being able to exchange banter with him made me . . . sad. Marcus gave a sidelong grin and slid his hand closer to mine, dragging a fingertip down the side of my pinky. When Damian's half-naked form appeared in my peripheral vision, I pulled my hands away, gulping.

The werewolf crossed his arms over his chest and his pecs did a little dance. "For wanting our help to stop this bitch, you sure as hell aren't giving us a lot of detail."

Marcus's gaze dropped down and then shot back up to Damian's face. "I'd be delighted to fill you all in on everything I know about her. But first, would you be so kind as to take one of my shirts? Your nipples don't entice me to speak."

Damian smirked. "Are you that self-conscious about yourself, Vamp, you can't stand the sight of a half-naked man?"

"And are you that full of yourself to think the sight of you bothers me?" Marcus grinned, and I got distracted imagining what he looked like shirtless.

Damian waved him off and retreated to the closet, yanking one of the shirts from a hanger.

Marcus turned to me, dipping his lips down to my ear. "If you're that curious, I can certainly satiate your imagination."

A breath hitched in my throat, and I took a step back. He smiled down at me, watching me squirm with obvious amusement.

"Marcus, now is not the time to joke around. What did you mean when you said you promised yourself to her?" I asked.

His smile faded and he sighed, playing with his shirt sleeve. He traced his thumb over the part of his wrist where he'd bitten for me to drink. "It'll all make sense once I explain." He walked to the center of the room.

Damian buttoned up the black shirt he'd borrowed from Marcus, which due to his size couldn't be buttoned up all the way, and the sleeves stopped mid-forearm. Rose and Adam took seats at the small table in the corner of the room while the supernatural beings all stood at full attention.

"I met Isabela over a thousand years ago when I was sailing through the Caribbean." Marcus paused, walking over to a duffle bag resting on the desk against a side wall. He picked up a black piece of fabric, handing it to me with a single nod.

Perplexed, I stared at it before realizing he'd handed me a sweatshirt. Rose smiled at me from across the room, and I attempted to ignore her, slipping the shirt over my head. His scent was all over this thing, and it made me shudder. I pulled the sleeves down so it covered my hands. The shirt was so large the hem almost touched my knees.

"When I met her, she was lonely. Longed for companionship after living off the grid for the better part of a century."

My body went rigid because I knew exactly where he was going with this, and I wasn't sure I wanted to hear it.

"I couldn't offer an eternal partnership, but I did spend

a good amount of time with her."

The thought of my great grandmother and him having a tumble in the sheets multiple times made my stomach flip. I dropped my face to my hand, rubbing feverishly at my forehead in an effort to hide my reaction.

*It was a long time ago. . .*

He peered at me pleadingly, like a scolded puppy. To be honest, he and I were nothing more than friends. So he boned my great-great-great grandma. Good for her.

"How does this have anything to do with your deal?" I flipped my hand into the air, the baggy sleeve flying past my hand.

Marcus interlaced his fingers and let his hands rest in front of him. He paced back and forth, looking between all of us as he spoke. "Over time, Isabela grew jaded. Ravenous for revenge. A revenge I wanted no part of."

Adam perked up. "Revenge for what?"

"As I told you before, Isabela used to be the Aztec goddess of love. She had a husband, and they were deeply in love. That was until another god, the god of the night, pined over her for her beauty. Repeatedly he asked to be with her, even if for one night, but every time she denied his advances. To lay with him even once would be betraying her husband."

I wrapped my arms around myself, remembering what little Isabela told me. Strangely, I felt a bit sorry for her. She'd been dealt a poor card and had to live with that guilt for multiple lifetimes.

"So the god took what he wanted and she became

pregnant. When she still showed no desire to be with him and now fully despised him for forcing himself on her, he cursed her to live for all eternity confined to darkness, forced to feed on human blood to survive. He then killed her husband."

Frankie gripped Damian's arm with a pain-stricken face. He rubbed her hand comfortingly. Celeste looked bored, more than likely having heard this story before.

"And the child?" Rose asked with a frown.

"The god wouldn't dare kill his progeny, proof that he got what he wanted. Isabela too couldn't bring herself to destroy her own flesh and blood but also couldn't live with the constant reminder of what was done to her. She left the baby on the doorstep of a childless human couple."

I pulled at the sleeves uncomfortably, knowing though this story sounded like a myth, it was part of my history.

"Is there a way to break her curse?" Damian asked, his tone grave.

"If there is, she never told me." Marcus looked at me and I bit at my thumbnail.

"You promised to be her companion. Didn't you?" I didn't have to read his damn thoughts to come to that conclusion.

He licked his lips, and the fact he hesitated to answer told me all I needed to know. "It was the only deal I knew she'd take. Otherwise, she would've continued to summon you."

Celeste stepped forward, pointing at the ground. "You're going to abandon us because of one puny human?"

I cocked an eyebrow. This "puny human" better not have been me.

"She's not just any human, Celeste. I made the deal. If we stop her, it won't matter." He unlocked his hands and stood firm, puffing out his chest.

"And you trust her when she says she won't summon her anymore?" She flicked her hand flippantly.

"That's why you're going to charm her." He glared at her.

Celest shook her head. "She is far more powerful than me. The charm won't do a damn thing, liege. You know that."

"Excuse me!" I yelled, stepping between the two vampires. "Charm me?"

"Her gift is a form of mind control. She can coerce you to ignore the call if Isabela were to break her word."

I couldn't help laughing. Every waking moment became crazier than the last. "You think for one second I am letting this thing into my head?"

"Don't worry about it. It won't work anyway." Celeste shifted her stance to one foot, jutting her hip out, and crossed her arms in a huff.

"Celeste, that's an order. Do it. Now," he growled, pointing a finger from her to me.

Celeste cleared her throat, moving some of her platinum blonde hair behind her ear. As she trudged forward, I shuffled back.

"Marcus." I looked over at him pleadingly.

"Let her do this, Freya. The only other alternative is to handcuff ourselves together so you can't go anywhere." He shrugged. "I'm game if you are."

My expression turned emotionless. It was alarming how

well he knew me already. "Fine. But I swear, Celeste, if you make me cluck like a chicken every time someone says the word 'pocket watch' or something, I'll be extremely pissed."

"You'd be lucky if that's *all* I did." She smirked and placed her hands on my shoulders. Her eyes stared me down and soon I felt numb. "Freya, are you listening to me?"

I couldn't blink, couldn't move, couldn't think. It was kind of peaceful in a way. "Yes."

"If Isabela tries to summon you. You will ignore her and remain wherever you are. Do you understand?"

I nodded.

"Say that you understand."

"I understand."

She blinked, removed her hands, and I was back to myself again. I thought I remembered everything that happened, but it seemed hazy. Celeste stood in front of me, waiting for me to say something.

"Did you do anything?"

Seemingly pleased, she nodded once and looked over at Marcus. "It's done."

"It's going to be sunup soon. Celeste and I must rest."

Everyone started to shuffle away, and Adam caught my gaze. I used my head to reference the door, and with hesitation he obliged, walking ahead.

I stepped up to Marcus, tugging his shirt sleeve to get his attention. He looked down at me with a weak smile.

"I'm not letting her take you for forever. You know that, right?"

He fully turned toward me, the smile widening. "I can't

say I've ever had too many people, let alone a human, wish to protect *me*."

"You're my best shot at surviving this. Watching out for my own interests is all." I couldn't let the moment get too serious. The declaration of me needing his help was more than enough.

"Serious can be good from time to time." He peered down at me, the smile fading.

Biting my lip, I nodded and turned for the door.

"I'll see you tomorrow, Freya. Until then, I shouldn't have to tell you to be careful." His brow crinkled.

I took a moment to gaze at the scar over his eye and nodded in agreement.

# CHAPTER 17

"This is ridiculous." I sat on my couch, one leg draped over the armrest in a slouch. Damian sat rigid in a nearby chair while Rose sat on the couch next to me. We'd been staring at different spots in my apartment silently for the past ten minutes. After spending an entire day in here, we'd quickly run out of things to talk about.

Damian sat up straight, rubbing his palms against his eyes. "Ridiculous or not, we can't risk you whisking yourself off to Isabela on a whim."

"I don't need to be watched, Damian. You look tired as hell, just go. Celeste did her little witchcraft on me, and Marcus made the deal. It's bad enough I had to use vacation time from work to play keep away."

Rose stared off into space chewing on her cuticles. I slapped a hand against her arm to bring her back to earth and she jumped. "Yes! What Freya said."

Damian sighed, removing his phone from the confinements of his brown suede jacket. His jaw squared off, jarred by whatever he read. Dragging a hand through his hair, he stood, glancing at his phone one more time. "Are you sure you'll be alright?" His hand gripped my shoulder, stiff as a board.

"Go, Damian." I looked at the door, still remaining in my lazy position on the seat cushions.

He hesitated but soon succumbed to my pleas. "Rose, watch her. Make sure she doesn't do anything stupid."

Rose held two fingers up. "Scout's honor."

Without looking at her, I reached over and extended a third finger.

He hesitated again but gripped the phone tightly and turned to leave.

As soon as the door clicked shut, I turned to Rose with a mischievous grin. "So want to do something stupid?"

"Does the fact your life is in peril really do nothing to your nerves?" Rose stared at me blankly.

I scooted to the edge of my seat. "I want to follow Damian. He'll be around to help without even knowing it. Did you see the way he looked at his phone? Something's up that he's not telling us."

Rose tapped her finger against her lips, pretending to think my proposal over.

"Any day now." Standing, I didn't wait for Rose's answer and grabbed my jacket. With that stride of his he's probably half a mile away by now."

"You really think I'd say no?" She leaped to her feet, scrambling to grab her own jacket as I whipped open the door.

"Exactly why I'm already halfway there," I said with a knowing grin.

We rushed down the stairs and tripped over each other when we exited the building. I wanted to make sure Damian wasn't still hanging out right outside the door, but Rose hadn't bothered to check first.

I glowered at her over my shoulder. "The whole point is for him to *not* know we're following him."

She offered a sheepish grin. "Right."

I spotted Damian further down the street, turning a corner. Rose ducked into an alleyway, pushing her back against the brick. I looked around to see if anyone witnessed her deranged act and yanked her back onto the sidewalk.

"What are you doing?"

"Isn't that what they do in the movies when they're tailing someone?" She looked so innocent I wanted to pinch her cheeks.

Snickering, I said, "Did we switch bodies at some point?"

"Pretty sure I'd notice the stark contrast in skin pigment and boob size."

We both smiled and continued to follow Damian. His path took us further and further away from the city and to the outer surrounding woods. The change in scenery almost made me regret my decision—almost.

"What if he's burying a body?" Rose asked. "I'm not sure I want to be witness to that."

I stuck out my bottom lip, contemplating her words. "It's a possibility, considering he's a werewolf."

"Don't joke like that, Freya."

"Oh, you know me—always joking in times of distress." Or backpedaling in an effort to pull Rose out of a crippling fear.

In the distance, I could make out the faint sound of steady drumming. Rose squinted her eyes at me, and we turned our heads for a better listen.

"I think it's coming from this way." Wasting no time, I walked to our left and the drumming grew louder.

As we got closer, an orange glow bounced off of the surrounding trees, and the distinct smell of burning wood filled the air. A group of people gathered around a huge bonfire. Some played drums, flutes, and rattles, while others sat cross-legged on the ground.

"Are they Native American?" Rose whispered.

I couldn't fully process what I was seeing and thought we took a wrong turn at some point while following Damian. Who had pow wows in Pittsburgh? But then, he emerged from the crowd in only a pair of jeans. His tanned chest had several painted designs all over it, and he raised his hands into the air. I quickly ducked behind a bush, dragging Rose down with me.

"Freya, what the hell is going on?"

"You think I know?"

They all started chanting in a language I couldn't understand.

"I think they're speaking Navajo."

"How can you tell?"

"It sounds like words my grandmother used to say when I was little."

They began to dance in a circle around the fire, their bare feet kicking up dirt with every shuffle and stomp. Frankie appeared from the sea of people wearing a tan-colored skirt and a piece of fabric that covered her chest, her abdomen bare. When she turned to the side, I had to do a double take. Either she had a small bump, or she ate an entire deer for dinner.

An older man with long, gray hair pressed a hand against Frankie's belly, then raised both fists into the air. Everyone let out harmonized shrills in unison while Damian approached her, dropping to his knees. While the rest of the group continued to dance around the fire, Damian placed both of his hands over Frankie's stomach and bowed his head.

"Oh my—is she pregnant?" Rose batted me with her hand, not bothering to look over, and her finger almost poked me in the eye.

"Either that or they're celebrating her taking a victorious dump." I swatted her hand away.

Frankie placed a single hand on top of Damian's head and dropped her chin. She grinned widely as Damian lifted his gaze. He stood, wrapping his arms around her hips, and hoisted her into the air. She squealed and danced with the others around the fire, still cradled in his grasp.

The glow of the flames mirrored off Rose's shiny, dark locks. "How many surprises are these people going to have?"

"Endless." The dancing firelight entranced me. The fact werewolves could also get pregnant piqued my curiosity. With such a celebration, I'd venture a guess it wasn't a frequent occurrence.

When they all began to shed their clothes, I tensed.

"If this turns into an orgy, I will never forgive you." Rose clapped a hand over her eyes, but then parted her fingers to see.

They all morphed and changed, but not into werewolves. They were owls, foxes, eagles, crows, and coyotes. All animals spread out and took off into the woods in their new forms. If I could have unhinged my jaw, it would've dropped straight to the ground.

"Apparently, you *do* need a babysitter," Marcus purred from behind us.

I spun around on my knees, launching a fist in his direction, which he caught mid-air. He yanked me to him and kept me from falling flat on my face by pressing his other hand into my shoulder.

"What the hell are you two doing here? Especially after dark?"

The sun had gone down. When did that happen?

"Damian was with us, then he got this text and looked so concerned. We wanted to make sure everything was alright, so we followed him."

"*She* wanted to make sure everything was alright," Rose added, and I glared at her.

Traitor.

"And I am sure you put up a fight to stay in the apartment, hm?" Marcus smirked.

She pointed at him and cleared her throat, gaze dropping. "Ya got me there."

"How did you know I was here?"

He let go of me with a sigh. "'I sensed it' is about as good of an answer as I can offer you."

"You *sensed* it? You sound confused." I studied his expression, but he was always too good at keeping it blank.

"I've never been able to sense a mortal's location before. Considering your little venture and the fact there is no one around now to hear your screams, I'd say it was a fortunate surprise."

How dare he make me feel guilty for simply looking out for a friend? Damian could've been in trouble. Maybe the assailants would've been armed with knives made of . . . silver.

"Well, I've seen just about everything I needed to see here." I pressed my palm into my knee to hoist myself up.

Marcus stood too, sliding his way in front of me. "Oh no. You were so curious as to Damian's whereabouts, we're going to wait right here until they get back from their little gallivant through the woods."

"Did you know Frankie's pregnant?" Rose asked.

My head darted in her direction. "Rose!"

She rolled her shoulders. "What? I don't owe her anything."

Marcus canted his head, running a hand over his chin. "Pregnant? I wasn't aware their kind could procreate." I dared say he looked remorseful.

"Is that the same for all supernaturals? I mean, like, vampires can't, right?" Rose flipped her hand around in the air nonchalantly while she spoke. "At all?"

I gave her a seething gaze for the second time. She had no filter tonight.

Marcus chuckled, peering at me with his chin tilted

downward. His eyes caught with mine through the messy shambles of his hair and it made my groin clench. "Don't worry. I've had many lifetimes to get over the idea there will never be a Marcus Jr." He brushed past us, heading for the dancing flames. "We might as well wait by the fire. I'm sure you two little humans are freezing. What kind of jackets are those anyway? They look about as useful as a bucket full of holes."

We glanced down at our thin, cropped leather jackets and frowned. He had a point. We trotted behind him, and I squatted near the fire, holding my palms up to it. Rose flopped down on the dirt, repeating the same action with her hands after rubbing them together.

"So what's the deal with Celeste?" The words flew out of my mouth like vomit. Why I cared was beyond me.

"What do you mean?" He eyed me quizzically.

*Why don't you read my thoughts, Hot Shot?*

*I told you, it doesn't work that way.*

My eyes narrowed into slits, and I picked up the nearest rock, hurling it in his direction.

From where he stood, he barely got his arm up in time to block it from colliding with his face. He lowered it, glaring at me, but then his lips tugged into a playful grin. I couldn't help but smile right back.

Rose cleared her throat, and I looked over, noting the uncomfortable rigidness of her body. "So Celeste. How you two met is what Freya was going for. Right, Frey?"

I sucked on my lip for a moment before nodding. "Exactly. Since we probably have all night, right?"

"Very well. I met Celeste in 1864 during the Second Schleswig War. I've fought in dozens of wars throughout the ages, mostly because it's part of my nature. I can't escape it any more than a musician can escape the urge to make music."

Rose looked over at me with a pout. I waved at her, which was silent communication for "I'll fill you in later."

"I fought on the Danish side while Celeste's brother fought with the German Confederation. She was so desperate to ensure her brother would survive battle, she disguised herself as a man and fought alongside them. I knew she was a woman, but I didn't dare say a word for fear of the repercussions were she to be found out."

My throat constricted.

"To cut a very long story short, I watched her fool thousands of men for weeks, only to see her brother die. She was so anguished by his death, she got distracted and was shot multiple times, but somehow she didn't fall."

"Was she already a vampire?" I re-positioned myself to sit on my heels.

He nodded solemnly. "And I had no idea. Part of her gift." He tapped his temple.

"I couldn't stand the idea of her being alone after witnessing such a thing, so I offered her a place among my small band of vampires."

"Like a companion?" Rose asked.

"Not exactly. Think of a companion as what you'd call a boyfriend. She and I were colleagues, confidants."

"Have you guys banged?" Again, I went with the word puke.

"You have quite the obsession with my sexual prowess." He flicked his tongue against his teeth.

Thankfully, I didn't have to dignify that with a response because several naked bodies emerged from the woods.

Marcus's attention turned to the group. Damian and Frankie soon showed, hand in hand. To say the werewolf looked shocked when he spotted Marcus would have been a gross understatement.

"Marcus?" Then he saw me, and I gave a small wave. "What the hell are you guys doing out here?" The surprise wore off, quickly replaced by anger.

"You seem rather defensive, Damian. Is it because you've been hiding the fact you're not a werewolf?" Marcus glared at him through the crackling fire, embers making the surrounding air glitter with orange.

I stood. "Then what else could you possibly be?"

Damian's chest heaved and he scooped his clothes into his hand, followed by the others as they neared the fire. Funny how nudity seemed so commonplace now.

"Go on, Damian. Tell her what you are." Marcus coyly clasped his hands behind his back.

A growl formed at the back of Damian's throat and his nostrils flared. "You obviously already know."

"I want to hear you *say* it."

"Bloody hell! We're Skinwalkers," Frankie chimed in, holding a protective hand over her abdomen.

# CHAPTER 18

"*Skin*walker?" Rose asked, looking about three seconds away from expelling whatever she had for dinner onto the ground.

One of the other members of their tribe walked up to Damian, motioning between us all and speaking to him in that same language again. Damian responded with a shake of his head, talking back to him in the same tongue. The man walked off but glared us down all the while.

Frankie looked impatient. "We're from a line of Navajo people who can shift into multiple creatures. Not only wolves."

"Creatures, yes. Even other people if you so desired." One of Marcus's eyebrows twitched, and Damian's fists clenched.

"We don't anymore." Damian cut the air in front of him with his hand. "It's forbidden."

"But you still *can*?" Marcus wasn't backing off, still standing there with his hands clasped behind his back.

"Theoretically, yes." Frankie clenched onto her stomach. "But he just told you we are forbidden from it. Every time a

194

Skinwalker shifts into another human, it curses them. Possibly death."

"You can shift into someone else? Voice? Hair? Everything?" Rose was breathless.

Damian's gaze dropped to the ground. "As long as we've physically seen the person, it's possible, yes."

Rose turned around, took two steps away, bent over, and hurled. There it was. Called it. I walked over to her, pulling her hair from her face and rubbing her back.

"Why did you say you were werewolves?" Marcus widened his stance, squaring off his shoulders. "Why not tell the truth?"

Damian pointed at Rose. "Because of that. Skinwalkers aren't exactly seen in the best light. We're more misunderstood and terrifying than a werewolf."

Marcus nodded and I continued to comfort Rose, half listening to the conversation.

"And your mate, she's pregnant?"

Frankie's face widened, looking at Damian sidelong.

"How did you know?" Damian stalked forward, and Marcus held up a single hand to stop him.

"It's quite obvious, what with the way she clutches her midriff like the entire universe is within it."

Frankie's face melted, her palms pressing into her belly.

"Seems to be it's *their* entire universe," I chimed in, walking back over after Rose waved me away.

"Shifter pregnancies are extremely rare. It's the only way to carry on our line. We were beginning to worry it'd die off with those of us you see here," Damian said.

"Well, congratulations." Marcus zoomed in front of Damian, his face lingering near his. "We're supposed to be on the same side here, Walker. Lie to me again, and I'll be sure it *does* die off with you."

My face crinkled and I reached forward, grabbing Marcus by the crook of the arm. "Marcus!"

He glared at me over his shoulder, his expression a mix between apologetic and furious. Damian's hand launched out, grabbing Marcus by the collar.

"You threaten my kid again, I'll cut you into so many pieces there's no way you're coming back from it."

Marcus shrugged his hand off and turned to walk away. "Freya, a word."

I rested a hand on Frankie's shoulder, who'd thankfully re-clothed herself, offering sympathy before turning to follow him. "What the hell is wrong with you, threatening a baby?"

He dragged his hands through his hair with a sniff. "Of course I wouldn't kill it, but I needed to make sure he knew he can't decide to be trustworthy when it's convenient."

A peculiar relief washed over me. "You wanted to speak to me, liege?"

He squinted. "Don't call me that. You're not my soldier, you're—"

I raised my brows, trying to not think. It'd be unfair game if he could hear my thoughts on what I *hoped* he'd say. Rainbows. Car alarms. Mosquitos. "I'm what?"

"A pain in my ass."

"You get used to it. Ask Adam."

"Right. Adam. I want you to go to his place, lock yourself in, and do not leave until I come for you."

This felt like déjà vu all over again. "Marcus—"

His hands slid to each of my cheeks with a touch so tender it almost made me nuzzle into his palms. "Don't make me beg."

"Would you?"

His eyes searched my face. "You'd be surprised."

*. . . For people I care about.*

I tried to hide my breath hitching, pretending I hadn't heard that fleeting thought from him. So many questions clogged my brain, but I pushed them aside. At least until I was far enough away from him, he couldn't listen in.

Marcus still touched my face when I yelled over to Rose without moving. "Hey, Rose, you up for a game night?"

"That is probably the singular best thing I've heard in days. Yes, yes, a million times yes."

Marcus let his hands fall away, and I caught sight of his brief but grave expression. "The night just started, where will you be?"

"I have to check in with Isabela." He forced our eyes to meet.

I wasn't sure what it was I felt. Jealousy? Anger? Solemnity?

"Right. We must keep up appearances." I backed away from him, gulping, and ran my hands through my hair several times.

He stood motionless, tightening his jaw.

"Tell her I said hi." Not wishing to prolong the torturous

moment any further, I turned my attention toward Damian and Frankie.

"Congratulations, you guys! I'm so, so happy for you!" Their faces bordered on appreciative while their eyes looked at me like I was a deranged hyena. Probably because my excited tone sounded exaggerated.

"Also, great to meet all of you! Sorry I didn't have time to get all your names."

The rest of the tribe also looked at me like I was crazy, while I walked backward, almost tripping over a fallen log.

Marcus appeared beside me, and I jumped. You'd think I'd be used to it by now.

He peered down at me, the corner of his lips twitching. "You're worried."

"No, I'm not." *Of course I am!* I didn't want him to kiss her, to hold her hand, to act sweet to her. None of it. My chest tightened. I hated hormones.

"It doesn't mean anything, Freya."

He'd heard my thoughts. I wanted to crawl into a meerkat hole and become Queen of Meerkat Mansion right then and there. He didn't budge when my fists collided into his chest with annoyance. "I loathe the fact you can hear my occasional thought and I have no idea when it's going to happen."

He held his hands out to the side defensively. "Would you rather I could hear them all the time?"

I paused, stewing on that. "Yes. Yes, I would. Because then I at least would know what I was dealing with."

He traced a finger across several freckles on my face. I

closed my eyes, but then batted his hand away. "Do what you need to do, Marcus. You know where I'll be." I turned away and didn't re-open my eyes until I knew I couldn't see him anymore.

***

"Okay, never have I ever . . . talked back to one of my teachers." Adam glanced around the table where we sat, bottles of empty beer covering half of it.

I sighed, tilting my head back, and took a swig. Surprisingly, so did Rose.

"Wait, Freya, when? And Rose?"

I wasn't sure why he was so surprised. "Oh, come on, you remember that. Eighth grade? Mrs. Shea? She liked to whack you on the knuckles with a ruler if you got an answer wrong. One day I got tired of it, snatched it from her gnarled fingers, and whacked her right back." Shrugging, I took another sip for the hell of it. "By today's standards it would've been abuse."

"Mine is far less gratifying. It was first grade and this conniving little brat of a girl who hated me convinced me I should shoot a spitball at the teacher to be part of the Cool Club. So I did."

We all laughed, and I picked at the label of my bottle. I could feel Rose's stare burning a quarter-sized hole in my head.

"Never have I ever liked someone but fought every possible compulsion to hide it," Rose stated.

I lifted my eyes only to see them both staring at me. "That was random, Ro."

199

"You better take a damn drink, woman." She pointed at the bottle I clutched for dear life.

Out of the corner of my eye, I saw Adam's bottle lift and used it as a distraction from my own heated moment. "Who, Adam?"

It was his turn to abuse the label on his bottle. "I never told you this but, I had the hugest crush on you when we first met."

My plan worked because Rose's attention turned completely on him. Though I hadn't expected the conversation to take this turn.

"Me? I was eight when we met. I was skinny as a rail, teeth as crooked as my soul, and looked like Pippi Longstocking. In fact, I specifically remember screaming like a dying cat when we first met because I was switching foster homes . . . again." I started to laugh, but soon silenced myself, noticing Adam wasn't sharing in my amusement.

"All that aside. I admired you. To go through what you had and still be as strong and confident as you were? Even at ten years old, it was amazing to me."

Awkward times a gajillion. "Why didn't you ever say anything?"

"Because over time I realized what I felt wasn't romantic but was this overwhelming desire to protect you. Besides, given your track record over the years, I most definitely wasn't your type." He smirked and then gave me a genuine smile.

A smile that made my heart melt because I knew he spoke the truth. Still didn't make me feel any less of a jerk.

Rose pressed a hand to her chest. "Unrequited childhood crushes are absolutely adorable, but don't think either one of you are ignoring the pressing question. Freya is going to admit the truth before the night ends."

She wasn't going to let this go. "Fine. I find Marcus attractive. Happy?"

Rose settled back in her chair. "And?"

"Aaaand I may have imagined what it's like in the sack with him a time or two. So sue me." Rose was in the wrong line of work. She should've been a cop, for cripes sake.

Adam looked up as if praying for a beam of light to teleport him away.

Rose leaned forward, slamming her fist into the table, causing all of our bottles to bounce. Mine almost toppled over, and I grabbed it swiftly. "And?!"

I stood from the table, my chair knocking over. "What is this? 'Thirty-Six Questions?' I thought we were playing 'Never Have I Ever?'"

"It's 'Twenty Questions,'" Adam chimed in, which further infuriated me.

"Whatever!" I walked away, tilting my head back to drink.

Rose stood and followed me, soon standing in my path with her palms pressed together in front of her. "Do you remember the first day we met?"

I eyed her suspiciously. Where was she going with this? "Of course I do. I was talking to my boyfriend at the time, and you had to give your two cents about our communication skills."

"That's right. I have an instinct for these types of things.

Call it a blessing, call it a curse. The point is, do you remember what I said?"

After licking my lips, I sighed, the bottle cradled between two fingers falling slack at my side. "You said it wasn't going to last because I looked at him the way a vegetarian looks at a piece of meat . . . unenthusiastically."

"Exactly. You guys lacked passion, spark—"

"I also remember telling you why I stuck around longer than I should have." I gave a sly grin, remembering precisely why I stayed.

"He was a great lay, whatever, my point is you look at Marcus like he's a pretty, green broccoli floret."

I narrowed my eyes. "What is with you and making vegetarian references?"

"Freya!" She grabbed onto my shoulders, growing impatient.

"He's a fucking vampire, Rose. A *vampire*. I'm trying to get over whatever this is because, guess what? I'm going to grow old, and he's going to stay the exact same way. There isn't a point to how I feel because it would never work."

She frowned, her hands falling away.

"Yeah. Forgot about that small detail, huh?" I rolled my shoulders, turning away, not daring to look in Adam's reaction.

Plopping down onto the couch, I rested the bottle on my knee, slouching. Adam soon joined me, sitting close enough he could pat my free knee with his hand.

"I know what you're going to say." I stared at the wall rather than look at him.

"Oh? What am I going to say?"

"That I'm an idiot for falling for him."

"Like we can help who we fall for? I can't say I'm happy to hear it, but I'm also not surprised."

The words took a few moments to process before I looked over at him. He canted his head, patting my knee a few more times before moving his arms to rest on the back of the couch.

"It makes sense. He's tall, dark, and handsome with a sense of danger about him. He's not a complete douchebag like other guys you've dated, so I can see the appeal."

"He's also not human," I said without expression.

"Yeah, that part I don't get." He looked over at me, half smirking.

A knock sounded from the door and I froze, staring at it. Noticing my unease, Adam rose from the couch, holding his hand out to me to stay put. He walked over, peering through the peephole and made a "tsk" sound.

"He really does have impeccable timing." He undid the locks and opened the door to reveal Marcus. His face looked troubled, and he stepped over the threshold, glancing around the room frantically until he spotted me on the couch.

He sunk to his knees in front of me, and I sat straight up. His fingers curled around my knees and he peered up at me.

"Marcus, what is it?" He was scaring me.

"Before I say anything, know we're going to find a way around this." His grip tightened on my knees. Rose and Adam stood near us, their faces as frightened as I felt.

"Just say it." I gripped onto the edge of the seat.

"To break the curse Isabela needs the blood of her descendant." He paused, no doubt gauging if I realized what those words meant.

"So I do a little prick of the finger and she can be rid of a thousand-year-old curse?"

His jaw squared off and he leaned forward. "*All* of your blood."

# CHAPTER 19

My thoughts were far too jumbled to make sense of what he'd said. I hoped the gut feeling boiling in my stomach was false. I stood, ignoring Marcus's hands putting pressure on my legs to stay put.

"What does that mean?" The answer was plain, but I needed to hear it out loud.

"She doesn't want a reunion. She wants—*needs* to kill you. For her own selfish reasons." Marcus's hand opened and closed, his teeth clenching.

I barely noticed Adam moving toward me but felt his hand once it touched my arm.

"Did she say that? She's had a dozen opportunities to do it; maybe she's trying to psyche us out by threatening her." Adam, always the optimist.

Rose looked like she might hurl again. Her hand reached out to the side, finding the armrest of the couch, and she sunk down on it.

"No. It's because she has to wait." Marcus barely had time to take a breath before Adam chimed in again.

"For what?"

I bit down on my lower lip, repeatedly letting it roll past my teeth. "February twenty-ninth."

All eyes shot over to me like lasers, bewilderment consuming their faces.

"Your birthday?" Adam asked, taking a step back.

"How did you know that?" Marcus widened his stance.

"She told me my birthday was unique." I still didn't make eye contact with anyone. The idea of dying never really scared me, but for some reason fear rubbed at my spine like an Indian burn. "Not only was it a leap year, but the night I was born three different occurrences happened with the moon, and I happened to be her descendant to put the cherry on top."

*You're not going to die.*

Marcus peered at me with an intensity that could have caused a tsunami.

"For Christ's sake," Adam started, glancing down at his phone. "Your birthday is in three days."

"I certainly hope you all remembered to buy me presents, especially this year." A weak grin was all I could muster.

Marcus shoved his hands in his pockets. I could tell by how uncharacteristically quiet he was he hadn't told us the whole story.

"Let's say for the sake of argument she gets her way," I said.

Marcus opened his mouth to speak and I raised a finger, pressing it over his lips.

"She gets her way. The curse is lifted and then what?" I

dropped my hand away and stood in front of him, silent.

"She'll become more powerful than she is now. No longer reduced to life in the shadows. No more need to drink blood to survive. The power will make her dangerous and ravenous for revenge." His voice barely above a whisper, but the words dug so deep it was impossible not to hear them.

"This is bullshit! Why would the Aztec god of night make a clause like this if he meant to truly curse her?" Adam shouted, panic lacing his tone.

"He probably never thought it was possible. It's been thousands of years, their ancestral line could've easily died off at some point, but it didn't. And for someone to be born on the exact night with all of those anomalies? It's unheard of. He made the clause to further torture her. To give her hope." Marcus yanked his hands from his pockets, turning away from me. He interlaced his fingers and rested them on the back of his neck, his elbows sticking out on each side of his head.

"How did she know Freya existed?" Rose asked, and it sounded like she'd reverted back to a three-year-old version of herself, her voice squeaky and soft.

"I have no idea." Marcus stared out the window. It started to rain at some point after he arrived, and the water blurred the night sky. "She's been in exile for the past century because she gave up on life. Little did she know a petite red-haired girl who could give her what she wanted was out there, bouncing between foster homes."

"Lucky for me she didn't find me until after we met then, huh?" For a brief moment, I forgot Rose and Adam were there.

I stared at Marcus's back, and his glance steadily turned to me over his shoulder.

*I've been wondering lately if . . .*

My ability to hear his occasional thought seemed to fade over time, and this particular one disappearing into the gloom of the storm outside made me antsy.

I crossed the room and stood between him and the window. "You wonder if what?"

I caught sight of Rose and Adam sharing a troubled glance over Marcus's shoulder, but I focused on the scar over his eye.

"If we were somehow fated to meet." He looked down at me, those blue eyes intensifying.

Silence fell across the room as Marcus and I stood there trying to make sense of one another. A vibration thrummed against my chest from my increasing heart rate. Rose was right. And it shouldn't have surprised me, but at some point these past few days, my feelings toward him changed. My timing could've been better, considering I was about to die.

The chill of Marcus's touch caressed my neck, his hands resting at each side of my nape. He used his thumbs to tilt my chin upward. "We have three days. We'll figure something out."

For crying out loud. Please tell me he only heard the latter part of that thought.

"It's getting close to sunrise. I need to go. Tomorrow night, I'll meet with the others and discuss what we're up against." He caught my gaze one last time before his hands fell away.

He went to turn, but I grabbed his shoulder. "Marcus, don't think for one second you're sacrificing yourself for me. I won't let you be a martyr on my account."

"If I disregarded Caesar's orders on my safety, what makes you think I'll follow yours?" Despite the tension hanging in the air like smog, he half smiled.

I took another step forward, closing the remaining distance between us. My breasts brushed against his ribs, and I could hear him gulp. "Because I'm not Caesar."

He smirked, nodding before he stepped away. "I'll inform you all of the plan once we've come to it tomorrow." He looked between Rose and Adam. "That is, if everyone is volunteering to contribute?"

"You know I'm in," Adam said, lightly knocking his knuckles against the back of the couch.

"I'll help in any way I can," Rose said and wrapped her arms around herself.

Marcus nodded once. "Be safe, be vigilant." He opened the door and peered over his shoulder.

*I curse the sun for making me leave you.*

And then he was gone. I trailed my fingers down one side of my neck, still feeling the remnants of the coolness he'd left there.

"Are you okay?" Rose asked.

Was I? I wasn't sure anymore. "About as okay as one can be when their mortality is supremely challenged, I guess."

"You know neither of us will let you die." Adam's concerned expression made me feel uneasy.

"That's precisely what I'm afraid of," I said with a sigh. "I'm going to sleep."

\*\*\*

My phone felt heavy in my palm. I'd been sitting on Adam's couch for the past fifteen minutes, trying to decide whether or not to text Damian. I also had no idea how I was going to sneak under Adam's radar. I blew out a breath and worked my thumb across the number pad.

> Me: Can we meet?
> Damian: Now who's being cryptic.
> Me: I'm serious. I have a favor to ask and I need to ask it in private.
> Damian: Park in fifteen?
> Me: Bench?
> Damian: You know the one.

I turned off the screen when Adam's shadow passed by me. He glanced down at my guilty face.

"Who were you texting?"

I couldn't lie to him. Not with everything going on. "Damian. I need to talk to him."

"Okay. I'll go with you." Adam reached for his jacket and I didn't move a muscle.

"Alone."

He slowly let the jacket fall onto the back of the couch and glared at me. "Why?"

"This is one of those moments I need you to trust me."

In a nervous twitch, I tapped my phone against my knee.

"I do trust you. But with the current state of the world right now, I don't trust *it*." He grabbed his jacket again and threw it on. "I'll walk you to wherever you're meeting him and then stay out of ear shot. Deal?"

I didn't deserve Adam. How he managed to stay my friend this long and not lose his mind remained a mystery. "Thank you."

\*\*\*

Just like last time, Damian made it to the bench before I did. But unlike last time, we'd been through so much together our dynamic was different.

"What's on your mind, Spitfire?" He glanced up at me once I reached the bench, squinting his dark eyes from the sun.

"First of all—" I sat on my hands to warm them from the chill in the air. "I wanted to say a sincere congratulations to you and Frankie."

He grinned, his gaze dropping to look at his palms. "Thank you. I'll tell you though, having it in your brain that you'll never be a dad throws you for a whirl when you suddenly realize . . . you will be."

I chuckled, moving my butt around on my hands. "I bet."

"Is there a reason Adam is skulking around that garbage can?" He didn't look in Adam's direction, but I knew he was trying to be out of sight.

"Doing what big brothers do best. He's better at that

than being a spy, obviously."

Damian smirked. "So what favor do you need?"

Ah, yes. The part I dreaded most. "Marcus is going to call a meeting tonight with all of you. About Isabela. He found out in order for her to lift the curse, she has to kill me on my birthday."

He turned to face me, his expression falling. "Jesus, Freya."

"Marcus will no doubt bring up some harebrained idea where he sacrifices himself to ensure I stay alive. If he does, I need you to shoot it down." I gave him a sidelong glance and bit at the inside of my lip to keep it from trembling.

"You make it sound so easy. Did you think about the fact he probably already knows you're against it?"

"I have. And that's why I need you to stick to your guns with this, Damian. What good will it do for him to get himself killed or sign over his life to her? I'll be alive, sure, but what if she doesn't die?"

"Let's say I went along with this . . . he'll expect an alternate plan."

"Tell him you'll decapitate her with a katana for all I care. You're a smart man, I'm sure you can think of something."

He shook his head and leaned back on the bench, resting his arms across the entire length of it. His chin lifted as he stared at the sky. "You care about him, don't you?"

My mouth grew dry and I still couldn't look at him. "I need you to do this for me. Please."

"Since you asked so nicely, I will *attempt* to dissuade him. I can't make any promises though."

I gave him a hug. His body stiffened beneath my arms, but soon he returned the embrace. My sinuses burned and I peeled away, sniffling.

"I'll uh—let you get back to your mate." It came out more like a question rather than a statement. "I don't think I'll ever get used to saying that. Can I just call her your lady?"

Damian chuckled before standing up. "As long as you don't call her bitch, I don't care what you refer to her as."

I rose to my feet, holding a single finger up. "One last thing. I didn't dream up you saying you *could* shift into another human being, right?"

He laughed again, shaking his head. "No dream."

"That's what I thought. Still as creepy as the first time."

He jutted his head toward Adam still crouched behind one of the green metal garbage cans lining the sidewalk. An old woman walked with a cane, her eyes cast downward. "You better go get him before he scares the hell out of that old woman."

I did a hitch step before jogging over and gave Damian one last wave. Marcus would probably still insist on doing anything he could in order to save my life, but he didn't know what kind of hellcat I could really be when I didn't get my way.

# CHAPTER 20

"Do you have any threes?" My tone went from unenthusiastic to downright bored.

"Go fish." The tip of Adam's tongue stuck out of the corner of his mouth, and he reshuffled the cards in his hand.

I slapped my hand down on the pile of cards at the center of the table with a sigh, slipping the four of clubs in with the others.

"This is what I've been reduced to. Playing Go Fish to keep from losing my mind." I scratched my forehead in annoyance.

"Hey. At least I had a deck of cards. There's just something about the physical contact of the paper against your fingers a computer can't hold a candle to."

Groaning, I plopped my cards onto the table and stuck out my bottom lip. "You know I am going stir crazy, right?"

He didn't bother looking up and continued to shuffle his cards. "Yup."

"And you know at some point I'm going to insist you let me leave, right?"

He stared me down. "And *you* know I will shoot you with a tranq dart if I have to, right?"

"I hate you."

His eyes floated back to his cards with a wide grin. "No, you don't."

I couldn't help but laugh and threw my cards at him. "Stop being so damn likable!"

Chuckling, he lifted his arms to block the projectiles.

My phone buzzed and I stood, whipping it from my pocket. It was a text from Damian. Was I prepared for this? Holding my breath, I opened the message to read.

> Damian: After an hour of debating, he refused to listen to me. He plans to give himself over to Isabela for all of eternity if it comes down to it. Thought you'd want to know.

My entire body went numb, and I almost dropped the phone. Adam was by my side like a flash of lightning, resting his hand on the crook of my elbow. "Freya? What's wrong?"

"I've—" I started, the word "eternity" looping in my brain. "I have to go talk to Marcus. Before he does something ridiculously stupid." The shock soon sizzled into anger, and I grabbed my leather jacket from a nearby chair.

"You know I have to come with you, right? Especially now, you're all frantic. Not thinking clearly."

I went for the door, but Adam moved to stand in front of me.

"I really do need to do this one alone. If Isabela somehow manages to nab me in the few minutes it takes to get to his hotel, then she can have her fill." My chest pumped up and down, and my breathing quickened.

"Frey—"

"Adam!" The look on his face when I shouted his name stung like whiskey on an open wound. I couldn't remember the last time I'd raised my voice to him.

His lower jaw shifted forward, and he slowly began to nod. He stood aside, allowing me to pass.

I stepped outside, turning to look at him, my eyebrows crinkling in dismay.

"I really hope he's worth it." He slammed the door right in my face. I probably deserved that.

My eyes pinched shut, and I fought back tears, raising my fist, but letting it drop back to my side. Adam would need time before mending this moment, and time was something I didn't have. I needed to convince Marcus to abandon his plan.

*** 

I marched out of the elevator, heading straight for Marcus's hotel room and knocked repeatedly against the door. Ten seconds passed and I switched to two fists. Finally, the door swung open, and he stood there glaring at me. Not bothering to wait for an invitation, I shoved past him and paraded around the room.

"Is Celeste here?" I asked, poking my head into the bathroom, pausing a moment to gawk at how ginormous the bathtub was.

"No. She's not." He flicked his finger forward, shutting the door, and peered at me. "Care to explain you almost knocking a hole through my door?"

"We need to talk."

He must've just returned from the meeting because he was still in a pair of sleek black dress pants and a deep red button-down shirt.

Slipping his hands in his pockets, he took a few steps forward. "About?"

I crossed the room, tilting my chin up to look him straight in the face. "Who do you think you are, making choices that have to do with *my* life without consulting me?"

His eyes narrowed and he leaned forward, the tips of our noses almost brushing. "Much like human males, we vampires don't enjoy playing guessing games. Why don't you come out with it?"

I stood my ground. "I know your plan to give yourself over to Isabela."

He leaned back with a sigh. "I wondered why Damian was so concerned for my well-being. You two had a conversation, I take it?"

"Don't do it, Marcus. There has to be another way. There always is."

He studied my face, a glint forming in his eyes. This moment would be perfect to hear his thoughts. Any time now.

"She can't win. You know that. It'd be detrimental to not only humans, but supernaturals alike. I could possibly put an end to it by sacrificing my life in exchange for yours."

"We are talking an entire eternity here. She doesn't exactly seem the type to stick to her word. She could lure you into some kind of pact, kill me, and then not only will she have her gigolo, but ultimate power to go with it."

A hint of a smile played on his lips. "Gigolo?"

He didn't want to take this seriously? Fine. "I'm going to talk to her. I can be pretty convincing when I want to be. Maybe I can talk her into letting her only living relative live."

"Like hell you will." His face turned predatory, and he removed his hands from his pockets.

"Yeah? I can sacrifice too, Marcus. She's my grandmother, my problem. I've appreciated your help, but it is my friends who could be affected by all this, and I should be the one to protect them."

"My life is damned. You still have the rest of yours to live. Don't be foolish!" His shoulders hunched forward, his words growing more frustrated by the second. "You hate vampires. One less to worry about."

My heart leaped into my throat. "I do hate vampires. And I tried hating you. I really did. At first, I hated when you were around, but I also hated when you weren't." My voice cracked as my throat felt like sandpaper.

He stood there silent as the grave, and I felt compelled to deafen the silence by doing what I did best . . . ramble.

"I was content being alone, having Rose and Adam to fill that void. You stir things in me that irritate me but make me weak all at the same time. I haven't fully figured this out, but Marcus I will be *damned* too if you give yourself to Isabela before—"

His mouth engulfed mine, swallowing the rest of my words. I returned the kiss, my mouth mingling with his.

Though he was cold, it did nothing to dampen the fire surging through my veins. My fingers gripped onto his hair while his arms wrapped around me, his large hands pressing between my shoulder blades and lower back. A hunger had been building within me, and I was at the point of starvation.

He pulled away from the kiss, and I almost tripped forward. He stared down at me, his eyes the brightest blue I'd seen them since the day we met. I wasn't sure if he was waiting for the a-okay from me or . . .? A corner of his lips slid into a grin, and he scooped me into his arms, carrying me over to the bed as if I weighed nothing more than a pillow.

I half expected him to toss me, but he rested me gently atop the comforter and stood upright. The lion's gaze locked with mine, his fingers making quick work of his shirt buttons. He peeled the shirt away, revealing his pale yet chiseled-to-perfection body. I sat up on my elbows to get a better view. He had a warrior's build, and I wanted to feel the weight of him immediately.

He tossed the shirt aside, smiling as he ran a hand through his dark hair, giving it a tussle. My heart beat against my chest like a jackhammer when his hands began to work at the clasp of his pants. In one swift motion he rid himself of clothing and stood at the end of the bed in all his vampiric, naked glory. He playfully did a slow turn, allowing me to devour him with my gaze. He had the whole package topped with a pretty red ribbon.

I bit my fingernail, eyeing the ass I'd seen so many times

through the shield of pants, and it was every bit of rounded, muscular perfection I'd imagined it to be. There wasn't one ounce of him that didn't scream carnal, masculine sensuality. He crawled across the bed, grinning wickedly.

"Your thoughts are going to make me blush," he purred, his hands trailing up my still very clothed legs.

His chilly fingers slipped under the hem of my shirt, sliding it up as he continued to crawl. I lifted my arms up so he could easily remove it, goosebumps littering my skin. He dipped a hand behind my back, undoing the clasp of my bra with one flick of his fingers. I shimmied my shoulders, letting the straps fall, and he tossed the garment aside.

His stare lingered on my breasts before he dropped his head, taking one of them into his mouth, kneading the other with his hand. He lifted his head, peering up at me, the look in his eyes anything but innocent. His fangs sprung out and I'd forgotten for a split moment what he was, a breath hitching in my throat.

He dipped his head down again, beginning a descent down my body of licks, kisses, and the occasional graze from one of his fangs, never letting it break skin. He licked a complete circle around my belly button and a shiver ran down my spine all the way to my groin. Using his vampire-like speed, he ripped the pants from my bottom half, leaving me naked beneath him.

He sat back, his eyes unabashedly surveying my entire body, that predatory grin returning. I shivered, partly from his teasing caresses, and partly because I yearned for extra special attention.

"Marcus." It came out like a pleading whisper.

He smiled, bringing himself down on top of me, supporting his weight with his forearms on each side of my head. "Like I said, you've become greedy."

"I never took you for a tease." I spread my legs, trailing my big toe up the side of his muscular thigh, bucking my hips.

He lowered his mouth to mine, taking a moment to lightly lick my bottom lip before I felt the tip of him pushing slowly against my entrance. His eyes locked with mine as he pushed himself forward. It felt amazing, yet torturous. With a growl, he filled me to the hilt, and my back arched from the bed. It overwhelmed me at first before my muscles relaxed around him, my fingernails digging into his back.

He began his steady pulse within me, keeping our eyes locked, and I wrapped my legs around his waist, deepening the connection. Keeping with his well-timed thrusts, he lifted one of his wrists, biting into it. He held it so it wouldn't drip and stared down at me expectantly.

I gave him a bewildered expression considering I didn't need healing—at least not right now, check with me again in the morning.

"Trust me," he said, and I obliged by parting my lips.

He turned his wrist, the blood trickling down onto my mouth. I used my tongue to lap up what didn't make its way onto my lips, feeling the surge I'd felt during the fight. The adrenaline would be used for other activities this time however. His mouth dipped down toward my chest, but he didn't lose the momentum of his thrusts. He extracted his fangs, delicately plunging them into the plumpest part of my breast. I gasped. The mixture of brief pain followed by immense pleasure as he fed off me from such a sensitive spot coursed through me.

What happened next was what I could only describe as a . . . connection. His blood coursing through me, and my own flowing into him, bonded us somehow. He pulled away, retracting his fangs, and lowered his mouth toward mine. Our blood mixed again, stained on each other's lips as we kissed.

My turn. Reading my every thought and desire, Marcus wrapped his burly arm around my waist and flipped us over. I lay on top of him, my hair falling in a fiery cascade as I gazed down. Pushing myself to sit up right, I let my hands run through my locks, before tracing my fingertips down my chest, smearing some of the blood down my breast and stomach. He grabbed onto my hips, and I began to rock back and forth atop him. This man who had the power to snap me like a twig lay beneath me, completely under my control and at my will.

His blood rushing through my veins coupled with our act made every nerve in my body ignite. He didn't feel cold anymore; he felt like a normal heat mixed with the tingle of a mild, electric shock. I tilted my head back, continuing to buck my hips as I dragged my hands down my neck, eyes closed.

He sat up, my breasts pressing into the tautness of his chest, and I flittered my eyes open. He pressed his palm into one of my butt cheeks, guiding my movements. His lips found my neck, sucking it without teeth, and I longed to feel them there again.

Answering my unspoken wish, I soon felt the plunge of his fangs in my neck and gripped onto his shoulders, my nails breaking skin. He grunted from the sudden invasion but only held onto me tighter, our hips rolling against one another in perfect unison. My insides quivered and quaked. When he took one last hard pull of my blood, the vampiric kiss sent me straight over the edge. He pulled back, allowing my chin to tilt upward as I shivered through my release, my insides clenching around him in approval.

He motioned me back toward the bed and moved over top of me. Sitting back, he gripped onto my hips, pulling them so they were in a high angle and began to thrust into me. After a few moments, he let out a moan that sounded like a guttural snarl, reaching his own peak.

When he pulled himself away, I still felt every touch, every movement we'd performed, and it continued to tantalize my skin, my insides. I'd never done hard drugs before, but I wondered if this is what it felt like. Marcus's hand cupped my cheek, and it warped me back to planet Earth.

"Being high on drugs couldn't begin to compare. I assure you." He gave a wicked grin. "We should continue this in the shower."

I blinked, running my hands over my arms. "Continue?"

He brushed the hair from my eyes. "Didn't account for my stamina? How naïve of you, Hellcat."

He slid from the bed, holding out a hand to help me. I

took it, and he gave one firm tug so that I was off the bed and standing on my tiptoes in front of him. The sheets were soaked with blood, far too much to feign I'd been a virgin to the maid. "Marcus, it looks like a murder scene in here."

He interlaced his fingers with mine and led me toward the bathroom. "Shh. I'll take care of it. I've been covering my tracks for thousands of years, remember?"

The two of us, naked as the day we were born, paraded through the open space of the hotel room, blood staining our faces and chests. The coolness of the tile against my bare feet gave me a shock. He let go of my hand momentarily to turn on the faucets for the shower, and I caught a glimpse of myself in the mirror. My hair was in disarray but still somehow managed to look sexy. The puncture wounds from his two bites still remained as he had yet to heal them, and I let my fingertips graze each, feeling the oddest sensation like I'd been claimed.

He appeared behind me, dipping his chin into the crook of my neck. "A woman like you could never be claimed, Freya. Unless of course, you gave me permission." His eyes caught mine in the reflection of the mirror, and I desired him all over again.

The steam from the heat of the warming shower soon clouded our view of one another, and I turned around to face him, wrapping my arms around his neck. I kissed him with a newfound appreciation and could never have imagined needing, wanting someone who wasn't human. He backed me into the massive shower, the hot water cascading over my head, trickling down every curve of my body.

The blood from our bodies made the water circling the drain turn a light shade of brown, reminding me of the movie *Psycho*. He turned me toward the wall, my palms pressing against wet marble. He kissed the back of my shoulder before taking me from behind, his chest pressed against my back, his hands gripping my hips for leverage.

We finished in the shower, wet, clean, and satiated. He healed his bite marks, and we fell asleep wrapped in each other's arms like two normal lovers who'd given themselves to each other. I didn't want the night to end. Didn't want to deal with the enigma that was Isabela. I'd found a different sort of happiness I didn't think I was capable of having. She wasn't going to take that from me.

# CHAPTER 21

The room felt empty, my vision foggy. I slid my hand all around the bed, disappointed when it didn't hit another body. The sheets were new, no evidence of our unique occurrence last night to be found. I sat up, curling the sheet around me, naked, and still feeling the aftershock. Under normal circumstances, I'd have been taken aback, waking up alone, but I knew why he couldn't stay. The thought made my heart clench. We would never be able to wake up together. No morning breath. No staring at each other sleeping with the sun peeking through the windows. That is . . . if we lived through the ordeal with my deranged grandmother.

I rolled over onto my back and caught sight of something red resting on the nightstand. Sitting up and scooting to the edge of the bed, I smiled to myself. It was a single red rose and a hand-written note.

Freya,

I was tempted to let the sun take me this morning. It took everything I had to pry myself away from you. You looked so peaceful, as if all of this chaos festering around us didn't exist. If I should meet my death, I can die with the memories of last night, and for that, I am eternally thankful to you.

Yours,

Marcus

A single tear rolled down my cheek. I should've known better than to try and reason with him. He's a fighter and always has been. Putting himself in harm's way for those who couldn't do it for themselves was part of his nature—but I was a fighter too.

A loud knock sounded at the door, making me jump, the note falling into my lap. I stood up, clutching the sheet around me, and peered through the peephole before whipping open the door.

"Damian?" He knew it was daytime and therefore had to have known Marcus wasn't here.

He welcomed himself in, pushing past me, and didn't bat an eyelash toward my attire.

"He's not here," I stated, pushing the door shut with an ominous click.

"I know. I came to talk to you."

"How did you know I'd be here?" My grip on the sheet tightened.

He dropped his eyes to my makeshift dress and then leveled his gaze with mine.

"Yeah, don't answer that." I ran my hand through my hair, trying to make it look less like I stayed up half the night having sex.

"Freya—" He hesitated and shoved his hands into his jean pockets.

An unsettling feeling formed in the pit of my stomach. "What is it?"

"They took Adam."

I felt numb. My knees felt weak, and I reached for the wall for support. "Please tell me by *they* you don't mean Isabela's goons?"

He pursed his lips together, walking toward me. "A note was left. Along with—" He removed something from his pocket and hid it within his palm. "This." His hand opened.

"Is that a damn finger, Damian?" Fury possessed me, and I gripped my head in pain at the mere thought of Adam in danger.

"We don't know if it's his. It could be to get a rise out of you." He closed his fist around it again, tucking it out of sight.

My breathing turned shallow and I shot him a glare. "Well it worked. Messing with me is one thing, but when you threaten my family, you get the claws." I knew what I had to do to rectify the entire situation and no one was going to like it. Not even me.

"She promised not to call on you, but she never said anything about not trying to lure you. Don't let her win by getting irrational, we have time. We need to make a game plan."

"I already have one." I turned toward the door, resting my hand on the handle.

"What's going through that head of yours?" He stepped up beside me, trying to capture my gaze.

"Have everyone meet back here tonight." I opened the door, stepping aside.

"We'll get him back." He dipped his head down so I was forced to look at him. His expression was so concerned it contorted his face. "Don't let this cloud your judgment."

"It's not clouded, Damian. In fact, it's clearer than it has been in a really long time."

He nodded solemnly before stepping outside. I went to shut the door, but he turned around. "I really hope you know what you're doing."

"I do." I shut the door before he had a chance to say anything else.

I pressed my forehead to the white-colored wood, holding back every fiber of my being to keep from sobbing. They'd taken Adam and possibly cut off one of his fingers all because of me. His presence in my life automatically made him a target. I now knew exactly how Batman felt and why he couldn't let anyone in on his vigilante lifestyle.

Deciding it was time to put more on than just a piece of linen for clothes, I changed into what I'd come over in. I contemplated waiting for Marcus to come back but realized telling everyone my plan would be that much harder if I had to be alone with him before everyone else arrived. I'd wait it out in my apartment and go over the plan repeatedly so there was no chance of failure. It had to work flawlessly.

I texted Rose the address to Marcus's hotel, asking her to come to the meeting. Against my better judgment I texted her about Adam and didn't answer my phone when she called immediately after. An invisible thread held my sanity together, a thread that could snap at any given moment, and I needed to keep my head in the game. Talking to her always seemed to tug at my vulnerabilities.

When the sun faded away, replaced by the brightness of the moon and stars, it was time. I purposely left later to ensure Marcus and I wouldn't be alone. Besides, I wasn't exactly known for my punctuality. No sooner had I arrived on Marcus's floor, the door swept open and he stood at the threshold.

A lump formed in my throat from the sight of him, and an ache pooled between my thighs. I stepped up to him, gazing up at his stupidly handsome face.

*What are you scheming?* His thought flowed through my brain as clear as if he'd spoken it out loud. I'd been used to them sounding distant and no louder than a whisper.

*Let me explain before you freak out.*

I willed the thought back to him and he stepped aside to allow me entry. As I walked past, his arm delicately wrapped around my waist and he nuzzled my ear. And that is exactly why I needed to be alone before this announcement. He let me go and I moved to the center of the living room.

Everyone stood around, murmuring to each other. Rose ran over and grabbed onto one of my shoulders. "What the hell is going on?" Her eyes were wide, frantic.

I cleared my throat, glancing around before speaking. "Everyone, it would seem to me none of us can find the best solution with Isabela. The solution being her death. She's too strong in every way imaginable. I propose we entrap her. Force her to live the rest of her days behind a stone wall."

"Trap her in a cave," Rose said with a hint of amusement.

It was an idea we unknowingly spawned back when I wanted to kill Marcus.

"The idea has merit, but what's to stop her from going after you yet again if she were to one day escape?" Damian asked, his arm wrapped around Frankie's shoulders.

I stared at the floor and took a deep breath. "The only way Isabela will ever break the curse is by spilling my blood herself. That can't happen. And to ensure it doesn't I have two options: I can either die by someone else's hand or be turned into a vampire."

The room fell so silent you could hear a pin drop.

Marcus stalked over, glowering down at me. "Absolutely out of the question. Are you out of your mind?" His nostrils flared, his words booming across the room.

Everyone else started stammering their disapproval. There was so much shouting and words being exchanged I couldn't make out what anyone said. I clasped my hands over my ears. "Would you all shut up!"

They did, and the space fell silent as the grave again. I moved my hands away from my head and Marcus stared down at me, shaking his head.

"Marcus, it's a solid plan. I need you to do this."

"I will *not*. There's a reason I've never turned anyone else into this thing I am. Don't ask me to do that to you." His eyebrows crinkled and he peered down at me pleadingly.

"Should I ask Celeste, then?" Inside, I was dying from that look on his face, but I had to play the tough guy here.

"There has to be another way. You shouldn't have to condemn yourself to an eternity of darkness and blood sucking," Damian snarled, glaring at Marcus like he'd been on board for the idea.

"That's my choice to make."

Rose stepped up to me, her trembling hand grazing my arm like it'd burn her. "Have you thought about what it would mean? How life would change?"

I nodded and stared at the floor. "I have. But I've also thought about what would happen if Isabela won. I'd be dead, and you and Adam would likely follow. You know me. Do you think I'm okay with that? That I'll accept it?"

Marcus remained silent, standing rigid in the corner. If he'd been thinking anything, I couldn't hear it.

Damian dragged a hand over his face and paced the length of the room. "This is fucking crazy."

Frankie and Celeste were quiet too, as if they felt out of place in the discussion. Regardless of their feelings toward me, the concern was plain on their faces.

"Every minute we stand here debating is another minute closer to Adam being dead. Please. Let me do this." My sinuses stung, and I bit the inside of my mouth to keep my lips from trembling.

There was no hiding the shock on everyone's faces, though Marcus tried to mask it by planting a hand over his mouth and digging his fingers into each of his cheeks.

"Adam?" Marcus asked.

"Isabela took him." I sniffed.

Damian's eyes went wide and unblinking before he nodded and turned his gaze toward Marcus. "Do it."

Marcus's expression fell, and he clenched his fists, closing the distance between him and Damian with two long strides. "You think I take orders from you?"

Damian puffed his chest. "She's right. As much as I hate what she'll become, it's the only way for her to live. You think you can handle that? Her *actual* death?"

The corners of Marcus's jaw popped and he looked away, grabbing onto the back of his neck.

Rose wrapped her arms around herself and shook her head frantically. "I'm not on board with this, Frey."

Her words already made me start to die inside. I gripped her bicep. "I hope one day you can realize why I had to do this."

The skin between Rose's eyes wrinkled and she placed her hand over mine. We shared a silent moment, and it was the closest thing to an agreement I'd get out of her for now.

Everyone turned their heads toward Marcus as he was the last part of the puzzle. I hadn't thought convincing him would be easy, but I grossly underestimated the turmoil it'd fester in my gut seeing his tortured gaze.

He glanced around the room before stalking over to me. He grabbed my hand, leading me toward the bathroom and away from everyone else. Once inside, he slammed the door shut, rattling the mirror.

"Why are you doing this, Freya?"

"Have you not listened to a word I've said?" My words came out impatient and haughty.

"Of course I have. You *know* why I can't do this. If I'd had the choice to become this creature, I would've said no a million times over. You *have* the choice."

"They left Damian a note along with a piece of a finger. A finger, Marcus!" My lips grew dry as I remembered it resting in Damian's palm.

"For fuck's sake," he huffed, dragging a hand through his hair.

I stepped forward, gently placing my hand on his arm. "She can't win. This is the only way, Marcus, please."

He gazed at the ground, arms stiff at his sides. "You'll never see the sun again."

"I've worked nightshifts at a bar for the past three years, mostly sleep during the day, and have you seen my skin?" I pointed toward my pasty, pale, freckle-ridden skin. "The sun hates me."

He clenched his fists, still not looking at me. "You'll have to drink blood to survive."

I shrugged. "I've gulped yours down several times. It's not so bad."

"*Human* blood."

A lump formed in my throat. It was the part that bothered me the most. "I'll get over it."

"Do you know where I go every day before sunrise?" He peered down, walking toward me.

"I'd been meaning to ask—"

He cut me off and kept walking until my butt hit up against a nearby wall. "Under the foundation of the building. I have to find a cold, dark, and merciless spot with no windows, completely separated from the day."

We stood toe to toe. When I made up my mind, not even scary intimidation techniques would work on me.

"Sounds . . . cozy."

Marcus groaned, turning his back on me, and stepped away again. "You will have to watch everyone you care about grow old and die while you remain on Earth exactly as you are now."

"At least they'll have a chance at life! A *chance* to grow old." I closed the distance between us again, taking his hands in mine.

"You will never bear children." Out of all the negatives he mentioned, that one looked like it pained him the most to say.

"I never wanted to pass on this kind of crazy anyway." I smiled, but he didn't seem to find it as humorous as I did.

"You ask me to turn you into the very thing which took everything away from you." There went that tortured expression again.

"Humans took a lot from me too, but not all of them are monsters." I placed my hand over the coolness of his cheek.

"I'd be lying if I said a small part of me didn't wish for this very moment. You asking me to change you. But now that it's happening, I know it was complete selfishness on my part."

"If Isabela wins, I'm dead. My family is dead, and she gets to have the one person who made all the chips fall into place. We both knew going into this how immortality has a way of dampening a relationship when a mortal's involved." I kept attempting to make light of the situation. He wasn't having it.

"I care enough for you to let you go. We'll trap Isabela and then I'll walk away. Let you forget about me." He curled his fingers with mine, staring down at our hands locked together.

"And there's another one of those shreds of humanity you have left after all these years. Those shreds make me less frightened to go through with this. Plus, I could never forget about you, Marcus. *Never.*"

He slipped his arms around me, pulling me toward him and dipping his face against my collarbone. "I don't deserve you."

I nuzzled my cheek against his beard. "That's not for you to decide."

He pulled back, resting his hands on each of my shoulders. "There's something else you should know." His lips thinned. "You would be sired to me."

"Well, sure, you'd be *siring*," I air quoted, "another vampire. Is that not the definition of the word?"

"It means something different in this case. We'd be connected. Bonded. Able to feel everything the other felt even if we weren't around one another. Sense where the other one is. It's a defense mechanism to allow us to protect each other."

My entire body tingled in response to his words. "Apparently we can already hear each other's thoughts. Seems like the next logical step."

He cupped my face with his hand, staring down at me with a tender expression that made my heart soar. "I fear you will never forgive me for this."

"I already have forgiven you. You're not forcing me into this, and you haven't asked me to do it. You'd be doing this because I asked *you*."

He tilted his down and gave me a gentle kiss. "It

wouldn't be like I've bitten you before. I'd have to continue until you are on the very brink of death."

My breath caught in my throat. "And then?"

"You'd drink my blood and trigger the transformation. It hurts like hell, Freya." He moved his hand to the back of my head, continuing to stare down at me.

"Watching Isabela get her way would hurt a lot worse." I clenched my jaw.

Marcus's nostrils flared as we stared at each other, his hand idly kneading the back of my neck. His fangs sprung out, and he slowly dipped his mouth toward my neck. His nose brushed against my nape, and a single drop of liquid fell onto my skin. A tear. He pushed away from me and wiped his shirt sleeve under his nose.

"I won't do this."

I blinked rapidly. What just happened?

He bolted into the room, and everyone looked between me and him expectantly. He was silent as he stormed past them and left the hotel room, shutting the door behind him with a loud *bang.*

# CHAPTER 22

The sunlight seeped through the window, waking me. The harsh brightness stabbed me in the skull, my eye sockets throbbing. I sat up with a groan, breath hitching from a stiff back. I'd slept on the couch all night, and memories of what transpired before sunrise flooded my brain like a hurricane. After Marcus left, I went numb. I was an idiot to think he'd drop everything and turn me into a vampire, no questions asked. It was like asking a guy to put a baby in you. A life-altering decision that I admittedly should've handled with far more grace. There wasn't time for pleasantries. My birthday was right around the corner, and Isabela could be torturing Adam at this very moment.

"Glad you managed to get some sleep," Rose's voice sounded behind me.

I jumped and clapped a hand over my chest.

"Forget I was here?"

"It's nothing personal, Ro. I feel like I've been through a pinball machine. I'm trying to piece together everything from last night. And why does my face feel so tight?" I dragged a hand over my face, sniffling.

She sat down beside me on the couch, raising a hand to secure the hair from my face. "Because you've been bawling your eyes out for the past several hours."

"That would do it."

"You didn't talk to anyone after Marcus left, you just walked home. I followed you and stayed with you all night. What happened?"

"Isn't it obvious? He turned me down." Recalling the look on his face when I'd first asked him stirred up anxiety all over again. I stood, rubbing my hands over my cheeks furiously to rid them of dried tears.

"You're asking him to fill a very big order, Freya." She stayed seated on the couch, staring up at me like a frightened doe.

"Do you think I don't realize that? Of course I don't want to be a vampire! But I'm out of options."

"He's probably worried you'll resent him in the end."

"He is." I nodded, staring at the floor. "He said there's been a part of him that hoped I'd ask him to change me, but now that I have, it made him feel selfish."

She let out a breath. "Wow. That's . . . deep."

"He doesn't realize denying me what I ask because of what he feels and how he fears I'll feel about him afterward is also selfish given the stakes at hand."

She stood and walked over to me, wrapping her arms around my shoulders in a tight embrace. I rested my chin on her shoulder and returned the hug in kind with a sigh. "I'm going after Adam."

She pushed back on my shoulders, digging her fingers into my flesh. "What? You can't do that! They're way too powerful."

I wrenched away from her grasp, scooped my jacket up from the back of the couch, and threw it over my shoulders. "I'm done debating with everyone. Either you come with me or you don't, but either way I'm going." We stared at each other, and I mentally counted to five before turning for the exit and grabbing my keys from a bowl near the door.

She groaned. "Son of a bitch. Freya, wait! I'm coming. I'm coming."

***

"Are you sure this is the right place?" Rose asked in a loud whisper. She could've talked normally and it would've been quieter.

I slapped a hand over her mouth and lowered my voice to a true whisper. "I've been here before, remember?"

Her eyes shifted before the metaphorical light bulb sprung to life, and she nodded vigorously. After removing my hand, I pressed my shoulder in the corner we'd been lurking around, peering into the darkness. What I wouldn't give for a pair of night vision goggles right about now. I looked at Rose behind me and proceeded to point at both of my eyes and then to the other side parallel where we stood. After twirling a circle in the air with my finger and then pointing forward, I widened my eyes.

Her mouth formed a tiny "O" shape, and she flailed her arms in front of her face in a huff. Perhaps we should've established signals before embarking on this crazy adventure. I rolled my eyes and motioned with my hand for her to follow. We didn't make it far down the hallway before the sound of boots dragging against the concrete floor alerted me. I pressed my back against a nearby wall, grabbing Rose's jacket to bring her with me. There was a good foot and a half of shadow for us to hide in if we stayed absolutely still.

When the figure neared us, it stopped to sniff the air. One of Isabela's vampiric goons. His head was shaven on each side, leaving a strip of fuzzy brown hair down the center. His features were narrow and gangly like a rodent's, and the way he twitched his nose only added to his rat-like physique. I willed my breathing to remain steady given my increased heart rate, and Rose buried her face into my shoulder, attempting to do the same.

The vampire stood there for what seemed an eternity before he took a single step forward . . . and then another. Patience was a luxury I hadn't been able to afford in a long time. I slid my hand down the side of my calf until my fingertips brushed against the top part of my boot. The vampire slid forward, and before he had a chance to lock gazes with me, a stake was in my hand and I plunged it into his chest. His eyes rolled into the back of his head before he collapsed to the ground in a pile of gelatinous red goo.

Rose looked over my shoulder and gagged, covering her nose and mouth with her hand. She scurried past me as the smell of vampire remains permeated the air. The scent had been so overwhelming when I'd killed those vampires years ago, I couldn't tell you what it smelled like now. The nerves in my nostrils may have been burned to hell that night.

"Rose, wait!" I tried to whisper.

She'd got so far ahead of me she was bound to run straight into trouble. I slipped the stake back into my boot and ignored the feeling of cold blood smearing my ankle.

Once I'd caught up to her, I almost collided into her back. She stood frozen, staring ahead. Before asking what the hell her problem was, I peered over her shoulder. Three vampires huddled in the hallway, the lead one scraping his long nails against the wall like Freddy Krueger.

"Oh, shit," I said, grabbing Rose's arm to coax her backward.

I couldn't tell you what the plan was for this daring rescue attempt. Freya Johansson, former vampire slayer turned eccentric supernatural sympathizer, armed with one singular stake. Rose Morales, badass cocktail waitress turned eccentric vampire slaughter survivor, armed with . . . extremely supportive words. We were screwed. What was I thinking?

"Rose, run! Get out of here! I'll hold them off." I pushed her toward the entrance we'd snuck through.

"What? No! You can't take them all on by yourself."

"Now, Rose!"

Her forehead crinkled before she took off in a sprint. I rolled my shoulders, craning my neck to one side until it cracked. Narrowing my eyes, I sunk to one knee, taking the stake into my hand. The lead vampire gave a final slash at the wall with his claws before they all appeared in front of me. Given Marcus's lessons, I'd been fully expecting it and pre-emptively started an uppercut motion from my spot on the ground.

The stake landed in the underside of one vamp's chin. He made a gurgling sound of annoyance, but it wouldn't kill him. I yanked the stake from his face and shoved it into his chest. The vampire dematerialized, and before I had a chance to recoil my hand with the stake in it, the other vamp wrapped his arms around me from behind. The stake embedded itself into the pile of goop, and the sound of jaws snapping, attempting to bite me, flooded my eardrum.

I pulled my neck away as much as I could, digging my nails into the vampire's arm. His strength overpowered me, and all I could think to do was the one thing Marcus told me not to. Life had few choices lately. I balled my hand into a fist and slammed it into the vampire's family jewels. The vampire growled and loosened his grip enough so I could drop to my knees. I did some form of a ninja-like somersault I'm sure looked more like me flailing my arms and legs around. Peering down at the stake nestled within vampire guts, I scrunched my nose, dipped my hand into the red jelly, and secured the weapon.

A boot collided into my face, causing me to fall onto my back. My vision blurred from the blunt force, and I willed my wits to come back to me before the striking pain of my hair being pulled damn near out of my skull brought me back. One of the two vampires dragged me across the ground on my ass, and I tried to stab its hand with the stake but couldn't get a good angle. The pain started at my head and traveled all the way down to my hips as the vamp picked me up by my hair and slammed me into a wall. I stared in horror as the stake fell from my hand and bounced away.

I threw my knees, my feet, my fists, any available limb at the vampire, but he didn't budge. He leaned forward, and I prepared to be bitten, but instead he took a long, hard whiff of my neck.

"You have another's blood in you. A *very* old one at that." His lips slithered into a grin.

I'd go bald before this guy got to his point. Honestly, couldn't he hold me up by my neck like a normal bad guy?

"What vampire gave you their blood?" he demanded, his soulless black eyes flickering.

Marcus. My heart wept at the mere thought of his name. Thinking about those intimate moments together would do nothing for my present situation, so I lied straight through my teeth. "Her name is Celeste."

"Celeste. I have not heard of this Celeste."

I ground my teeth together, trying to pry his fingers from my hair. "She's not exactly a people person."

"Release her. She's mine," the vampire whose junk I bludgeoned demanded.

Quickly, I eyed the stake on the ground before he let me go. In two swift motions, I scooped the stake into my palm, turned, and stabbed him in the back over where his heart would be. Taking a moment to rub my scalp was a bad idea given the other one vamped across the room and slammed his arm into my chest, sending me flying into a wall horizontally. I coughed, sending dust from the floor flying, and lay motionless, trying to find my life for a moment.

"Did you honestly think you could simply walk in here, take us all out, and get whatever it is you came here for without a scratch? We know who you are, Freya. Isabela will be so pleased." He stalked forward, and I tried to move. I really did, but my body wasn't having it.

"I can imagine her pleased face when I deliver salvation to her on a silver platter. All I need to do is—" His words were cut short by his head separating from his body. I blinked, watching it fall to the ground before it and the rest of his body turned into slime.

Standing there was a petrified Rose with a rusted saw blade in her trembling hands. Her cheeks filled with air, and she dropped the blade, clamping a hand over her mouth and bending forward. I winced, finally able to get to my feet.

"Wow, Ro."

She waved her hand at me. "Don't get all thankful on me. I'm *not* making this a habit. Come on, let's get out of here. This was a horrible idea."

She started to walk away, but I stayed put, fixing my gaze on the hallway.

"Freya, no. We need everyone's help. We're no good to Adam dead or captured."

I bit the inside of my cheek, knowing she was right. Where there were four vampires, there could be four hundred for all we knew, and Isabela could *not* capture me. I needed Marcus's help as much as it pained me to admit. He could help me rescue Adam, but regardless of alternatives he thought we had with Isabela, I knew I still needed to become a vampire. If he couldn't bring himself to do it, maybe someone else would.

***

"You could've picked a better meeting spot." Rose grimaced and yelped when a rat scurried past her feet.

We were in an abandoned building in a deserted part of town. I'd managed to find a room not already inhabited by a hobo.

"We need seclusion and privacy."

"I'm shocked she agreed to meet you here." She poked a wet spot on a nearby wall and scrunched her nose.

"Because she's such a lady?" I slapped her hand. "Why would you touch anything in here? That was probably piss and you contracted hepatitis. Congratulations."

Her face fell and she wiped her hand on her jacket. "Oh, she's by far no lady, but she seems . . . sophisticated?"

I canted my head at her, putting my hands on my hips. "Are we talking about the same person?"

"This *better* be good, Johansson. I'm an immortal and this place still makes my skin crawl." Celeste's voice echoed through the empty space, the moonlight pouring in through a nearby window making her platinum blonde hair iridescent.

Rose secured her hair over her ears and moved behind me like a kitten.

"Trust me, I wouldn't have called you if it wasn't important."

Celeste stuck her bottom lip out, sauntering her way over

to us. Her pale knees poked out from the holes in her skinny jeans, boots kicking up dust as she made exaggerated steps. "And here I thought we were becoming besties."

Ironic I was about to propose far more than best friend status with her. My mouth grew dry, and I clenched my fist so tightly my fingernails dug into my palm.

Celeste leaned her body to the side, eyeing Rose hiding behind me. "Hey there, Rose. Long time no see."

Rose gave a wave that resembled an Obi-Wan Kenobi gesture. "Yo."

One of my eyes squinted and I whipped my head over my shoulder, mouthing the word "Yo?" I'd never heard her say something like that before. Rose shrugged and rubbed her lips together, curling hair behind her ear that didn't need securing.

"I need you to make me a vampire." I rushed my words, fearing I wouldn't say them if I prolonged it anymore.

Celeste blinked rapidly, rubbing her knuckles across her bull-like nose ring. "I'm sorry. You need me to *what?*"

"You were there. I don't need to repeat why this needs to happen. Marcus won't do it, and you're the only other vampire I . . . trust." That last word felt like ash forming in my mouth.

"Are you out of your damn mind?"

"Yes."

She squared off her jaw and scratched her scalp. "If Marcus refused you, it's because he doesn't want to see you turn into this. He's obviously grown fond of you."

"That's precisely the reason I need you to do it. Take out

the middleman of emotions." I'd been frustrated but moved by Marcus's hesitation to turn me. My own words stung, making me sound like I thought Marcus was a coward.

"I can't do it, Freya." For the first time since we'd crossed paths, Celeste's expression bordered on sympathy. She bit her lower lip and her eyes squinted.

"If you don't, people will die," Rose chimed in, stepping out from behind me.

"I realize the risks. But you two don't understand the debt I owe Marcus. To go against his wishes? To destroy the only mortal I've ever seen him care for? It'd be as big a betrayal as killing him."

Rose's breath hitched.

My sinuses burned and I stormed forward, dropping to my knees in front of her. "Do you want me to beg? This has to be done. Just do it."

Celeste rolled her eyes. She grabbed the collar of my jacket and hoisted me to my feet with little effort. "Stop it. Respect his wishes and trust he has a plan. When I was a new vampire, I came so close to dying countless times. He found me, took me under his wing, and I got to live among people like me. Until I could stand on my own two feet, they all kept me safe. Do you understand?"

I stared at my boots. "You owe him your life."

She nodded. "Yes."

Rose pushed past me, grabbing onto Celeste's shoulders. "I don't want to see her turned into one of you, but even I can see this is the only way *any* of us has a chance of surviving this."

Celeste cocked her head to the side, looking at Rose, and surprisingly not prying away from her grip. "Your passion for your friends is admirable, but my answer stays the same. Have faith, ladies. We're to all meet up at the hotel tonight to discuss what we're doing. He wouldn't deliver anything less than solid."

Celeste and Rose stared at one another for a moment before Rose let her hands fall away. She turned her gaze, rubbing the back of her neck. Celeste cocked her head to the opposite side, still watching her, and then turned her head.

"You're brave, Freya. I haven't given you enough credit, for what it's worth."

I made a tsking sound, blowing out a puff of air. "No offense, but right now, it's worth zilch."

She bowed her head. "I'll see you two tonight." Then she vamped away.

I held my head in my hands. Marcus better have one hell of a plan.

# CHAPTER 23

I stood outside Marcus's hotel room, staring at the golden number on the door, wondering if he was peering at me through the peephole. Murmuring voices muffled through the wood of the door, but I couldn't make out who they belonged to.

"For crying out loud," Rose said behind me, reaching forward and knocking her knuckles against the door several times.

I tossed her a glare over my shoulder.

"We don't have all night. Time for you to put your big girl panties on," she said, breaking eye contact once the door opened.

Marcus stood there, a hand raised and resting on the doorway. Our eyes locked and I forgot how to breathe, how to live.

"Marcus," Rose greeted.

"Rose," he responded, not taking his eyes off me.

She cleared her throat and walked forward. He pushed the door open enough for her to slip through. I took a step, prepared to follow her inside, but his own movement forward sent me into the hallway. He shut the door behind him and crossed his arms over his chest, glaring down at me.

"Are you glaring at me?"

"You asked Celeste?"

The back of my neck became clammy. I should've known she'd spill her guts about the entire ordeal.

"She wouldn't have had to, or have you forgotten I get glimpses of your thoughts?" He stood there like a towering statue.

My mouth opened, but no words followed. I put one hand on my hip and the other clapped over my forehead. "Yes. Yes, I did. I was willing to be sired by Celeste for the rest of eternity. That's how dire this entire situation is."

His eyes formed slits. "You went behind my back to become a vampire despite my continued efforts to convince you otherwise?"

Piercing my heart with a stake would've paled in comparison to the tightness forming in my chest. "Lying to you was the last thing I ever wanted to do, but this is bigger than us. More important than us."

Those icy blues dropped to the floor, and the right side of his mouth twitched.

"Marcus. . . ." Taking a step forward, I reached a hand up to grip his arm, but he turned away from my touch.

I may be saving Adam, but I'd lost Marcus. And why could I not hear even the most fleeting thought from him?

He shoved his hands in his pockets and lifted his gaze. "Do you trust me?"

CARLY SPADE

Was this a loaded question? ". . . Yes?"

He turned around, wrapping his hand around the doorknob. "Then come inside and listen to the plan." He raised a finger. "Which doesn't involve you becoming a vampire."

Right when I thought I'd had him convinced. "Fine, Marcus."

Everyone else was already there, but it was Celeste's gaze I caught first. She puckered her lips and shrugged. Figures I'd get the empathetic version of Celeste for a grand total of thirty seconds.

"I think we can all agree the only way out of this is to trick Isabela," Marcus started, moving to the center of the room.

"We should also be prepared for silver. Considering we're all affected by it and she's not," Damian chimed in.

I raised my arm. "I'm not."

Rose mimicked me. "Neither am I."

Celeste held her hand out to me like presenting a delectable meal and raised her brow.

"No. No mortals. It's too risky. *Especially* not Freya," Marcus demanded.

My blood boiled and I took a step forward, but Rose grabbed onto my bicep, coaxing me back.

"Isabela will smell shit from a mile away if we all show up." Celeste flicked something from her fingernail. "She'll immediately team up with her goons and destroy Pittsburgh looking for Freya. We'd be lucky to get a scratch on her before she disappears."

"I should be there." I threw my hands out at my sides. "Whatever the plan is, it can account for me dodging out of harm's way at the opportune moment, right?"

"Everyone be quiet! We've already hatched a plan. Freya *will* be there but . . . not," Marcus said.

"What the bloody hell is that supposed to mean?" Frankie asked, folding her arms over her chest.

Damian took a few steps forward, flexing his arms, his eyes focused on the ground. He lifted his chin and took a deep breath. "I'm going to shift into Freya."

"Damian, no! You know what could happen if we shift into people." Frankie gripped onto his arm, demanding he look at her.

"*Could* happen. And it's a curse. Not death." He finally looked down at her, and she grabbed both of his hands, pressing them between her own.

"My love, please. What if the curse puts you to sleep or makes you lose your memories? We have a pup on the way, remember?" She placed his hands over her belly, and he grimaced like he'd touched a hot iron.

The conversation was private, and I felt like an intruder.

"It's why I need to help in any way I can." He widened his stance, lifting his hands to cup each side of her face. "For the future of our kid, Francesca. Isabela has to be dealt with. Freya was willing to sacrifice her life, the least I could do is risk a curse that may not exist."

She cried, nuzzling her face into his palm while slowly beginning to nod.

"It'd be more than simply appearing as her. You'd have

to move like her, talk like her, if it's going to convince Isabela long enough for us to trick her." Marcus's tone was grave.

Celeste slapped her hands on her knees, hoisting herself to her feet. "I guess that's where I fall into this grand scheme. I can coerce his mind into thinking he's Freya." A devious smile spread across her lips.

Damian stared at her, his eyes unflinching before he gave a firm tilt of his chin. "I'll do it. But you better return my brain to normal after this is all over, She-Fanger." He pointed at her, nostrils flaring.

"It's settled, then," Marcus said. "Tomorrow night, Damian will shift into Freya, go to Isabela willingly as if we let her go as promised. The rest of us will follow to take care of any stragglers. There's a cave she will take you to for the ritual. We will need to time this precisely if it's going to work."

"What about Adam?" I asked.

Marcus glanced over his shoulder but didn't fully turn to face me. "I'll look for Adam before joining the others outside of the cave. Think you can handle it, you two?" He looked over at Celeste and Frankie.

"Count Frankie out. It's too risky," Damian said.

"You're a bloody fool if you think I'm not taking part in this. Have you seen anything more ferocious than a mother protecting her own? *Nothing* will happen to me."

Frankie's and Damian's gazes battled before Damian relinquished with a growl.

I stepped up to Marcus, cupping his elbow with my hand. He pinched his eyes closed.

*What you do to me, Freya. . . .*

The intrusion of his sudden thought made my breath hitch. "Please let me help you find Adam and then I will take him and Rose out of sight, as you wish."

"It's too—" he started to say, and I tightened my grip on his arm.

"Are you really going to decline two of my requests? If you're not willing to make me a vampire to save my family, then you sure as hell better let me help you rescue them."

He stared down at me, the corners of his jaw popping, before he gave a curt nod. "Alright. But you *will* get as far away as possible once we find him. Do *not* be a hero."

"Understood." I slipped my hand away and continued to look up at him.

His hand rose for a fraction of a second before he turned away. "Everyone meets back here tomorrow night. We all know what our roles are."

Everyone filed out, followed lastly by Rose and me. I paused at the doorway, looking over my shoulder at Marcus, who'd busied himself by pouring a drink into a tumbler.

*Please look at me.*

His face twitched and his hand tightened around the bottle as he poured. His eyes never lifted. I slipped out in the hallway. Rose waited for me, her brows crinkled.

"You okay?" she asked, bending her face down so she could gage mine.

"I'm not going to get as far away as possible once we find Adam. She *will* have silver. If I don't help, all of us are going to die."

Her face grew solemn, and she rubbed a hand up and down my arm. "I kind of figured you'd say something like that."

***

The next night, we all met again in Marcus's hotel, ready to take on an ancient Aztec vampire goddess.

"Can I clarify Damian is going to look and sound precisely like Freya?" Rose asked, her wide eyes unblinking.

"Yes," Damian said, words clipped.

"This is crazy," she responded, dragging her hands through her hair.

"Ro, we're standing in a room full of vampires and skinwalkers. It can only go up from here, right?" I gripped her shoulder, offering a weak smile.

"You still haven't said how we trap her in there." Celeste sat in a chair, her legs wide, elbows rested on the seat between them, bent forward. "With her powers I'd think she could blast through anything we try to seal the entrance with."

"These past few weeks as I've spent time with Isabela, I've managed to tap into some of her thoughts and found a singular weakness I believe we can use against her. The very reason for the curse itself." Marcus glanced around the room.

"My great, great grandfather, you mean?" I asked, a walnut-sized lump forming in my throat.

"Yes. Tezcatlipoca was the Aztec god of the night. Isabela at some point trapped him inside an urn that she keeps on her person at all times. If she's distracted enough, I think we can manage to steal it. Release him to deal with her. Considering he's been trapped in there for centuries, I highly doubt he'll object."

"We're supposed to trap one god only to release another?" Damian asked.

"Tezcatlipoca isn't dangerous. Immoral and misguided perhaps, but no more menace to society than you or myself." Marcus tossed Damian a sly grin. "Is everyone clear on what their jobs are?"

Silence deafened the room, everyone resorting to solemn nods. Marcus caught my gaze, and his demeanor seemed to have changed since last night. His expression void of anger or sadness. I looked away.

"Celeste, do you have clothes I can borrow?" I pinched my lips together.

She arched an eyebrow. "For?"

"I don't think a nude me showing up on Isabela's doorstep would be very convincing, do you?"

"I see your point." She disappeared into the other room.

I nervously picked at my fingers with my thumbnails. "This is going to make things awkward between us, isn't it?" I couldn't even look Damian in the eyes.

"Well, I don't know, given the chance, would you become one of your friends for a day if you could? Suddenly know their mannerisms?"

I scrunched my nose. "Probably, not, no. I like a little mystery. And did you just say we're—friends?"

He leaned down, lowering his voice to a whisper. "I

won't tell anyone if you don't."

I gave a sidelong grin before Celeste appeared at my side, holding out a pair of gray sweatpants and a track jacket. "You're bigger than me. It's the only thing I could find you wouldn't bulge right out of."

Snatching the clothes from her hand, I debated on whether to take those words as a compliment or not.

"Perfect. Get to kick ass in style," I said sarcastically before dipping into the bathroom to change.

When I came back out, Damian stood in the middle of the room in a pair of boxer briefs with Celeste right next to him. Sighing, I walked over, clutching my clothes to my chest.

"Everyone ready?" Damian asked, his fists clenching.

"Ready as I'll ever be," Rose mumbled, backing away the furthest possible distance she could.

Damian grunted, the veins in his arms bulging out. When he shifted into an animal, the transformation was instantaneous. This was another manner entirely, and I fought the urge to run away screaming. The sound of his bones cracking, grinding, and shifting pounded through my ears as he yelled in a fit of agony.

I looked at Frankie. "Is this supposed to be happening?"

She kept her gaze turned away from Damian and nodded. "And you thought shifting into an animal was unsightly. When we shift, we change our entire bone structure. It's not pretty."

It was a horrifying sight to see a man's body morph into a much smaller female one. He collapsed to his knees, gripping his ribs, his breathing became erratic. A hand slipped into mine, gripping it. Marcus. I'd been so horrified by Damian I hadn't seen him step up beside me. His large hand engulfed mine. His eyes were glued to Damian, but his gesture comforted me.

I attempted to drown out the sounds of Damian's body ripping itself apart and putting itself back together again, but the sight of long, red hair sprouting from his head squelched that idea.

He remained on his hands and knees, his breathing normalizing until there was now a naked woman there instead. When he stood up, I may have fallen backward were it not for Marcus's sturdy frame behind me. I stared at Damian, who looked like me, but with a glower I would've never been capable of pulling off. He didn't try to hide any of my vital parts, and I shoved the clothes into his—my arms.

"Do you have no decency?" I found myself shifting my glance elsewhere, even though it was me, and I'd seen it many times before. It felt wrong somehow.

"Suddenly so modest? Not like anyone in this room hasn't seen it before," my own voice said to me and he proceeded to dress.

"You haven't seen me naked, Damian, and do *not* look down, just dress yourself faster, would you?"

Rose stood frozen like a scarecrow, arms wrapped around herself, staring at the other me.

He chuckled, and the way he dressed himself looked far more manly than it should have. His stance was too wide, and he stood rigid. I now knew why Marcus insisted on Celeste screwing with his head. Speaking of the She-Devil herself, she approached Damian, pressing her hands to each side of his head.

"Damian."

"Yes?"

"You will not lose sight of yourself, but while you are in this form, you will move like Freya. Your facial expressions, speech inflections, mannerisms, it will *all* be like her. Do you understand?"

"Yes."

Celeste released her hands and took a step back. Damian shook his head, the way he held himself changing within an instant. He sauntered past me and stood toe to toe with Marcus. Marcus rolled his shoulders staring down, his lips thinning.

Damian nodded once, turning to face the rest of us. "You all ready to do this?"

\*\*\*

Once we reached Isabela's makeshift compound, Damian, Celeste, and Frankie split off from me and Marcus so we could find Adam before all hell broke loose. A pity I wouldn't get to see Isabela's face when she realized it wasn't me.

We faced a large, metal slab of a door, and I tugged Marcus's jacket sleeve. He peered down at me. Though he was immortal, he looked exhausted with his heavy eyelids and scowl.

"Are you not going to talk to me anymore?"

He raised a hand, brushing his fingertips against my temple. I fought the temptation to drag my lips across his fingers, the urge to feel his touch overwhelming. I'd given him the space he needed, but if either one of us didn't make it out of this, I couldn't stand the thought of coldness being the last emotion we showed one another.

He dipped his head and kissed me, holding each side of my face. I wrapped my arms around his neck and gave into him. When we broke away, he pressed his forehead against mine with a sigh.

"If only we'd have met under different circumstances," he said, the ocean blue of his eyes begging me to dive in.

"I don't think we'd have ever met were it not for this circumstance." I half smiled.

He took a step back and dragged a hand over his beard. "When we're inside, follow my lead and don't say a word. We must remain as quiet as possible."

"I can do that."

We walked inside to pitch-black darkness. I blinked my eyes rapidly, attempting to quicken my pupils dilating. Gripping onto Marcus's jacket so he could lead me, I shuffled my feet across the ground behind him. We passed through several corridors, and I started to feel queasy. What if he wasn't here?

*He'll be here. It is her way to ensure you'll come.*

After another corridor, a faint scent seeped into my nostrils. I halted, grabbing onto Marcus's elbow, my stomach fluttering with hope. We switched our path and entered a vast room. It smelled like dust, mildew, and the faintest hint of blood. The sight of a body slumped in a chair in a far corner made the past day's events a distant memory. Sprinting forward, I forgot all about being quiet when the recognizable blonde hair came into view.

"Adam. Are you hurt? Let me see your hands."

My words were scattered and panicked. His hands were tied behind him around the chair.

He weakly lifted his head, squinting in the darkness. "Freya?"

"Yes, it's me. Marcus is here too."

Marcus stepped behind him, and in one swift motion, ripped the ropes away.

Adam rubbed at his wrists. Relief washed over me when I saw that all of his fingers were intact. I dropped to my knees in front of him and cupped my hands to his face.

He winced, pulling his head back. "Your hands feel like death."

And somehow, he still maintained his sense of humor. Tears rolled down my cheeks and I hugged him.

Marcus stepped in front of us. "There's a gold-encrusted urn Isabela keeps around her at all times. Have you seen it?"

Adam licked his dried, cracking lips. "Yeah. She keeps it in a case in her chambers. I think it's three doors down on the left. Or two doors down. I can't remember."

Marcus gripped my arm to guide me up to my feet. "I'm going to get the urn. You do what you promised me. We have Adam. Take him and get as far away from here as possible." His eyes searched mine, frantic when I didn't answer right away. "Freya?"

"Yes. Yes, alright. Please be careful."

His cold lips pressed against my forehead. "I've survived over a thousand years. This is child's play." He squeezed my arm before turning away and vamping from the room.

Adam walked up behind me. "Jesus. Your birthday is today."

I wrapped my arms around myself and nodded.

"Did they come up with a plan?"

Turning to face him, I slipped my phone from my pocket and opened a new text window. "They're going to fool Isabela into thinking I'm giving myself up."

"How the hell does that work? I just heard him say for you to get away as far as possible."

I finished my text to Rose and put the phone away. "Damian shifted into me to go there in my place."

The realization melted down his face like the world's slowest dominoes. "Is that—that's . . . possible?"

"Saw it with my own two eyes." Withholding from Adam my request to be turned into a vampire not only once, but twice, tortured me. But with what we were about to go through, the less he had on his mind, the better.

He frowned. "You're not going to stay away, are you?"

"I can't, Adam. They're underestimating her. I need to be there when they realize it. I told Rose to meet up with you at your apartment. Hunker down. Protect each other so I don't have to worry about you guys."

His brow furrowed and he stepped forward. "This isn't only your fight. You're crazy if you think I'm not going to be right there beside you."

I sighed. Had I expected a different reaction? Really? I opened my mouth to argue, but my phone buzzed. There were several texts from Rose:

Rose: Like HELL I'm not going 2 be there.

Rose: Where R U?

Rose: If u found Adam, I bet anything he's saying the SAME thing 2 u.

Pinching my eyes shut, I pressed the call button and put the phone to my ear. It took one ring for her to answer, and she went into a barrage of debates.

"Do you have that saw blade handy?" I asked.

# CHAPTER 24

How we'd managed to follow Celeste without her detecting us was still beyond me. Following one of the werewolves seemed riskier given their keen sense of smell, and I took the chance on a vampire. We'd been crouched behind the same bush for the past half an hour, watching Celeste and Frankie guard the cave entrance.

"What's the plan to infiltrate the compound?" Rose asked in a whisper.

"It's a cave," Adam responded deadpan.

"We wait until they both go inside, sneak in, and wait for the opportune moment to surprise the living shit out of Isabela," I added, gripping a nearby tree so hard I broke a piece of bark off. *Snap.*

I dropped to the ground, hiding myself behind the bush; Adam and Rose followed suit. Frankie glared over her shoulder, eyes scanning the area, and I pinched my eyes shut, wishing I was invisible.

"You can open your eyes. They didn't see us," Adam said, lightly elbowing me in the arm.

"What if this doesn't work? What if Isabela grabs you the second you reveal yourself?" Rose's eyes glazed over.

"That's not an option." I'd laced my words with an extra layer of tough-guy bravado, but truth was, there was a big possibility of this *not* working.

"Here's an option. You hang back unless absolutely, positively necessary. She doesn't know I know that's not the real you in there. I'll go in once Celeste and Frankie are in and buy more time," Adam said, crinkling his brow.

I stared at him as if the words would change. "You're out of your damn mind if you think I'll be on board with that."

"I've heard crazier options," Rose said, cocking a brow at me.

Bless her for not blabbing my request to be a vampire when Adam had no clue.

"What are you going to do when you get in there, huh?" I asked. "Put up your dukes and challenge her to a duel?"

"Hell no. I said distract her, not commit suicide. I'll be a Chatty Andy."

This was crazy. I was supposed to be the one risking life and limbs for *them*, not the other way around. "No, Adam. No. I can't risk losing y—"

"Freya," Rose said my name with the soft coo of a dove. "You know Isabela can't know Damian is you. If she wins. We *all* lose," she continued, sliding a hand across the ground until it rested on top of mine.

"Let me do this," Adam said and slid his hand over, then slapped it on top of Rose's.

I chewed on my bottom lip until the taste of copper

coated the tip of my tongue. Pinching my eyes shut, I sighed. "Damn it all to hell. Fine." Once I slapped my hand on top of the theirs, we all exchanged a glance of determination bordering on paralyzing fear.

"They're going in." Adam pointed.

They walked side by side into the dark cave entrance. Once they disappeared into the blackness, I motioned to them with a flick of my wrist. "Let's go. Stay behind me until we get further in. Regardless of how we do this, do *not* try to kill Isabela. Yeah?"

"The bitch is yours. We get it." Rose blinked her eyes lazily.

Normally I'd applaud such sarcasm. Having no idea what we were about to walk in on left my head all fuzzy.

We moved through the entrance of the cave. I dragged my fingertips across the cool, damp rock walls and stopped, motioning for the other two to halt.

"Did you think I wouldn't take precautions? Not suspect you and your band of failures wouldn't try to rescue her?" Isabela's voice echoed through the cave.

"Can't blame a gal for trying," Celeste responded.

"You don't have to do this. There has to be another way," Frankie added.

"Alright," Adam whispered. "I'm going in. Stay. Back. Freya. You promised."

I hadn't promised a thing in actuality, but something told me semantics would be a touchy subject given the current situation. Nodding, I attempted to glue my boots mentally to the cave ground, willing them to not move as I watched Adam walk further away.

I looked down at my hand; shimmering dust coated my skin. "What the hell?"

"Is that—" Rose grabbed my hand, bringing it closer to her face.

"Silver. Oh my God." I went to bolt forward, but Rose grabbed onto my shoulders, and shoved me against the opposite wall.

"You're not going in there. We talked about this." A side of Rose I'd never seen before. A very strong side.

Grimacing, I tried to pry her death grip from my shoulders, but she only latched on harder. "Since when are you the friggin' She-Hulk, Rose? Ouch."

"Since I've been given the task of keeping a very stubborn, skillful redhead from making a huge mistake."

I opened my mouth to retort but snapped it back shut. "Touché."

"Let her go, Isabela, and no one has to get hurt," Adam's voice sounded.

Isabela's cackle was so loud they could probably hear it downtown. "Well, well, aren't you quite the friend?"

"This is about more than just my friend."

"Adam, don't be stupid!" My own voice coming from Damian echoed off the cave walls.

It was an unsettling thing to hear, and for a moment I thought I'd become a ventriloquist.

"As truly touching as this is, I find it amusing you think I care about anything else other than being free of this dreaded curse," Isabela hissed.

Rose was pulled from my sight with such speed, it hadn't registered she'd been grabbed. Once my hair settled back down from the wind gust, fury raced up my spine. One of her goons vamped her away, her shrill cry piercing my ear drum from within the cave. The plan was officially changing.

Without a second thought, I ran into the cave, my chest heaving. The look on Isabela's face when her dark eyes landed on me was almost as satisfying as a cold beer after a torturous day at work. Almost. Her entire body shook, eyes increasingly widening, glancing between me and the fake Freya.

"What *is* this?" Isabela shouted.

Celeste looked over at me, her nostrils flaring. I imagined smoke plumes sprouting from her nose with that ring.

"Your real question should be which Freya is the real one?" I played a villainous grin across my lips, watching her anger grow with every passing second.

My back flew into a nearby wall, Isabela's demonic face glaring up at me, her hand clamped around my throat, lifting me from the ground.

Her eyes turned red, veins bulging from her forehead, and her fangs sprang out. "That's easy enough to determine."

Between choking gasps for breath, I reached into my jacket, grabbing the stake I'd hidden there. Celeste launched at Isabela from behind, but the ancient vampire swatted her away like a fly. She fell in a slump to the ground, struggling to get back to her feet. Adam and I caught gazes, and I shook my head as much as I could, hoping he'd get the hint. He bounced around and dragged his hands through his hair. Damian stood still, clenched fists at his side.

Isabela grabbed my forearm and sunk her teeth into my flesh. I stifled a scream and slammed the stake into the top of her head. She dropped me and I scurried away, pressing the sleeve of my jacket against the gaping bite wound. She growled, tearing the stake from her head with a spray of blood.

"You Freya, the *real* Freya . . ." She licked my blood from her lips. "Are a disgrace to my bloodline if you thought that would kill me."

"I wasn't trying to kill you, my dear Grandmother. I was buying time."

Her eyes narrowed into slits.

Marcus leaped from the darkness and landed in front of me, casting a shadow from the glowing torches.

"About time you showed up. Where have you been?" I hovered at his back.

"Going with the plan unlike some stubborn mules," he growled.

"Oh, Marcus. I never pegged you for a lovesick idiot. You are still bound to your agreement. You *will* be mine," Isabela screeched.

"Not if you're dead." He extracted his fangs, and an inconvenient twinge sprung in my abdomen.

I grabbed onto his arm before he went full alpha vampire mode. "There's silver powder everywhere."

He shot a look at me over his shoulder. "What?"

I'd thought my words were rather clear but didn't have a chance to repeat myself before Isabela flew into his chest, sending him toppling to the ground. Celeste appeared in front of me, pushing me back toward a corner.

"Stay out of sight and let us handle this," she said.

"You all are going to get yourselves killed. She's got the entire cave covered in silver powder. Why do you think you feel so weak?"

Her face fell. "We're still stronger than you, not to mention immortal. Stay. Put."

She vamped off to help Marcus, who'd got to his feet and regained his composure enough to give Isabela a run for her money, despite his weakened form. Damian ran to me and touched my bloodied arm.

"Damian, this is ridiculous. She knows which one of us is real. Shift into something else."

His lips pursed together. "I . . . tried."

"You tried? And nothing happened?"

He shook his head and the realization sunk in.

"You're stuck as my twin?"

"I really hope not."

"You and me both, buddy."

Rose's shriek cried out from across the cave as the vampire who'd grabbed her held her in a bear hug. Her legs kicked around frantically. Adam ran over, and I pushed Damian aside to get to Rose before Adam did something stupid.

"Freya!" my own voice called to me from behind, but I ignored it.

I sprinted across the space, leaped onto a rock protruding from the ground with a single foot, and launched myself onto the vampire's back, wrapping my legs around him like a damn spider monkey. He dropped Rose, grabbed onto my shoulders, and in one swift motion hurled me over his head. I landed on the ground, conveniently right on my injured arm, with a grunt.

"Oh my God!" Rose yelled, running over to me.

"I love you two, I do! But what about 'stay away' is so hard for you to do?" Frustration clouded my words, and I looked around at the battle we were undoubtedly losing.

Frankie had shifted into her wolf form, protecting Damian in his weakened form of, well, me. Celeste fought Isabela with Marcus but kept getting thrown every which way, and every time it took her longer to get back to her feet. Marcus held his own, but the strain on his face was an expression I'd never seen. I didn't like it.

The vampire pushed Rose aside and advanced on me, making me backpedal across the dampened floor. This felt all too familiar. Laying on my back, I threw my boots into the air and shoved them into the vampire's chest. It was like pushing into a brick wall, and I winced in pain. He grabbed the collar of my jacket and started to drag me across the floor, leading me to the moonlight spilling through the circular opening in the cave ceiling. I shimmied off the jacket, falling to my hands and knees.

Adam let out a battle cry and charged past me. With terrified eyes I pushed to my feet, gripped the back of his hair, which was the only thing I could manage to grab, and hurled him backward. Instead of slicing into Adam's abdomen with his claws, the vampire only swiped through air.

We were all out of breath. Out of energy. Out of options. I wasn't certain how much longer I could keep this up. With the silver laced throughout the entire cave, I couldn't be certain how much longer our supernatural counterparts would last either.

My legs gave out, and I fell to my knees with a huff of breath. This wasn't like me. I was a fighter. No. Had . . . to get . . . up. As I pressed a shaky hand against my knee and rose to my feet, the vampire sent the back of his hand across my face. The sound of bone colliding into bone reverberated.

Before I could make sense of what happened, the cool night air kissed my cheeks. The stars sparkled in the sky, and the moon was the brightest I'd ever seen. I wiggled my fingers, feeling the blades of grass beneath me, littered with dew.

"Freya," Marcus's voice whispered.

He peered down at me. I was cradled in his arms, and I managed a weak smile. "Did we win?"

"Not yet, Hellcat."

His voice sounded strained. I wished I could see his face, make out his expression.

"Then what are we doing outside? We need to get back in there. The others, they'll—" I went to move, but his arms around me tightened.

"I've come to the bone-chilling conclusion there is too

great of a possibility of us losing this."

My heart beat against my chest like Thumper's rapid feet. "We can't give up. Too many lives—" Attempting to move again proved moot.

He lowered his face, the moonlight highlighting it in all of its chiseled, masculine glory.

"What you asked of me earlier . . . is it something you are still willing to go through with?" His expression was no less pained than last time.

Was I? Now that the reality of it happening was on the table, it squeezed my insides like a sponge. Drinking human blood. Reduced to the darkness. Immortal. Marcus. The grip on the sponge lessened, and I propped myself on an elbow, bringing our faces inches apart.

I ran my palm down the hair scattered over his chin. He pressed his hand over mine and shut his eyes. A tear rolled down his cheek as it had before, and I leaned forward, kissing it away.

"I forgive you." The words were a whisper across the clouds.

I heard the hiss of his fangs escaping before he sunk them into my neck, hugging me to him. I closed my eyes, gripping onto his arms for support. As more and more blood left my system, I got dizzy and could barely feel my legs. My body slowly sank, and Marcus held me all the way down. His fingers kneaded the back of my head as he continued to drink. I'd got so weak I could hardly open my eyes. He stopped abruptly and rested my head onto the grass.

Soon, cold liquid dripped onto my lips, and Marcus's

fingers stroked my forehead. My breathing grew shallow, and I felt so sluggish I couldn't remember how to make my brain communicate to my body.

"You must drink," Marcus whispered, continuing to caress my skin.

Weakly, I forced my tongue to lick my lips and covered the wound on his wrist with my mouth, drinking him in. After only a few moments, a pain like I'd never felt before burst through my ribs. I cried out in agony, and Marcus held me to his chest. The pain, which felt like someone carving my insides out with a hot knife, traveled up my neck and into my skull. I clutched my head, my cries morphing into straight wails.

Marcus pressed his lips to my ear. "Hate me all you need to right now, but don't you dare hate me afterward."

*Like I already hate myself.*

I didn't often shed tears, but the pain that coursed through my entire body would've made anyone pass out from shock. Sobbing, I haphazardly punched Marcus's shoulder several times, and he let me, only embracing me tighter. The sound of my erratic heartbeat was so loud it made my eardrums ache. And just like that . . . the pain stopped and a final breath escaped my lungs.

# CHAPTER 25

At first, I didn't feel any different. When my eyes caught Marcus's gaze, however, so many sensations, emotions, and feelings swarmed through me. None of it made any sense. My chest pulsed and panic washed over me. I tried to breathe through my nose but couldn't. Marcus firmly grabbed onto my shoulders and gave one light shake.

"Look at me!" he beseeched, and a calmness came over me like snuggling a security blanket.

"I can't breathe, Marcus."

"You don't have to anymore. No breathing, no heartbeat." He took my hand and delicately placed it over my chest. What once pumped blood through my veins now remained a hollow shell.

He trailed his fingertips down the side of my face, his expression pained. "Aside from the mild panic attack, how are you feeling?"

I furrowed my brow, trying to sort out everything I felt. "There's so much going on. I feel fear, confusion, but also admiration, concern . . . sadness." My eyes locked with his, and he leaned forward, pressing our foreheads against one another. The coolness of his skin was a normalcy now, mingling with my own chill. "Those last few—they're coming from you, aren't they?"

"Yes." He lifted his chin, kissing my temple. "I could feel your overwhelming anxiety, so I fought everything else except the calm in hopes it'd soothe you."

"It worked." I tilted my head so our noses touched.

"I'll explain everything and more to you later. We have to get back inside." He rolled up his shirt sleeve, flexing his forearm muscles.

I tried to read his thoughts to figure out what the hell he was doing but heard only a faint buzz. How'd he shut off his mind like that? "What are you doing?"

"You can take my blood—for now. It'll satiate you for a time, but it's more like a crumb than a meal."

"We can survive like that? Off of each other?"

"It's *barely* surviving, Freya. If we are in a pinch, it would keep us alive. All things I'll explain to you later. Trust me, I won't leave you in the dark."

His hand motioned for me, and I walked forward with labored steps. It all happened so fast my new mind couldn't keep up. Couldn't process I was different. So . . . very . . . different. I stood in front of him, staring down at his pale arm beckoning me, and my teeth ached.

"Don't worry about hurting me." He tugged me to his chest. "We'll go over all of it later."

It was like being taught how to swim by getting thrown in.

Awkwardly, I opened my mouth, my fangs springing out without another thought. I brought his arm to my mouth, licked my lips, and plunged my teeth into his flesh. He tensed and grunted, which told me I hadn't done it gently. His blood was the elixir of life, tumbling down my throat, and I didn't want to stop. Just a few more drops.

"That's enough for now." His words passed through my ears like a floating cloud.

I gripped onto his arm, sinking my fangs deeper until he pushed me way. My lips dripped with crimson and he stared heatedly down at me. A peculiar kind of lust melted within me, and I couldn't decipher whether it was him or me . . . or both.

*We've so much to discuss.*

His thoughts felt like a massage to my brain, sending a ripple down my spine and caressing my hip bones. The puncture holes my fangs had left disappeared almost as quickly as they'd been put there. I'd been in such a state of shock I didn't realize he'd walked past me.

"Come on, Freya. Let's finish this."

My eyes blinked rapidly to fight back tears as I looked at him over my shoulder. He stood there with his hand outstretched. I sifted through the emotions coursing through me like a tornado, searching, searching for regret, but came up empty. Neither of us felt it. For the first time in days my shoulders relaxed, and I slipped my hand into his. He gave it a squeeze before he vamped us both back inside the cave with an extravagant *whoosh*.

A breath would've hitched in my throat if I'd had any.

Celeste crawled on her hands and knees toward Rose and Adam, who were hunkered down in a corner. Adam held Rose behind him and waved a torch back and forth at several approaching vampires. Most of Frankie's white wolf coat was stained red with blood, and Damian, still as me, sliced the air with a dagger at an imposing Isabela.

When we'd arrived, all actions seemed to halt simultaneously. Anger swelled within my chest, accentuated by the fury boiling in Marcus's core.

"Look who finally decided to return. I thought I'd have to kill one of these imbeciles," Isabela spat before appearing in front of us.

She attempted to reach for me, but Marcus grabbed her by the throat before she had the chance. Isabela screeched and stabbed a dagger through Marcus's arm. He groaned with pain, nearly dropping to his knees. My own arm burned like I'd stuck it into an open flame and left it there. I winced, attempting to hide the connection we shared.

*Silver.*

Every cell in my body went into overdrive. Before I knew what I was doing, I vamped to the opposite side of the cave. Adam noticed, and his eyes went wide behind the flicker of the torch held in his hand. Isabela vamped over to me, shoving me against the wall.

"No!" she wailed, her fingernails digging into the flesh of my chest. Her nostrils flared, chin dipping down, and she took a long, hard whiff.

Wait for it. . .

It was like watching water simmer to a pulsating boil.

Her hands began to shake, eyes searching my face in fury, and then she slashed a hand across my face. "No!"

Marcus yanked the dagger from his arm with a predatory growl that could've caused an earthquake. I grimaced, gritting my teeth to suppress the pain. The three slash marks over my cheeks sealed shut. Marcus launched at her. She threw a furious backhanded swing at his face, which would've sent any human flying halfway across the room. His head flew sideways, his feet stumbling, and he rubbed his jaw.

"You did this! I should have known you were lying through your teeth," she snarled, hands splayed open and stiff.

"Yes, but you didn't. And what once was yours is now of *my* bloodline. The vampiric one, if I need to be clearer." His head dipped lower with each passing word, until he was nearly bent in half, their noses inches away from touching.

*Marcus, where's the urn?*

*I have it covered.*

Isabela appeared behind me, her claws clutching at my throat. I tried to pull away from her, but even with my newfound strength, I wasn't any match for her.

"Or perhaps I will spill her blood anyhow, in case there was a clause in his curse." Her chin grazed my shoulder as she spoke, and despite the situation, I found it amusing she had to stand on her tiptoes to accomplish a threat. "Would not be the first time he made some foolish mistake. Tell me, what do you think will happen when you release him? That was your plan, correct?"

Marcus squared off his shoulders in a huff, and if he had fur, it would've bristled all down his spine.

*When I give the order, use every bit of strength you can to duck and push away from her and call out to Celeste.*

*I'm going to take it you have a* new, *new plan.*

*Now!*

Letting out a yell, I lurched myself forward. It worked—kind of. I succeeded in breaking away from Isabela's grasp but took her right along with me. We tumbled to the rocky ground of the cave, my knees colliding into the hard surface beneath me. I hopped up to my feet in time to face the fury that was Isabela.

"Celeste!" I yelled.

Celeste furrowed her brow but raised herself to her knees and tossed the urn to me. I'd been known as the world's worst butterfingers, so imagine my surprise when I reached my hand out and caught the sucker like a receiver in football.

"How could you let him curse you with the very thing that has cursed our family line since the dawn of time?" Isabela screeched, her expression pain stricken.

"I didn't let him. I asked him."

Marcus wrapped his arms around her from behind in a tight bear hug and lifted her from the ground. She kicked her legs feverishly, Marcus grunting as he tried to hold on.

*We need the dagger.* Marcus's thought traveled across my brain.

*The silver one?*

*No. We don't need any more damned silver. There's one in the ritual space with the moonlight. I'll distract her.*

The moon cast a glint on the blade, the dagger resting there, silently waiting. I ran over and scooped it up, holding it like a kitten and wondering what the hell I was supposed to do with it. The three vampires still advanced on Rose and Adam. With the new weapon in my hand, I leaped forward, threw my arm horizontally, and decapitated all three with one swing. Rose and Adam stood dumbfounded, the color drained from their faces.

"I'll explain later." I wiped blood spatters from my face with a jacket sleeve.

*Pour the ashes in the same spot she was to sacrifice you. When I get her over there, you cut any part of her you can reach. Only her blood can release him.*

*How do you know all of this?*

He struggled to contain Isabela. She threw the back of her head into his face and clawed at his arms. He tossed me a look of exasperation instead of projecting his thoughts.

*You know what,* I thought, *we'll talk about it later.*

I knelt to the ground, illuminated in a circle with glittering moonlight. I pried the top of the urn off and turned it upside down. As the ash billowed out, it cast a gray puff of smoke, making me cough. The last thing I wanted was dead guy remnants in my nostrils.

Isabela shrieked, and I turned around in time to see her yank herself away from Marcus's grasp. She came straight for me, but this time I could follow her movements rather than be blindsided on which direction she'd approach. I dodged out of the way and lifted my foot, then slammed it into her abdomen. She landed in a crouched position on one knee—

the "superhero" pose—and glared up at me, her black hair whipping behind her.

*Follow my lead, I'm going to flank her from the left, you take the right.*

Marcus appeared on her left side, and Isabela stood to her feet. He threw a strike she easily deflected, and I followed suit with a strike from the right. This progressed into a paranormal Bruce Lee movie, Marcus throwing strikes and kicks from one side while I mirrored on the other. No matter what we did, Isabela would counter. This wasn't working. She was too fast, too strong.

*That's what a human would say.*

He gave me one quick look with those glacial eyes, strands of delicious chocolate hair dangling in his line of vision before he stopped all movement and threw his forearm out in front of Isabela. She'd expected another strike and her throat collided into it, sending her to her back.

"Freya!" Rose's voice called out.

For a moment I panicked, forgetting she was still there. She tossed me a sword and I caught it with ease, staring at it dumbly. "Where did you find this?"

"I don't know! It was . . . over here."

"Stay out of sight!" I tossed the sword around in my hands like I knew what I was doing with it. It didn't seem to affect me, so it couldn't be made of silver.

"Don't have to tell me twice, sister," Rose said, ducking behind a boulder she and Adam found.

*I* may not have known how to use a sword.

Marcus didn't have to look at me. He held his hand out

behind him, and I tossed it. He caught it in one swift motion, twirling it like the badass Roman soldier he once was.

*I still am. Just with a few upgrades.*

My lady-parts tingled and soared to all-out static shock when Marcus slashed several times through the air as Isabela leaped to her feet. His movements were fluid, and his eyes darted constantly, watching her.

"You cannot win! Stop being foolish."

The debt. The promise Marcus made to be with her forever if she didn't call on me.

*I'm yours. This plan will work. Trust me.*

The tingly feeling radiated all the way down to my toes.

"Siring a baby vampire does nothing to detract you from your promise. You are to release her and spend eternity with me. That was the deal," Isabela said, continuing to dodge Marcus's slashes.

I ground my teeth together and leaped forward, jumping onto Isabela's back and wrapping my arms and legs around her. A move I was a fan of as of late. My distraction worked momentarily, Marcus managing to nick her in the thigh with the sword. She yelped and I extracted my fangs, sinking my teeth into her neck with the ferocity of a wildcat.

My fellow wildcat, the lion, sprung forward and followed suit, sinking his own fangs into her shoulder. We both hung on as she attempted to whip us off her. Celeste leaped forward, plunging her fangs into her arm. Frankie in her wolf form slid forward and clamped her jaw onto her leg. Despite my best efforts to tell them to stay the hell away,

Rose and Adam joined in on our family affair, grabbing onto any available portion of her that wasn't being bitten.

Marcus's eyes met mine, both of us staring at the other feeding off the vampire who started it all. I knew in that moment that I'd never be the same. My body, my inner self felt the same, but I was a different version of myself. A version I'd have to acquaint myself to at some point or another. At some point, but not today.

Isabela tilted her head back and let out a blood curling scream, tossing us all back and forth, trying to get us to let go. Rose and Adam staggered backward onto their butts. She kicked Frankie in the face several times before she whimpered and trotted away. The vampires all held strong, but my muscles grew weaker and I couldn't keep the pressure.

Isabela broke my limbs free and tossed me into a nearby wall. I landed on the floor with a grunt and probably would've broken a rib as the old me. Marcus and Celeste still clung to her shoulders with their powerful jaws, moving her closer and closer to the spot we needed her. Her back was to the moon, and she was so preoccupied, she didn't notice.

*Keep her back turned!* I thought.

*You catch on quickly.*

They almost had her there when she got the upper hand by twisting her head to the side and using Celeste's body to strike Marcus in the chest, which broke both of their holds. She was so close.

A gigantic grizzly bear launched into Isabela's side, pinning her to the ground, the blood oozing from the wounds we'd inflicted dripping onto the ashes. I blinked several times, watching the massive beast, its paws triple the size of my head.

Isabela cried out in agony and then set her gaze on me. "You stupid bitch! I gave you life! A chance to live it! All I wanted was to have a chance to live mine."

The ashes began to swirl in patterns similar to a tornado, and I stood to my feet, ignoring her villainous rants. "Technically, *he* gave me life." I pointed at Marcus.

Isabela turned her head, petrifying fear sliding down her face. Once the swirling subsided, a tall man with hair as black as a starless sky stretched his arms skyward. His skin was a darker olive tone than Isabela's, his eyes a chocolate brown, and he wore a long black robe. His full lips slid into a sinister grin as he stared down at Isabela beneath the bear's weight.

"Thank you. I will take it from here." His voice flowed freely and thick as if it'd been slowed down by the weight of time. He looked nowhere else but at her.

The bear grunted and slid away, its heavy steps vibrating the stone floor as it walked. I scrambled to my feet, watching Isabela mimic the same movement, turning to run away, but Tezcatlipoca, the Aztec god of night, held up a hand and she stood frozen.

"Ah, ah, ah. We've got *so* much to catch up on, my dear."

Isabela's body shook, and for a brief moment I felt sorry for her.

"You may all leave. Rest assured she will never bother you again," my ancient great grandfather said, glancing around at all of us.

Marcus nodded once and hooked his arm through mine to lead me out. Rose couldn't get out fast enough, barreling in front of us, and the bear shifted into Damian. The sight of his nudity paled in comparison to watching my mythical grandparents.

"Oh, and Freya," Tezcatlipoca started. "I look forward to getting to know my granddaughter. Vampire or not." He grinned.

Was that a threat?

We left the cave, and no sooner had we set our feet onto the grass outside, it sealed shut behind us, allowing no others in or out.

# CHAPTER 26

We all gathered in Marcus's hotel room for a post-victory pow wow. Or a temporary victory, as I saw it. Given Tezcatlipoca's words, I was skeptical Isabela would be the last of our worries. Marcus sat in a brown leather armchair in the corner of the room, his legs spread wide, clad in his usual business attire like he was Bruce Wayne. His tie was partially undone, each of his elbows resting on opposite armrests.

I bit my thumbnail, taking in the sight of him from across the room. My attraction for him previous to my transformation was to the extreme, though I wouldn't have admitted it then, but now—as a vampire—I melted into a puddle. He watched me as I walked toward him, his eyes twinkling with intrigue. Once I reached the chair, I slipped behind him, letting my hand drag down the length of his beard before resting on his chest.

He dragged his own hand across my knuckles. "Well, hello there."

Adam cleared his throat nearby, and I slipped my hand

away from Marcus like I'd been caught stealing.

"Can we talk?" Adam asked, barely looking at the vampire in front of me.

I peered down at Marcus, and he gave a small nod, motioning past me with his hand. "You can talk in the bathroom, if you wish. For privacy."

Tucking my hair behind my ears, I followed Adam to the bathroom. Once I stepped inside, I faced the door and shut it as slowly as inhumanly possible. I wasn't ready for this.

"Please tell me for the love of God, Freya, you didn't do what I think you did," Adam almost shouted.

Pinching my eyes shut, I turned and pressed my back against the door. There was no point in beating around the bush. The fangs extracted and I found the courage to catch his gaze. He looked mortified and confused. It was like he didn't know who I was anymore. A little piece of myself died. That is if there was anything left to die.

"Jesus." He backed away until his butt hit the sink, his face growing pale.

I retracted the fangs, holding my hands out in front of me defensively. "I would never hurt you, I—" I took a step forward, but he held his palm out as a gesture for me to stop, so I did.

"Give me a minute here, Frey. I mean, why?"

"I didn't have a choice. You saw how powerful Isabela was. She weakened everyone else with silver. If she would've got ahold of the human me and killed me, she'd have become unstoppable. This was the only way to avoid that." The tears stung my sinuses, but I forced them back.

CARLY SPADE

"To become a vampire. A blood-sucking, immortal, moon-walking vampire." His hands gripped the sink behind him so harshly his fingers made squeaking sounds against the porcelain.

Screw this. I vamped forward, directly in front of him, and gripped each of his shoulders, pinning him. "Adam, I would be *dead* right now if I hadn't done this. You and Rose would be *dead*. I couldn't live with that. Could you?"

He trembled, the corners of his jaw popping. He reached a shaky hand forward and touched his fingertips to my cheek. Flinching upon feeling the ice-cold skin where there had once been warmth, he eventually placed his entire palm on my face. I closed my eyes and removed one of my hands from his shoulders to rest it over his.

"I'm so sorry you had to do this," he said, before pulling me into a hug.

I wrapped my arms around him and rested my chin on his shoulder with a sigh. "From the day I was born, this has been my life. I just didn't realize it until now."

"Happy Birthday, by the way." He smirked.

I couldn't help but laugh, and tears rolled down my cheeks. Pushing away from him, I dabbed my eyes with my fingertips, still chuckling. "How fucked up is it my human birthday is also my vampiric one?"

He gave a lopsided grin. "Makes it easy to remember, I suppose."

Playfully, I punched him in the shoulder.

He cocked his head to the side. "You're still you in there."

I eyed him speculatively. "Of course I am. You don't lose your personality becoming immortal." At least, I hadn't thought so, considering I felt no different in that sense.

"Oh, I'm sure you'll change after a hundred years." He cupped my elbow with his hand. "But I won't be around to see it, so I guess it really doesn't matter, right?"

I stared at him. Feeding on human beings was a secondary downside to the immortality, which would make me watch my friends—my family—grow old and die. I didn't know what to say.

A light knock sounded against the door. "I'm sorry to interrupt you, but Rose is here," Marcus's soothing voice said.

Clearing my throat, I moved to the door and opened it. Marcus leaned against the doorframe with one arm raised high. He gazed down at me with those icy blues, and my stomach twisted into knots.

*Everything okay in here?*

I gave a half smile. *About as good as it can be.*

We could seriously have an entire conversation without ever opening our mouths. I was still unsure how I felt about that. I'd have to coerce him into teaching me how to shield my thoughts like he did. A smidgen of privacy with a significant other would be nice. Especially considering we were bound together for eternity. My throat constricted.

Marcus stepped forward and brushed his fingers against my arm. "As I said, we've got a lot to talk about." He stepped aside, revealing a fidgeting Rose.

I ushered her inside the bathroom and shared another

glance with Marcus before shutting the door behind her.

She dragged her hands through her hair several times before turning around to face me. "Alright, lay it all on me. Show me the teeth, show me the shifty trick, everything, before I lose my nerve."

I bit the inside of my cheek before vamping in front of her and springing my fangs out.

She jumped with a yelp and stumbled backward. "Holy hell!"

Retreating the fangs, I sprung out a hand to catch her by the wrist and keep her from falling. "You asked for it."

Her nostrils flared, staring down at our skin-to-skin contact. "You're ice cold."

"Yes. Yes I am."

"I'm so sorry, Freya." A tiny dribble of snot leaked from her nose.

Letting go of her hand, I took a step back and motioned between my two best friends. "You both need to stop apologizing. None of this. None of it—is your fault. It's Isabela's."

"I think I can speak for both of us when I say, we wanted to be able to do more for you. To avoid . . .," Adam said, folding his arms.

"I know. But it's not as if I'm alone in all of this."

"Marcus. He's the one who changed you?" Adam asked, his brow furrowing.

"Yes. But before you get all big brother on me, the first time I asked him, he refused. Do you hear me?"

Adam's arms fell to his sides and he stepped forward. "The first time?"

"When you were kidnapped," Rose said quietly.

"It doesn't matter now. What matters is Marcus only did it because he knew it was the only way out of this mess." I pointed a finger. "So don't even think about getting pissed at him."

"Would you have really gone through with Celeste?" Rose asked, kicking at an imaginary pebble on the tiled floor.

"Honestly? I think I'd have chickened out. The thought of being bonded to her for eternity makes my stomach nauseated." I smiled and Rose's eyes lit up. "Come on, let's get back out there. Are we all good . . . for now?"

They both nodded, and I squeezed each of their shoulders before we exited back into the main room.

"Where the hell are Damian and Frankie?" Marcus leaned against the bar.

"Damian texted. Said they were running late." Celeste sat in a chair, leaning forward with her arms on her knees.

"On texting terms with the walkers now?" Marcus asked.

I attempted to hide my smile.

"So?" Celeste said like an adolescent girl, partially sticking out her tongue and rolling her eyes.

The door to the room swung open and Marcus stood upright, rigid and defensive. Damian and Frankie appeared from the other side of the door, holding hands, and Damian gave an awkward wave, us all staring at them.

"Sorry we're late," he said, shutting the door behind him.

A fear washed over me. "Is the baby okay?"

"Absolutely fine. We were . . . testing something. Why don't you fill them in?" Frankie said, raising her eyebrows to Damian.

Damian dragged his hands over his beard and then through his hair, stepping to the middle of the room.

"There's bad news, good news, and more bad news." Damian paused. His eyes transfixed on the carpet.

"Out with it," Celeste spat.

"The curse is real. I can still shift but only into a bear."

"The last thing you shifted into," Marcus muttered.

"So, you're a wearbear now?" I asked, biting my lip in a teasing grin.

He gave me an unenthusiastic glare. "Don't call me that."

"I don't know it has quite the ring to it, and that grizzly form is friggin' scary as hell." I looked over at Rose and Adam who nodded their heads in agreement.

"It could've been a lot worse," Frankie said, rubbing Damian's bicep affectionately.

"True. I'll miss flying with you," he replied, turning to face his mate, lowering his face so he could press his forehead against hers.

"I'm truly sorry, Damian." All joking aside, I felt like a tool. It was because of me, after all, he shifted in the first place.

"None of this is your fault. You didn't have a choice what family you were born into, what day you were born on. I'm honored to have helped."

"You're a better person than me." I gulped, knowing my words rang true.

He smirked. "I don't know about that. Not sure I would've agreed to be turned into a vampire."

Damian and Frankie turned to talk to Marcus.

"I gotta say, I'm surprised you went through with it," Celeste said.

"I'm surprised you're surprised, considering I was willing to be sired to you for the cause."

"Bullshit. You wouldn't have gone through with it." She looked at Marcus sidelong. "We both know the other reason you did it."

"I'd be lying if I said Marcus wasn't a small part of it."

"By the way, did you feel affected by the silver in that cave? You didn't seem weakened at all." She scrunched her face.

I frowned. Would I have known the difference if I had in fact felt weaker? I wasn't sluggish or even tired. "I'm not sure." It was the best I could come up with.

She flicked her tongue against the back of her front teeth. "Interesting. Well, welcome to the damned, Freya. I sincerely hope you don't regret it." She gave my shoulder a hearty slap before turning toward Rose. "You, my dear, were *amazing* in that cave."

"You think so?" Rose grinned.

I smiled to myself before stepping away from them and over to Adam. He sat in a chair with his head cradled in his hands.

"You okay?" I crouched down so I could look up at his face.

"Are you staying in Pittsburgh?" His voice muffled against his palms before he lifted his face.

Marcus met my gaze this time before returning to Damian. "We haven't talked about it, but something tells me Marcus would move mountains for me if he could. If I want to stay in Pittsburgh, I think it'd happen. And I do want to stay."

He offered a weak smile. "Would you still work at the bar?"

"Uh, absolutely. I became a vampire, Adam, not a millionaire." We both laughed, and he used a knuckle to brush under his sniffling nose.

A pain twisted in my stomach like a worm eating me from the inside out. I pinched my eyes shut, rubbing a hand over my abdomen.

"You okay?" Adam asked, putting a hand on my shoulder.

I waved his hand off, gripping onto my stomach, clenching my shirt with my fingers. "I'm fine."

*You're not fine. The hunger will never go away.*

I risked looking over at Marcus. He patted Damian on the shoulder and was already making his way over.

Adam stared at me. "You don't look fine. I didn't know it was possible for you to get even paler."

Marcus was by my side in an instant, his hand cupping my elbow, coaxing me to stand.

"If you'll excuse us, Adam."

I stood up, attempting to hide the discomfort on my face, and Adam shot up like a rocket. "Marcus . . ."

The vampire paused, quirking a brow at him.

"Thank you."

"For what?"

"Because in some bizarre, fucked up way, you saved

Freya's life. And I get to have her crazy antics and sarcasm in *my* life that much longer." He shrugged and scratched at his arm. "So, thank you."

Marcus bowed his head. "You're welcome."

As we made our way toward the exit, I bit at the inside of my mouth to keep my fangs from extracting.

"We'll have to leave this little shindig a bit early, I'm afraid," Marcus said, glancing around at the group.

Rose's gaze caught mine and I gave her a reassuring smile. I opened the door and slunk out into the hallway so I didn't have to disguise my anguish any longer.

"Don't wait up," Marcus said.

"Wouldn't dream of it," Celeste responded.

Once we stood in front of the elevator, I collapsed into his arms. He held me, dropping his lips to my ear. "Freya, we'll need to get to ground soon. You really must feed."

I shook my head. "Yours. Please. I'm not ready, Marcus."

He sighed, pushing his nose into my hair before lifting his bare forearm to my face.

I grabbed for it like it was the last filet mignon on the plate, sinking my teeth into his flesh. His blood dripped down my chin like the juice from a pomegranate. His hand gently pressed into my shoulder, coaxing me to stop. This time I quickly found the strength to pull away. I licked every last drip of the red elixir from my mouth, gazing up at him.

"Why does your blood taste like chocolate?"

"Chocolate? I can't say I've heard that one before." He reached forward, pushing the down button for the elevator. "Do you like chocolate?"

I blinked once. "Don't most women?"

"I'm not sure. Maybe it was your subconscious telling yourself it tasted like something it didn't so you wouldn't—how do you put it—freak out?"

I squinted at him, waiting to see if his thoughts delved elsewhere. "I'll accept this answer for now. And if it is my subconscious, I hope it continues to fool me."

He snickered, the elevator doors binging open, and we slipped inside. He pushed the button on the panel labeled "B," and we stood in silence for what seemed an eternity. I looked at the descending lit up numbers and reached a pinky finger out to curl around Marcus's. He gave a sly grin before using only his pinky to pull me forward. Our chests collided and he kissed me, tangling his fingers in my hair.

He pulled away, holding me to him. "Everything's going to be alright, Freya. I promise you."

I nodded, licking my lips. "I know." For the first time in I couldn't remember—I believed myself.

When the elevator reached its destination and the doors opened to a darkened chill surrounded by concrete, I froze. He said we needed to get to ground. Those words hadn't fully registered. He meant we needed to get *under*ground to prepare for sunrise. Marcus waited outside of the elevator, using his hand to block the doors from closing, beckoning me with his other.

"I'm with you every step of the way." He forced my gaze to his, and a calming sensation swept from the back of my head all the way down to my heels.

I slipped my hand into his and allowed him to pull me

from the safety of the elevator. He led me through the dank basement of the hotel, the smell of mildew and dust invading my nostrils. We stopped at a back corner, and he let go of my hand long enough to crouch down. He slipped his fingertips into two corners of a block, and with little effort lifted the solid concrete square from the ground, resting it to one side of the hole.

"Am I able to do that? Lift a solid block of rock like a feather?"

He stood up, dusting off his hands and flicking a piece of dark hair that'd fallen into his eyes. "In time. You're not even a day old yet."

"Back to the days of infancy. Splendid. At least I can still wipe my own ass."

Marcus chuckled, cupping my face with his hand. "I'm glad to hear you still have your sense of humor."

I turned to face him. "Is that something that could happen? Losing what makes me . . . me?"

He shook his head, his eyes roaming over my hair. "No. You're too strong. Only the weak minded lose themselves to the darkness."

I looked down at the dark, lonely hole and my eyes shot back at him. "Do we seriously have to go down there? Why can't we stay in the basement? There's only a few small windows."

"It's true. We could probably make do, but the workers file in during the day. It'd be a pity for them to come across us sleeping in a random corner of the basement, don't you think?"

I frowned. "I guess I can see your point."

He slipped his suit jacket off before jumping into the hole. The foundation beneath stopped at his kneecaps. He reached out a hand, motioning with his fingers. "Be brave, Hellcat."

Whenever he called me that, it lit my very soul on fire. But I sensed apprehension on his part—pain. I tried to listen in on his thoughts, but he blocked me again in the most inconvenient moment.

"What's on your mind?" I crossed my arms, not budging.

He sighed and let his hand drop. "Someone possessing the ability to sense my feelings—my emotions—will take decades to get used to, it seems."

"Out with it, Roman."

He peered up at me through strands of unruly, dark hair. "I never wanted this for you." He gestured to the hole.

I rubbed my lips together, kicking at a crumpled piece of paper on the ground. "We've talked about this."

"Doesn't mean I feel any different. You're a treasure, Freya. You should've been given the chance to share it with the world. The *mortal* world."

"Then help me share it with the mortal and immortal world alike. Don't be my wet blanket, Marcus. Now of all times, I need you to see the glass half full with me, please."

A corner of his lips curled before he stepped up and out of the hole. I had to crane my neck back to look at him. He grabbed each of my hips, kneading them, and studied me.

"You willingly met your demise, and even the smallest part of the reason for it . . . was me." His eyes twinkled, his hand caressing the back of my neck.

"You made the idea of it irresistible."

He gave a full, genuine smile. "I'll spend every day of the rest of my unnatural life thanking whoever or whatever brought me to you."

"That's a hell of a lot of thank yous." I gave a light tug on his beard.

His head dropped with a sigh. "Sunrise is very close. We need to get down there." He slipped away, hopped back into the hole, and held out his hand.

I took it and hopped down with him. He guided me to lay on my back, and he sunk down, reaching out of the hole to grab the concrete slab to drag back into place. Complete darkness enveloped me, and I panicked, frantically seeking Marcus's hand, dirt and pebbles kicking against my fingers.

Calmly, he took my trembling hand into his. "You can see in the darkness now. You're suppressing it. Close your eyes and then open them again."

I did as he instructed, pinching them shut so tightly it stretched the skin across my cheeks. When I opened them again, I could see an outline of Marcus, and after a short while, the entirety of him. The world looked black and white in this view, but it beat not being able to see my own hand in front of my face. Marcus's calming mental melodies spread through me like melted butter.

I turned my head to the side to look at him. "I never realized turning someone into a vampire created such a connection. Books, television, movies—they all made it seem as if vampires made vampires simply for global domination or something."

He balled up his jacket and lifted up my head to slip it underneath me like a pillow. "It's ritualistic of sorts. We can't reproduce, so we create. There are those who abuse the system of course, but in the end, it only drives them insane. Can you imagine feeling what you're feeling times a hundred? If a singular vampire created that many, they'd constantly feel each and every one of them."

"I can't imagine feeling this times two, let alone a hundred. This is why you killed Catalina? The connection you two shared?"

"Yes." He found my eyes, and I was content simply staring at him for a few moments. "It was far too precious a gift to share with someone like her."

"How much longer can I go on feeding from you?"

He sighed, resting a hand behind his own head. "I'm unsure. Eventually, you *will* have to do what you dread most."

I turned my gaze to the concrete block above me. "Is it something all vampires can do for each other?"

"Only those who they've been sired to or sired. You could take Celeste's blood, and it'd do nothing for you. Just mine."

His words made my stomach flutter. *Just mine.*

"We should rest." He adjusted his legs.

"Can I wrap my arm around you, or do we have to lay on our backs with our hands crisscrossed over our chests?"

He reached out a hand and pulled me to his side. I rested my head on the comfort of his shoulder. His scent infiltrated my every sense, and it alone was enough to make me drowsy.

He kissed the top of my head. "Close your eyes and let the sun lull you to sleep."

And so I did. I drifted to sleep realizing he was my forever. For the rest of my immortal life, we would spend the centuries protecting those we loved . . . and each other.

# EPILOGUE

*Marcus*
*Two Months Later*

How a battle-ridden, jaded, and stubborn bastard such as myself deserved a companion like Freya, I'd never understand. I could live for another two thousand years and it'd remain a mystery to me. She'd begun to catch onto the ways of a vampire with increased ease. I dared say she'd become quicker than me in certain aspects. What she had yet to do however, was feed from a human. I could sense the hunger, the pain writhing inside of her, yet she still refused. Who was I to force her? I wouldn't.

She'd already been through enough, so it didn't take much convincing on her part to get me to come to Pittsburgh. Celeste, on the other hand, was like pulling a wisdom tooth without anesthesia. I'd lived all over the globe and had only spent the better half of a century in America. I wanted her to be around her friends until the day they passed into the next life. A thought Freya chose to keep hidden deep inside, and I couldn't blame her. It was a reality every new vampire came to at one point or another, and it never got easier.

She'd laughed in my face when I informed her I had millions in investments. When you live as long as I have, you learn and create the means to start an empire. I told her there was no need for her to work anymore given my net worth, but she insisted on having that one ounce of normalcy, and it made me care for her that much more.

Damian and Frankie were having a baby shower for their soon-to-be-born child. Given our recently developed friendship, we were cordially invited. I dragged my hand over the dozens of shirts I owned. Freya's arms slipped around my waist, and once her scent hit my nostrils, I instantly got hard. I'd been with plenty of women through my life, but she was the only one who could drive me crazy without showing me one inch of skin.

Reaching past me, she tapped a sky-blue-colored shirt. "This one. Brings out those baby blues of yours."

I smiled to myself, peeling the shirt from its hanger. I turned to face her and reached a hand over my head, grabbing at the fabric of my T-shirt, and in one swift motion, removed it, then let my eyes roam over her body, a vision in an emerald-colored, form-fitting dress. I flexed my muscles and grinned, watching her gaze drop straight to my abdomen.

"You better cut that out or we're going to be *very* late." She gulped, moving her hands forward to touch me but reluctantly recoiled them.

Never one to back out on a challenge, I stalked forward until her ass pressed into the nearest closet wall. She stared up at me, and I could feel the urge raging through her like a wildfire. I caged her with my arms, grinning down at her like the sly lion she loved to compare me to. "A quickie?" I perked an eyebrow.

She whimpered, sliding down the wall, and ducked under my arms. "You *know* there's no such thing as that with us."

She was right.

She cupped a hand over her ear. "I'm sorry, what was that?"

This little minx.

"You're right." I smirked, slipping on the shirt, doing up most of the buttons, and tucking it into my gray pants.

"I hope they're okay with this gift card. I mean, what do you get a shifter baby anyway? A four-legged onesie?" She stuffed the card into her purse.

"I wanted to run something by you." I closed the space between us.

"Right now? Can it wait? The shower starts in thirty minutes."

I took her hands into mine, and I needn't read her thoughts to know she raged with skepticism.

"I want to start a financial business here. An underground one, in fact. For supernaturals."

"Supernaturals?" She blinked her eyes rapidly. "Plural? There's more things out there than just vampires and shifters?"

"There's still so much of this world you are simply not aware of, Hellcat." I secured a piece of fiery hair behind her ear that had escaped from her ponytail.

"Well, what else is there? Fairies? Harpies? Goblins? What?" Her eyes went frantic with intrigue.

"You want me to spoil the surprise?" I plastered a devilish grin across my lips.

Her face fell, but she knew by now she couldn't pry it out of me.

"I want to call it Cassius Investments. It'd be nice to use my real name for once."

"True. Very true. But you should call it Cassius Enterprises."

I cocked a single brow. "Why enterprises?"

She twirled her hand in the air and gave a sheepish smile. "It's this comic I've liked since I was kid. Billionaire dude disguises himself as a rodent at night, fights crime. Anyway, point is for me, you should call it Cassius Enterprises."

I hadn't a clue what she was talking about, but every fiber of my being wished to please her. "Alright. Cassius Enterprises it is," I said with a chuckle.

She smiled wide and I moved over to the mirror. Checking myself out, I gave my semi-long locks a tussle with my fingers. I'd be lying if I said I wasn't still trying to have my way with her before we left, the tussle always drove her crazy.

Spying her reflection in the mirror behind me, I saw her cross her arms over her chest and try to suppress a grin.

*What am I going to do with you?* I heard her think.

I turned to face her, curling an arm around her hips, and

pulled her into me. "Anything and everything for the rest of our unnaturally born lives." Grinning, I bent down to kiss her. We were fashionably late, and I couldn't care less.

Be sure to check out Carly Spade's contemporary fantasy romance featuring a warrior Druid, magic, adventure and Celtic mythology:

# Power of Eternity

Out now!

Be sure to check out Carly Spade's slow burn, enemies to lovers contemporary romance amidst a Great White shark expedition in Australia. Witty banter. Adventure. And a hero based on Discovery's Shark Week host: Paul de Gelder:

# The Other Tide

Out now!

Want to be up on all the latest and greatest?
Click here to sign up for Carly Spade's mailing list for news
on upcoming novels, sneak peeks and cover reveals.

Head over to www.carlyspade.com to stalk—er follow 😌
Carly on social media.

# Acknowledgements

First, as always, I'd like to thank my husband for his continued support and constant willingness to be my sounding board. Vampires are definitely not his forte, but he still listened with enthusiasm and offered input.

To my critique partners: AK and Sarah. You both offered me some amazing input which truly made this story the best it could be. I'll always appreciate your honest feedback and love having you in my corner. You seriously rock.

To my beta readers, this was the first book I called out to the masses for beta readers and your input not only helped improve the story, but also ensured me other people would want to read this. Thank you for taking the time to read and report.

To my parents, for allowing me to watch *Interview with the Vampire* when I was honestly probably too young. It single-handedly made me fall in love with vampires and sparked my Anne Rice obsession. Sincerely, thank you for that.

To the readers, thank you for taking a chance on this

book. The entire idea behind it spawned from my love for vampire romance, but never able to find a read which incorporated all the elements I wanted to see. Many came close, but none gave me Freya & Marcus, and now I have them to read over and over again. 😊

CPSIA information can be obtained
at www.ICGtesting.com
Printed in the USA
LVHW032312260821
696159LV00008B/372